# Playing WITH THE Boys

# Playing WITH THE Boys

### a novel by

## liz tigelaar

razor
bill

Playing with the Boys

RAZORBILL

Published by the Penguin Group
Penguin Young Readers Group
345 Hudson Street, New York, New York 10014, U.S.A.
Penguin Group (USA) Inc., 375 Hudson Street, New York, New York 10014, U.S.A.
Penguin Group (Canada), 90 Eglinton Avenue East, Suite 700, Toronto, Ontario,
Canada M4P 2Y3 (a division of Pearson Penguin Canada Inc.)
Penguin Books Ltd, 80 Strand, London WC2R 0RL, England
Penguin Ireland, 25 St Stephen's Green, Dublin 2, Ireland
(a division of Penguin Books Ltd)
Penguin Group (Australia), 250 Camberwell Road, Camberwell,
Victoria 3124, Australia (a division of Pearson Australia Group Pty Ltd)
Penguin Books India Pvt Ltd, 11 Community Centre, Panchsheel Park,
New Delhi – 110 017, India
Penguin Group (NZ), 67 Apollo Drive, Rosedale, North Shore 0632, New Zealand
(a division of Pearson New Zealand Ltd)
Penguin Books (South Africa) (Pty) Ltd, 24 Sturdee Avenue, Rosebank,
Johannesburg 2196, South Africa

Penguin Books Ltd, Registered Offices: 80 Strand, London WC2R 0RL, England

10 9 8 7 6 5

Library of Congress Cataloging-in-Publication Data

Tigelaar, Liz.
  Playing with the boys : a pretty tough novel / by Liz Tigelaar.
      p. cm.
  Summary: When fifteen-year-old Lucy and her father move to Malibu, California, for a
fresh start, Lucy tries out for the varsity football team and feels strong and in control for the
first time since her mother's death—as long as her overprotective father does not find out.

  ISBN 978-1-59514-113-2
  [1. Football—Fiction. 2. Sex role—Fiction. 3. Fathers and daughters—Fiction. 4. Single-
parent families—Fiction. 5. Moving, Household—Fiction. 6. High schools—Fiction. 7.
Schools—Fiction. 8. Malibu (Calif.)—Fiction.] I. Title.

  PZ7.T4525Pla 2008
  [Fic]—dc22
                                                                              2007024121

Printed in the United States of America

*This book is dedicated to the Prettiest
and Toughest woman I know — my mom, Mary.*

## one

Lucy Malone had always felt that she was just one letter short of "lucky," and in her fifteen years on this planet, her theory had definitely been proven true. It wasn't just that she often found herself inexplicably trapped in bathrooms, had broken both arms (the left one twice), or had more freckles than she knew what to do with. It was more than that.

Lucy vividly remembered sitting in the hard wooden pew at their church just over a year ago, listening to friends and family members recount funny stories about her mom while Lucy sat there, desperately wishing she'd just had that missing *K*. Then maybe things would have turned out differently. She really could have been Lucky instead of Lucy.

And now, a year later, she was on a plane next to her father, Greg, flying over the Rockies or the Grand Canyon or somewhere the pilot had mentioned, only she hadn't heard, because Guster was blasting on her iPod, and once again, she felt totally unlucky.

Today was the day she'd been dreading for months; the

day she was moving from Toledo, Ohio, to Los Angeles, California. Well, Malibu to be exact.

All she knew about Malibu was that it was on the Pacific Ocean and everyone who lived there had blond hair and blue eyes and a great tan. Lucy looked down at her own milky white skin. She was beyond pale; she was *frighteningly* pale. One look at her skin could seriously blind someone. Maybe if she had a few more freckles they would morph into one giant one, which could fool people into thinking she was tan. She stopped herself. Had it really come to this? *Wishing* for *more* freckles? Maybe the altitude *had* gone to her head. They were, after all, at thirty-five thousand feet.

She shook her long, strawberry-blond hair in front of her face, something she did when she felt nervous. Her choppy bangs covered her green eyes as she fiddled with the earbuds on her iPod.

She pressed the silver button to recline her seat and stared out the small window at the fluffy, white clouds. She sighed and couldn't help but think of her friends back home. Most of them probably weren't even awake yet, sleeping in after staying up practically all night at her going-away party. And that had been after a long, preseason practice session with her soccer team. They'd invited her to practice one last time before leaving. Then this morning, she'd gotten up super-early, to finish packing her whole life into suitcases.

She loved (and by "loved" she meant "hated") how

parents (in her case, "parent," since now it was just her and her dad) used the phrase "family decision" when talking about things like whether to get a dog, whether to go on vacation, or . . . whether to move across the country. By the time her dad sat down to talk to her about it, the decision had clearly already been made. So much for the "family decision."

She remembered the moment so clearly. It had been April 14th. She'd just walked in the door from her best friend Annie's fifteenth birthday party, which had involved ditching their mini-golf plan to hang out with some cute sophomores, Tyler and Jason, at the pizza place across the street. She'd had two pieces of sausage-and-onion pizza, then instantly wished she hadn't. Unless Annie had a pack of Listerine strips, Lucy's chances of making out—which she'd only done two point five times (the point five was a loooong story)—had just plummeted from "potentially" to "no way in hell." Luckily, Tyler hadn't held it against her, texting her on the way home. She'd burst in the door, quickly hunting through her bag for the phone and pecking out a response. But before she could hit send on her reply, her dad had had her cornered.

"We need to talk," he'd said, in a tone that let her know this wasn't going to be a good conversation.

Panicked, Lucy had quickly scanned through the night's events, confident she hadn't done anything wrong. She hadn't had any alcohol, she hadn't so much as come in the vicinity of a cigarette, and she'd even come home ten minutes before her curfew, thanks to Annie's dad hitting all green lights . . . but her dad had looked as though he had something important on his mind.

"We're moving to California," he had stated quickly, as if saying the words faster would make them sting less.

"What?" she'd gasped, looking up from her text. She couldn't have heard him correctly. "What'd you say?"

"We're moving," he'd replied firmly. "To California."

Lucy had felt her knees buckle under her. She'd leaned against the wall for support as her dad explained.

"The firm's expanding, and they want someone to open a new West Coast office," he told her. Her dad was an architect who designed large planned communities, which often meant that all the houses were big, expensive, and looked exactly the same. "And besides that, I just . . . with everything that's happened . . . being here . . . it's hard. Everywhere I look, it just . . ." He trailed off.

Lucy knew what he meant. Everything reminded him of her mom. From the markings on the wall behind the pantry, where Lucy's mom measured Lucy's height and wrote down the date, to the yellow paint in the kitchen that her mom had been so excited about, to the flowers that she and her mom had planted in the yard two summers ago that were starting to bloom again . . . you couldn't be in their house without feeling that overwhelming sense that someone was missing. But was it really going to be better somewhere else? Lucy wondered. Somewhere they'd be even farther away from her mom's memory?

"But Dad," Lucy argued, "what about Aunt Kate and Aunt Mary?" Those were her mom's sisters, who lived less than two hours away.

"They understand that this is something I need to do," he answered simply. "It's a great opportunity, Lucy. We'd be even closer to my parents." Her dad's family lived in Arizona. "We could spend more time with them."

*What?* Lucy wanted to scream. *Your mom is crazy and your dad is crazier! You moved to the Midwest to get away from them!* But she knew better than to argue and didn't want to make him feel worse. Instead she just stood in the doorway, floored. How could it be possible that the day before, the biggest stress in her life had been who to include in her Top 8 on her MySpace page, and now she had to give up her entire life and move across the country and start over? She already felt as though she'd had to do that once after losing her mom. She certainly didn't want to do it again.

"Please bring your seat backs to their full upright position." The stewardess's chirpy voice resonated throughout the plane. Lucy was snapped out of her thoughts and back to reality.

*Seat back? Upright? Landing?*

This was it. This was really happening. She had a one-way ticket to California with no return in sight. Unless the pilot miraculously turned this plane around, there was no going back. Goodbye, Toledo. Nice knowing you. What did they say in L.A.? *Don't call us, we'll call you.*

Her dad turned to her. His hair looked grayer than she'd remembered it. The last year had aged him significantly.

"You ready, kid?" he asked, patting her gently on the arm. "Is your seat belt fastened?"

She loved when her dad called her "kid." He wasn't as amused when she called him Greg.

She simply nodded. "I think so." She wanted to be brave. She wanted to make this easy for him. She looked out the window, took a deep breath, and braced herself for landing.

A bright red convertible raced down the Pacific Coast Highway with Lucy's dad at the wheel. She knew he was trying to do something special by renting such a cool car, but as she desperately tried to keep her hair out of her face, it felt like more trouble than it was worth. Much like this whole moving-across-the-country thing.

She pushed the offending strands back again, convinced that by the time they reached the house, her hair would just be one giant snarl. She'd probably have to shave her head before the first day of school. That'd be a great way to make new friends—show up bald.

Her dad pointed to the left. "See? Over there? That's the Santa Monica Pier." Lucy looked in the direction he was pointing and saw the giant Ferris wheel spinning around and around. She swore she had seen it a million times in movies or on television.

"And look over there," he added. "That apartment building is built right into the cliff."

Lucy squinted her eyes and blocked the sun with her hand. Her dad was right. The apartments were built right into the rocks and hovered precariously over the highway.

"Wow," she said, mustering as much enthusiasm as she could. Her dad was trying. "It's amazing." And to be honest, it was—the ocean, the palm trees, the rollerbladers and bikers . . . The beach was packed. She watched as a cute male volleyball player spiked the ball. The opposing player missed it and the cute one celebrated with his female teammate. She jumped on him, tackling him to the ground.

Strange that other people could be having so much fun while she was so miserable.

"Wait until you see our rental place," her dad said, smiling. "You're going to love your room."

Lucy silently nodded and kept her thoughts to herself. It wouldn't do any good to whine or complain—it would just make a difficult situation harder. She wished she could tell her dad that she didn't want a new room, that her old one had been perfect. Her mom had let her splatter-paint the walls—a project that had ended in disaster for the carpet and resulted in brand new hardwood floors. After that, Lucy had been allowed to use paint and markers to graffiti her bedroom and make it personal. She'd painted the word *imagine*—her favorite word—on the wall above her bed, and her friends and a bunch of the girls from varsity had written notes and messages on the sliver of the wall next to her closet.

"What up, Slam?" Annie had scrawled on the wall only moments after Lucy had mistakenly run into the closed glass patio door.

Her old room was perfect, so unless *this* room had Orlando Bloom *and* Johnny Depp in it, she didn't see how it was going to beat what she'd had back in Toledo.

But shortly after they turned left across PCH and pulled into the driveway of their new house, Lucy was prepared to reconsider. Their place was *right on the beach!* She stared in awe as her dad parked in front of the garage; then she hurriedly grabbed her suitcases.

"Forget your bags." Her dad smiled. "I got 'em. Go check out your room, kid."

Lucy jumped out of the passenger seat, leaving the door open as she bolted for the house. The front door was ajar, as if the house was expecting them (or the realtor was *that* good). She ran through the house, barely noticing that it was already fully furnished. Whatever. She didn't care about stainless-steel kitchen appliances or a window the size of the entire living room wall that overlooked the surf. All she cared about was her bedroom.

As soon as she walked in, her jaw dropped. It was hands down the coolest room she'd ever seen. The walls were painted a light yellow, making the room warm and inviting. Straight in front of her, under a huge window, was a queen-size bed that rested on a large wooden platform. It appeared as if the bed were suspended in midair. Covering it was a fluffy red comforter; orange and yellow pillows with tiny circular mirrors were scattered all over it. Momentarily forgetting that she was in a state of mourning, Lucy ran to it and jumped on it. Her body bounced as she landed. She snuggled into the softness of the mattress and burrowed into the pillows. This bed would be perfect for sleeping until noon—something her dad rarely let her do, even in the summertime.

Then, suddenly, she noticed something above her. A loft.

Sitting up to get a better view, she saw that a narrow spiral staircase led up to another level. She jumped off the bed and tore up the staircase to a loft with a huge wooden desk, a giant wooden bookshelf that stretched from the floor to the ceiling, giant red beanbag chairs, and a brand-new white twenty-four-inch iMac on her desk. "So you like it?" her dad asked, walking into the room. He made his way up the spiral staircase into the loft and could tell by her expression that she was surprised. "I thought you would." He smiled.

She sank back into a beanbag chair as he took a seat at her desk and leaned forward, his brow furrowed. Lucy knew this meant he was going to say something serious.

"I know it's tough, Luce," he began. "Moving to a new

place, having to make new friends—but we need this, kid. *I* need this. A fresh start, you know?"

Lucy nodded, knowing that as hard as the last few years had been on her, they'd been even more brutal on her dad, who'd had to take care of both Lucy and her mom. Seeing him now, so vulnerable, with tears in his eyes, just broke her heart. She'd only ever seen her dad cry once—in the hospital, when they'd shut down the life support.

She stood up and rushed over, throwing her arms around his neck. She didn't really care about iMacs or mirrored colored pillows or houses right on the beach. She cared about him. Her dad. And she was determined to do everything she could to help him start over. Besides, if her room was any indication of what lay ahead for her, maybe California wouldn't be so bad. She just wished her mom were here to see it.

Lucy left her room and stepped out onto the deck off of the living room as the sun was beginning to set. She walked down a long set of wooden stairs that wound down to the beach below. It was weird to think that now she was living on the ocean. The vast, endless ocean. Her days of being a big fish in small pond were definitely over.

She glanced down at her watch and saw it was almost six-thirty. She did the math. That meant nine-thirty in Ohio. She supposed Annie would go to bed early since school started tomorrow, so she figured she better call now or risk not getting to talk tonight. Good thing she had unlimited nights and weekends. Thank you, AT&T!

Lucy kicked off her flip-flops, and her feet sank into the sand. About twenty feet out from the deck, she saw a fire pit with a few logs around it. The sight of something this cool should have made her happy, but instead, her heart sank. Annie would have loved this place. She could just hear her voice now.

"No freaking way!" she'd have squealed. "You actually *live* here?" Lucy couldn't really believe it herself. She grabbed her Razr phone out of her pocket and opened it. She'd begged for a Razr last Christmas, after she'd "accidentally" dropped her old phone—which, FYI, didn't text—in the toilet.

She was about to hit 2 on her speed dial—Annie's cell number—when something caught her eye. Something bobbing up and down in the water.

Lucy squinted and looked out to the horizon. She made out a surfer, paddling strongly as a huge wave approached. Right as the water swelled underneath, the surfer popped up perfectly, dropping down the face of the wave, then cutting back and forth inside of it. Lucy watched, awed. Growing up in Ohio, the closest she'd ever been to actual surfing was the third row at the local AMC, watching *Blue Crush*. As the surfer cut toward the beach, Lucy realized that she wasn't just watching a surfer—she was watching a *girl*.

## two

Once on the sand, the girl undid the Velcro strap around her ankle and shook out her dark, slicked-back hair, revealing it to be layered and shoulder-length. She wore small board shorts and a bikini top, and a dark tan emphasized her toned body. Her eyes were dark and soulful, and her face, like Lucy's, was covered in freckles. She noticed Lucy staring.

"Yeah?" the girl asked, expectantly. "Did you want something?"

Lucy instantly blushed. "Oh, nothing . . ." she stammered. "That was just . . . really, really cool."

Lucy cringed, instantly hated the sound of her own voice. *Really, really cool?* Lame. Could it have been *more* obvious that she wasn't from California?

The girl barely smiled. "Thanks."

"I'm Lucy," Lucy quickly said. "I just kind of moved here, like, five minutes ago."

The girl gave Lucy the once-over. "Yeah, you don't look like you're from here." Lucy's gaze tipped down as she, too, scanned her outfit. Madras shorts with cute slip-on gold flats had been semi-stylish back in Ohio, but Lucy wasn't exactly a cutting-edge fashionista, often relying on Annie and sometimes even Annie's older sister, Carrie, for guidance.

The girl sensed Lucy's self-consciousness. "Don't worry," she said, "Looking like you don't belong here? That's a good thing."

Lucy grinned, suddenly relieved. She liked this girl.

"I'm Charlie," the girl said quickly, as if she wasn't particularly interested in her own name.

"Charlie," Lucy repeated. "I've never heard that for a girl. That's really, really . . . cool."

Ugh! She'd said it again. She made a mental note: No more "really." No more "cool."

Charlie sighed. "Not if your last name's Brown."

Lucy had to ask. "Well, what's *your* last name?"

Charlie raised an eyebrow. It became obvious to Lucy that Charlie's last name *was* Brown.

"I'm sorry. . . ." Lucy cringed, not knowing what to say. Clearly, she'd hit on a sore subject. *God, Charlie Brown? What parent would do that?*

Charlie shrugged and grabbed her board. "Whatever. I gotta go."

Lucy thought fast. She couldn't just let this girl go without at least trying to make a new friend.

She tentatively called after her. "Um . . . maybe I'll see you around . . . or something. Meeting you was really,

really . . ." She trailed off.

"Cool?" Charlie asked, finishing her thought as she strapped her surfboard to her bike.

Lucy shrugged, embarrassed. "Yeah, I mean . . . you know."

Charlie gave her a funny look. "Not really."

She jumped on her bike without a word and took off. And as quickly as Charlie appeared, she was gone, leaving Lucy discouraged . . . and feeling anything but cool.

The following Monday, Lucy stood frozen at the doors of her new high school. Not literally, of course, because even at seven-thirty in the morning, it was "seventy and sunny, with the marine layer expected to clear by noon." At least, that was what the perky weathergirl, who looked as though she belonged on *Days of Our Lives* rather than on the morning news, had chirped for the fifth consecutive day in a row—which was now exactly how many days Lucy had lived in Malibu.

She looked down at her outfit—short, pin-striped shorts, with a flowy empire-waist tank top. It had seemed cute when she picked it out at the Urban Outfitters on the Third Street Promenade, but now it seemed as though too much of her arms and legs were exposed. Having grown four inches in the last two years, from 5'2" to 5'6", she often felt like a puppy whose feet were too big for its body.

"Knees and knuckles," her dad jokingly called her.

Now she shook her hair in front of her face, wanting to disappear. It was all supposed to be so different. She should have been back in Toledo, starting her sophomore year at Hillcrest with all her friends—instead, she stood outside a foreign, sprawling campus that sat on a hillside overlooking the Pacific Ocean. Who cared if it was beautiful? She didn't want beautiful. She wanted home. She wanted her friends . . . or if not her friends, *any* friends.

The bell rang. Kids hurried past her, some bumping into her as if she were invisible. Everything blurred together. She could hear a girl's voice, talking to a friend as she texted. . . .

"And then he was all whatever," she said breathlessly. "And then I was all *what-EVER!* Can you believe that? I mean, *whatever.*"

Lucy had no idea what she was even saying. Maybe she shouldn't have signed up for Spanish. "Valley Girl" could have been its own second language.

But no matter; she was sure she'd have plenty of time to contemplate her foreign-language choice when she was sitting alone at lunch in her exclusive school, picking at her fish sticks or fiesta salad or whatever disgusting food they served.

She sighed, glancing down at her schedule, knowing she had no choice but to walk in the double doors and get this over with. It was now or never. She took a deep breath.

"Okay, Beachwood Academy," she said to herself. "Here I come." She headed inside.

Starting with gym class didn't help. She hadn't known to bring clothes to "dress out" (since she didn't even know what "dressing out" meant), so the gym teacher, Miss Sullivan, had given her an oversized shirt and a pair of boy's shorts from last year's lost and found to change into. *Ew. Loaners.* Lucy hadn't wanted to put them on, but she'd had no choice.

Now, as she sat on the hard wooden bleachers, virtually swimming in an XXL, she couldn't have felt more conspicuous. The other girls were wearing little fitted tank tops with built-in bras, and Juicy Couture pants with cute phrases written on the butt, like ANGEL and SEXY. Lucy's shirt read 2003 TURKEY TROT. *Huh?* It might as well have said BIG GIGANTIC LOSER. She folded her arms across her chest, hoping to obscure the giant orange-and-yellow turkey on her front.

The bleachers rattled beneath her as a weird-looking emo girl stomped onto them and plopped down next to Lucy. Lucy's eyes darted toward the girl. Forget dressing out. This girl wore tight black jeans, horn-rimmed glasses and a too-small button-down shirt. She had giant earplugs in her earlobes, black nail polish, and, apparently, as she scooted closer to Lucy, no regard for personal space. There were endless rows of bleachers, and this girl was practically sitting in her lap. Lucy gave a half-smile and tried to subtly scoot closer toward the boy next to her. He had a mess of dark curly ringlets that had practically achieved Afro-like status.

As Miss Sullivan went over the rules of floor hockey, Lucy turned to the boy.

"Hi," she said shyly. The boy looked up from under his semi-curly, semi-Afro hair and gave Lucy a polite smile. He seemed to personify "dorky cool."

Miss Sullivan continued. "Now, when you hold your stick, you need to hold it tight. . . ." This elicited giggles from everyone on the bleachers. What was it about kids in high school that made them interpret everything as sexual?

"Sorry," Lucy said softly to the boy. "It's just, this girl is, um . . . kind of . . . in my lap. . . ."

The boy looked around Lucy to the emo girl, who was glaring at them both.

"Right." The boy nodded as he scooted further down to make more room for Lucy.

She smiled, grateful. "Thanks." She debated whether or not she should say more, then did. "I don't really know anyone—I just moved here," she continued, then added, "I'm Lucy."

"I'm Benji." He smiled, revealing a mouthful of braces.

"Excuse me?" Miss Sullivan called out, annoyed. "Would you two like to share your conversation with everyone?"

Lucy turned red as she looked down at her hands, her go-to avoidance move: stare at your hands as if they are the most fascinating thing you've ever seen and pray that the other person stops looking at you. She only looked back up when Miss Sullivan began dividing them into teams. As they were both called, Benji and Lucy stood up to take their respective places on the floor.

Miss Sullivan handed them both floor-hockey sticks and only Lucy a pinny. Lucy slipped the red mesh on over her head. It reeked of sweat.

"Cute," Benji commented.

"Let's go, people," Miss Sullivan instructed, "before the period's over."

Lucy rushed to take her place on the floor, running smack into the emo girl, who was standing right behind her.

"Oh, sorry," Lucy said quickly. "I didn't see you there."

The emo girl just stared her down. Lucy swore she heard her growl. Her head began spinning. She'd been in California exactly four days and she'd met a girl named Charlie, a boy named Benji, and a growling emo. *Could it possibly get any more bizarre?*

"Pickle," Miss Sullivan called out, "you start."

Lucy watched a spunky, athletic-looking African-American girl knock the hockey puck across the floor. Lucy shook her head. *Pickle.* But before she could think about it anymore, she realized the hockey puck was heading directly toward her.

At the end of fifty minutes, Lucy was relieved to lose the hockey stick and head to English. Wearing cargo pants and Vans, her English teacher, Miss Reese, looked as though she could pass as a student herself. And outside of school, Miss Reese insisted that everyone call her Martie. Martie quickly took attendance, as the class settled into their seats.

Lucy took a spiral notebook out of her backpack. Due to the move and rush to unpack before work and school, her dad hadn't had time to do their usual prerequisite back-to-school shopping, so she had only a half-used notebook from last year. Classy.

Martie called out, "Amy Andrews . . . Payton Baker . . . Nick Baldwin?"

A cocky guy's arm shot up into the air. "Yo." He gave a smarmy little wave.

Martie checked him off as here. "Charlie Brown?"

Lucy perked up. *Charlie?* She spun back around to look.

"Here," Charlie said as she picked at her black nail polish.

Lucy couldn't believe it. It was really her, the surfer. She was here. At Beachwood. In her English class. What were the chances?

Martie smiled, as if she were particularly fond of Charlie. "Welcome back, Charlie." From the front of the room, the pretty blond girl that Lucy had overheard talking and texting that morning—the *whatever* girl—sighed.

"Where're Snoopy and Woodstock?" Whatever Girl muttered to another impeccable-looking student next to her. Together, the two oozed popularity.

"It's getting old, Regan," Charlie spat. "Kind of like your ratty hair extensions." A few kids chuckled. That shut Regan up, as she self-consciously fingered her long, blond hair.

Martie seemed to suppress an urge to giggle. Instead, she gave a reprimanding, "Charlie," then continued. "Ryan Conner?"

"Yep," a male voice said. Lucy tilted her head toward the sound and realized she was sitting next to the cutest boy she'd ever laid eyes on in her life. He had sandy brown hair that was lightly gelled into what looked like the inklings of a tiny, messy Mohawk—the kind a preppy guy trying to be the slightest bit edgy would have. He was dressed in jeans, cheap black drugstore flip-flops, and a vintage Led Zeppelin concert T-shirt; he also had a Beachwood letter jacket thrown over the chair behind him.

Lucy stared, mesmerized.

From behind her, Nick poked her in the back with a pencil. "Take a picture. It'll last longer." Lucy quickly snapped out of it and blushed, embarrassed. She wished she actually could subtly take a picture with her camera phone.

"Regan Holder?" Martie called out.

Regan rolled her eyes. She'd already made her presence very known. "Obviously," she sighed.

Lucy barely heard her. She couldn't take her eyes off Ryan.

"Lucy Malone?"

*Annie has to see this guy,* Lucy thought to herself.

"Lucy Malone?"

He looked like someone who had been genetically engineered to be the perfect combination of cute, clean-cut, and ridiculously hot. If the government wasn't already cloning him, they should have been.

"Is there *anyone* here named Lucy?" Martie asked for a third time. Lucy realized Martie was talking to her, and jumped as if she'd been electrically shocked.

"Here!" she said, practically knocking her folder off her desk.

The other kids laughed. Lucy again blushed a deep shade of red.

Martie scanned the roster. "You're new, right?" Lucy nodded, wondering what had given it away. Probably the fact that everyone else looked straight out of an Abercrombie catalogue . . . or something more expensive. "And it says here that you're a sophomore?"

Lucy's eyes darted around. Wait—wasn't everyone?

"You know this is a junior English class," Martie explained, as she thumbed through the paperwork she was holding. "It says here you've already taken English 2. . . ."

Lucy nodded, remembering that her guidance counselor had said something about the school system in Ohio working differently, that she might be ahead in some of her classes, which meant fewer classes with the kids in her grade. *Great*, Lucy had thought at the time. *That'll make it even harder to make friends. . . .*

Martie smiled. "Well, welcome to Beachwood, Lucy. We're glad to have you here." Lucy could hear a few scattered chuckles. She slunk down in her chair, not wanting to stand out anymore than she already did as a badly dressed sophomore.

As soon as class ended, Lucy tried to push her way toward Charlie, the one familiar face she'd seen—but before she could even say hi, Charlie was swallowed up in a sea of rushing students and was gone.

The next morning, Lucy was drinking coffee at the kitchen table, trying desperately to wake up. She grabbed the Sports section of the *L.A. Times*, to read an article about the U.S. women's soccer team. Lucy had been obsessed with them since she was a little girl. Her mom had even taken her to an exhibition game against Norway for her birthday. She'd seen the soccer documentary *Dare to Dream*—about the 1999 U.S. World Cup Championship team—at least twenty-five times, and it still made her cry. The team's 2007 World Cup loss to Brazil stung, but watching Marta play had been amazing.

Running late, she stuffed the article into her backpack and remembered it during the middle of English, when Martie was giving a particularly boring lecture about the pluperfect tense. Putting it inside her binder, she pretended to be taking notes as she read about her old favorite players—hall of famers Mia Hamm and Julie Foudy . . . just reading the names took her back to another place and time, almost like a fairy tale, where the underdogs beat the odds and came out on top.

She scanned the article, soaking up every description and word until—

"Lucy!" Martie scolded.

Lucy's head jerked up. She wasn't sure whether or not she'd been officially caught. Martie approached quickly, too quickly for Lucy to successfully hide the article. And in an instant, Martie had snatched it up. Everyone saw. Lucy sank down in her seat—her new go-to position following any and all things humiliating—and spent the rest of class ferociously taking notes.

After class, she quickly gathered her books. Martie approached, article in hand.

"So . . . you like soccer?" she asked, almost suspiciously.

Lucy nodded. "I'm sorry about that. It's just, the U.S. team got a bunch of new players—"

"I know," Martie said excitedly. "That senior recruit from Huntington, right?"

Lucy smiled, impressed. "Yeah, the forward."

"I read it this morning. In the middle of our morning meeting," Martie admitted. "I was busted too." Lucy laughed. She didn't feel so bad now. "So, do you play? Soccer?"

Lucy nodded. "I used to. Back home in Toledo."

"You play freshman?" Martie asked, trying to gauge Lucy's skills.

"Varsity," Lucy admitted, a hint of pride in her voice. She'd been the only freshman who'd made the team that year.

"You know, tryouts are starting on Monday . . ." Martie hinted.

*Tryouts?* It hadn't even occurred to Lucy to think about joining the Beachwood team. She'd been so upset about the move, and so fixated on not looking like a dork, that she'd forgotten a part of her life that she loved could actually come with her. *Soccer.*

"Really?" Lucy asked. "I'd be able to?"

"Of course," Martie encouraged. "We'd love to have you. We only have a varsity team this year—we kind of spent last year rebuilding our program, recruiting new players. . . ."

"Winning state," Charlie added as she walked by, her backpack slung carelessly over one shoulder.

"Thanks, in part, to the extraordinary efforts of a certain forward," Martie indicated, putting a hand on Charlie's shoulder as she looked at Lucy. "Seriously, it'd be great to have you try out. If you're interested. And it's a good way to make new friends, too."

Lucy smiled. That sounded like music to her ears.

"That'd be . . . um . . ." She caught Charlie's eye and tried to avoid the words *really* and *cool*. She thought for a second. "That'd be totally awesome."

Charlie laughed and Lucy beamed. Suddenly, she was feeling more confident. Maybe she was getting better at this whole California thing after all.

## three

Lucy had been counting down the days and minutes to soccer tryouts. By the time Monday rolled around she was so excited, she popped out of bed, not even needing coffee to wake up.

"Someone's excited for school," her dad said as he buttered toast for the two of them.

"Soccer tryouts today," she reminded him. "You know what that means?"

He considered. "Practices, games, a lot of smelly Adidas shorts and dirt stuck in your cleats—"

"It means *friends*," Lucy interrupted. "If I make this team, I may actually make a friend."

"Knowing you, Lucy? You'll make a bunch."

Lucy held up her fingers. They were crossed. She really hoped so.

When she showed up on the field after school that day, she was happy to see a few familiar faces. Not that she had ever spoken to anyone besides Charlie, but there was Pickle from her gym class and a few other girls she recognized.

"Gather around, everyone," Martie said. The girls formed a semicircle around her. "I'd like to welcome back all our returning players and introduce myself and the team to those of you trying out." All the wannabe walk-ons looked around, hopeful, as the teammates from last year clustered together, already close. They seemed more like sisters in many ways than friends.

"Last year's state win was incredible," Martie recounted, giving the potential players an idea of what they had to look forward to. "Especially because we came from nothing, came out of nowhere to win. Now, this year, we have a reputation to uphold. We have a title to defend. We won't be under the radar anymore. Everyone's going to be gunning for us, so we're going to have to work harder than ever. And that hard work starts with . . . ?" She paused for the team to fill in the blank.

All the old players chimed in together. "Hell Week."

Lucy looked around, nervous. *Hell Week*? She'd never been part of any Hell Week back in Ohio—except the week of studying for midterms and finals.

"Hell Week's where the real fun begins." Martie smiled.

The next afternoon, Lucy found out that Martie's definition of "fun" was cruel, hard, endless torture. The girls headed up from the locker room after school, to meet in the parking lot behind the athletic field house. Together, they hopped in a van to drive to the beach. Lucy was the last to climb in and shut the door.

On the ride over, all the girls talked ninety miles an hour, about everything from what teen star was following Lindsay Lohan and Britney Spears' foray into rehab to a sale at ZJ's Boarding House they wanted to check out. Pickle was listening raptly to a story Heather was telling, about one of the football parties two years ago where some guy had tried to jump off the roof into the pool. Heather was a senior this year and had shoulder-length golden hair with corkscrew curls.

"God, why don't we ever get invited to those?" Pickle asked wistfully.

"Because we play soccer, not football," Jamie reminded her. "Football players and cheerleaders *only*."

Charlie rolled her eyes. "I'm glad they're willingly containing themselves. Then we don't have to worry about running into them on Friday nights." It was no secret that Charlie wasn't a huge fan of that crowd.

"Still . . ." Pickle sighed. "It'd be nice to see what the big deal is."

"Casey Peterson's D-cups," a cute brunette, Erica, piped in. "That's always the biggest deal at those parties. The guys throw quarters in her cleavage and she keeps the change."

"No way!" Max, a freshman spitfire, exclaimed. Max had short, choppy, bleached blond hair and just looked tough. Lucy had figured out that Max was short for

Maxine, when she saw the tryout roster.

"Not that I don't want to talk about Casey's D-cups the whole drive," a pretty Hispanic junior named Carla said. "But did anyone see *Real World* last night?" Her deep brown eyes sparkled as if she'd just received good news.

On the front bench of the van, Lucy spun around. She loved that show!

Forgetting her shyness, she rattled off a list of highlights that had the entire van of girls enraptured.

"And then Tucker said Marlo should just go back where she came from. The gutter!" Lucy quoted.

"He did not say that!" Heather gasped. "He's so homophobic, anyway."

"And obviously closeted," Jamie pointed out. "No one protests that much."

"I know." Lucy laughed. "It's like the same thing every season."

Carla giggled. "I know. I love it."

Pickle leaned over the seat, adding her two cents. "By the end, Tyler and Jason'll be making out."

"I'm so sick of that show," Erica complained. "I'm seriously not watching anymore."

"You say that every season," Heather pointed out.

"At least you're allowed to watch it," a sophomore redhead, Ruthie, chirped from the front seat. "My mom won't let me. Can you believe that? No MTV?"

Max recoiled. "No MTV? That's, like, globally unfair."

Lucy giggled and Max looked at her for confirmation. "I mean, it is, right? Does she even let you google?"

As Ruthie explained, Lucy listened and relaxed a little, genuinely enjoying herself for the first time in a long time. It was fun to be around these girls. Lucy hoped she'd be around them for a long time to come.

That all changed once they arrived at the beach. While the girls were still fun, practice was not. Martie announced they were going for a short three-mile run.

"Is that an oxymoron?" Erica asked. "Short? Three miles?"

"*You're* an oxymoron," Heather countered playfully, as Erica fake-punched her in the arm.

Karen, a pretty blond senior, scoffed. "Heather, that didn't even make any sense!"

As the girls took off running, Lucy took her place securely at the back of the pack, where she struggled to keep up. Her lungs felt as though they were going to explode; running on sand was about a million times more difficult than running on cement. Somehow Lucy made it through, coming in third to last, which was a small victory. At least she wasn't the very slowest.

After the run, Martie prepared to take them through various drills.

"Can someone grab the bag of balls?" she asked purposefully.

"I will," Karen offered. "Or maybe Heather should. She

loves to grab the balls."

A bunch of the girls snickered. Clearly, they enjoyed ribbing each other and giving each other a hard time. Charlie and Carla exchanged amused looks, trying not to laugh . . . but it was hard not to.

Karen's comment elicited a very real punch from Heather.

"Ow!" Karen yelped. "That seriously hurt!" She nailed Heather back in the arm.

"Girls!" Martie said sternly, and Karen instantly snapped to attention. Lucy giggled. Heather grabbed the balls and the girls composed themselves as Martie explained what they were doing next. Of course, when she said, "We'll do various touches on balls," everyone— Lucy included— burst out laughing again.

But soon, Lucy was hard at work, focusing on the ball in front of her as she tried to follow Martie's footwork instructions. Running behind Carla and Charlie, Lucy dribbled around orange cones in as fast and controlled a manner as possible . . . and then came the trapping drills.

Lucy *hated* trapping. Using her body to stop a ball careening toward her wasn't really at the top of her to-do list. In fact, it was a giant "to-don't" ever since she'd been nailed in the chest by a soccer ball three years ago. To this day she blamed that incident as the reason her boobs had failed to grow past A-cups.

Now, as a punt came right toward her, she backed up,

letting it fall to her feet rather than stopping it with her body.

"Lucy, go to it," Martie ordered. "You don't back away!"

*I do,* Lucy thought. But instead she just mumbled, "Sorry." She hoped Martie wasn't making a mental note of that weakness—but then she saw Martie taking literal notes. *Crap!* Had she noticed how many extra mountain climbers and push-ups Lucy had done? Had she written that down on her yellow pad? By the end of practice, Lucy was too tired to worry about it.

When she arrived home that night, thanks to a ride from Charlie, her eyelids were so heavy she was barely able to make her way from the car to her bedroom. She collapsed on the bed without eating dinner, doing her homework . . . or, worse, calling Annie. When her dad came in to ask how practice had gone, she could barely muster a response. All she could think about was sleep, but once she finally drifted off, she even dreamed of soccer.

The next morning at breakfast, when she was well rested and more alert, she gave her dad a rundown of the girls on the team.

"There's Charlie," Lucy explained. "She's the surfer I told you about. From the beach that day. She's kind of what Mom would call a tough cookie, you know? Like, hard to get to know. I guess she had this older sister, Krista, who graduated—and was totally best friends with Brooks Sheridan!"

From her dad's blank expression, he had no idea who that was.

"You know, Brooks Sheridan? The actress? She had all those straight-to-DVD movies? Remember *Girl for Sale*? And then Mom got me the sequel, *Boy for Sale*? Anyway, I guess Charlie and her sister were, like, the big stars of the team last year and now that Krista's gone, Charlie's the leader. Along with Carla . . ." Lucy told her dad how Carla was from East L.A. and commuted all the way to Malibu in order to play soccer and have a better education. "She was recruited, like, handpicked by Martie last year and got this, like, mondo scholarship—"

"Mondo?" her dad questioned. "Wow. You've already been living in California way too long."

Lucy kept going. "Charlie and Carla are funny together. They're kind of opposites—Charlie's, like, dark and sarcastic, while Carla's totally optimistic and, like, super-positive. Then there's Pickle. Her real name's Nicole, but everyone, like, calls her Pickle. She's a sophomore too—we have, like, three classes together—"

"What's with all the 'like's?" her dad asked.

Lucy sighed. "Do you want me to tell you or not?"

"No, no, go ahead," her dad urged, then added, "minus the likes."

Lucy glared, then continued. "Well, I heard she—Pickle—

was cut from the team last year. She tried out as a goalie, but then she played on this league all summer, as a fullback, and now she's trying out on the field. So it's cool because we're, like—" She stopped abruptly, realizing she'd said "like" again. "Sorry," she said quickly, then continued. "So we're both defenders—me and Pickle—"

"Pickle and I," her dad corrected.

"Pickle and *I*," Lucy emphasized. "And we get to practice together. I'm just happy because maybe we'll get to be friends or something. Oh, and there's Max."

"Max?" her dad questioned.

"Short for Maxine. She seems pretty cool, too." Just up from eighth grade, Max had been recruited by Martie this summer. With her short blond hair and slightly rebellious attitude, Max had so much confidence, she could even make the senior girls laugh. Lucy couldn't help but be awed by the younger girl's lack of intimidation—and by what a strong player she was. Every shot on goal that Max took, she made. Not to mention, she was *fast*. Max had been clinically diagnosed as hyperactive, although Lucy wondered if that was due to the twenty Pixy Stix she consumed daily.

"Well it sounds like this team was just what you needed, kid," her dad said, pleased, as he helped himself to more coffee.

Lucy nodded. "Yeah, I think it is." As she scooted her cup closer for a refill and watched her dad pour, she decided that the glass—or in this case, coffee mug—was definitely looking half full.

That afternoon, Martie divided the girls up into teams in order to scrimmage. Lucy was placed on a team led by Carla, as were Karen, Heather, and Jamie, who was an amazing senior defender. Lucy played stopper, nearly the last line of defense before the goalie, a position that always felt like it came with a lot of pressure—probably because it did.

Twice the other side scored, and both times, Lucy felt responsible. Carla instructed her to get more aggressive. "Don't wait to go to the ball!" she ordered. "Step up!"

Lucy was caught off guard by Carla's intensity. She'd expected that kind of tone to come from Charlie. She nodded obediently. "I know. Sorry."

Carla softened a little. "Listen, just clear it. If it gets anywhere near the box, just clear it!" She patted Lucy on the back. "You got this, okay? I'm being hard on you because I want you on the team."

Lucy nodded, blinking back tears. She knew Carla was just trying to help. She reminded herself that she could do this. That she needed to be aggressive. She remembered when she was eleven and scared to learn to snowboard. Her mom, a great skier, had stayed with her as she learned, encouraging her the entire time. As Lucy had taken face-plant after face-plant and had begun to cry, Lucy's mom had told her, "You're Tough Lucy! Tough Lucy doesn't cry.

She gets back up. She tries it again." By the end of the day, Lucy was not only staying up on her snowboard, she was actually turning!

Now, on the soccer field, Lucy told herself to be Tough Lucy. This time, when Charlie passed the ball across the field, in Max's direction, Lucy sprinted forward. This ball was hers to clear. In one swift motion, she booted the ball, hard. It soared past half field, traveling at least thirty-five yards, right into the feet of Heather, her one open teammate. Heather trapped it perfectly.

On the sidelines, Martie was stunned. Even the other girls gave Lucy a look.

"Whoa," Carla gasped. "Nice leg."

"And nice aim," Carla added.

Lucy beamed proudly. After a rough start, she felt like she'd finally shown Martie what she could do. Now she just needed to do it about fifty more times.

After practice, Lucy considered calling her dad for a ride, but knowing he was working late all week, she suspected she'd be waiting outside school for a while. She saw Charlie, Carla, Pickle, and Max walking to Charlie's car and could hear their conversation.

"Come on!" Pickle pleaded. "In-N-Out."

"But I want a salad," Charlie complained. "What about CPK? Then Max can get pizza." Max only ate things coated in cheese.

"What about Chili's?" Max said. "I could get chips and

queso, then nachos, then broccoli-cheddar soup. . . ."

"You are seriously disgusting," Charlie commented.

Carla noticed Lucy sitting on a bench by herself. She nudged Charlie in the side. "Hey Lucy," Carla called out. "Want to come get some dinner with us? We're going to Baja Fresh!"

"Really?" Lucy asked happily.

"No!" Pickle said. "Baja *again*? What, just because you're Latina, you can only eat Mexican food?"

"Hey." Carla shrugged. "I like to support the cause. Besides, a burrito sounds so freaking awesome."

"I'm in," Max agreed. "I'm gonna get mine covered in cheese."

"No Mexican," Pickle begged. "Come on . . ."

"Yeah," Charlie agreed, and then turned to Lucy who had walked over with her book bag and soccer bag. Charlie folded her arms across her chest. "What do you want for dinner? Mexican or something else?"

Lucy looked from Charlie and Pickle to Max and Carla. They were all waiting expectantly. "Um—I don't know . . ." Lucy said, meekly. She hated being in this position. Here people were actually being nice to her, but there was no way to make everyone happy. "Mexican's fine with me. . . ."

Charlie and Pickle threw their hands up in the air.

"Or not," Lucy quickly said. "I'll eat anywhere . . . or anything. . . ."

Suddenly, she noticed a car pull into the parking lot. It was her dad's Toyota Highlander Hybrid, the new car he'd purchased a few days ago. It was not nearly as flashy as the red convertible but more practical and environmentally friendly.

"Oh," she sighed, disappointed. "That's my dad. I guess I can't go to dinner after all. . . ."

Her dad pulled up and came to a stop but kept the car running. He rolled down the window. "I'm in kind of a hurry, Luce. I have a meeting I have to get back for. . . ." He gave a wave to the other girls.

Lucy turned to them. "Well, I'll see you tomorrow. Thanks again for the invite."

She hopped into her dad's car. "Did those girls invite you somewhere?"

Lucy shrugged, not wanting to complicate things. "Oh, not really," she said. "Just dinner. But I have a lot of homework. And besides, that way we can eat together."

"Oh," her dad said slowly. "I just—I have to get back for that meeting. Maybe we could pick something up really quick. What's good around here?" He thought for a minute. "Maybe Mexican?"

Lucy sat back in her seat, trying not to cringe at the irony. "Yeah, Mexican's great."

That night, Lucy realized she was in bad shape. She'd rolled her ankle but the trainer said it wasn't a sprain. She just needed to ice it. In fact, she decided, she needed an ice bath for her entire body. Her quads and hamstrings hurt from running up the sand dunes at the beach. Now she could barely walk up the spiral staircase to her loft without leaning at least half of her one-hundred-and-fifteen-pound frame on the railing. Her chest and triceps ached so badly from the push-up and reverse push-up drills that she cringed even when she was lifting a Diet Coke to her lips.

But still, the next day, as she changed in the locker room, with the buzz of the girls' conversations swirling around her, she couldn't believe she'd ever considered *not* playing soccer—even if every part of her body hurt. As she strapped on her shin guards and wrapped the laces of her cleats around the bottom of her shoes and double-knotted them, she reveled in this feeling. It was as if she was putting on armor that would make her invincible.

As she headed upstairs and outside, the sunlight felt warm on her face, and the smell of freshly cut grass engulfed her. It was better than the smell of bread baking or the smell of laundry detergent. This smell reminded her of everything she loved about soccer.

Of course, moments later, as the team ran suicide sprints, Lucy remembered what she hated about soccer. She could feel the sweat pouring off her as she ran from the white end line to the eighteen on the field, trying her best to keep up with the pack. Running, like trapping, was not her strong suit.

Martie cheered encouragingly. "Okay, girls. Now to midfield."

The girls quickly turned at the end line. Some ran while others jogged to the midfield line. Carla and Charlie had already hit the line and were running past Lucy in the opposite direction.

"You got it, Lucy," Carla shouted out.

"Thanks," Lucy gasped as she stayed tight on the heels of Jamie, who trailed right behind Pickle.

"Let's go, Lucy. Come on," Charlie said breathlessly as she passed.

As Lucy jogged back toward the end line, Charlie's encouragement made her push even harder. Sweat dripped into her eyes, stinging them. This was about more than just soccer. This was about not sitting alone at lunch or getting picked last in gym class. If she made this team, she'd be automatically accepted into a group of twenty girls, anxious to embrace her as one of their own. She'd have friends. They wouldn't be Annie or any other of the girls she'd known for practically her entire life, but at least she wouldn't be alone.

Lucy picked up her pace as she ran across the full length of the field. She didn't care how many suicide sprints she had to do, or how many squat jumps, or how many times she'd have to stop the ball with her chest. She was going to make this team if it killed her.

## four

On Friday, Lucy felt as though things were definitely looking up—with soccer, with school, with everything. She'd finally figured out the trick to getting her frequently jammed locker open (kicking it three times in the lower right-hand corner) and she knew the fastest way to all her classes—sometimes going outside and walking around the periphery of the school was actually better than trying to weave her way through the crowded hallways.

In study hall, Lucy sat down at a table in the cafeteria by herself. She took out *Madame Bovary* so she'd look engrossed in something. Suddenly, Benji, the Afro'd kid from gym, slid into one of eight open seats at her table.

"This seat taken?" he joked.

Lucy smiled. "Uh . . . let me think. . . ." She paused, then answered, "No."

As he sat, she noticed he was wearing a football jersey. "Whose back did you steal that off?" she joked, playfully because really, Benji didn't exactly fit the mold of your stereotypical football player.

"Very funny," he said sarcastically.

"Wait . . ." Lucy realized. "Are you actually on the team?"

"Yeah," he admitted. "I'm on the team. You're not the only hard-core athlete around here. I've seen you out on the soccer field."

"I wouldn't exactly call myself hard-core," she confessed.

"Maybe medium-core?" Benji offered.

"Is that like medium rare?" Lucy joked, taking a sip of her Diet Coke.

Benji gave her a funny look. "Do you even know what we're talking about right now?"

Lucy giggled. "I have no idea." She liked how sweet and friendly he was. Funny, too.

Benji smiled. "So, how're you enjoying gym class?" he asked. "Dodgeball to your liking?"

Lucy shrugged. "What's not to like about standing against a wall waiting to be decapitated by a girl who looks like a corpse?"

"Are you talking about Morbid? The emo chick from class?" Benji stood up. "Come with me to the vending machine?"

Lucy stood and followed him. They continued their conversation. "What's her deal? I'm not gonna lie—she kind of freaks me out."

"Don't let her. Her real name's Nancy." Benji inserted

quarters. "After you. We'll share."

Lucy surveyed her options. "Thanks." She pressed B3 for Doritos. Forget Cool Ranch. Nacho Cheese were her favorite.

Benji shoved a few more quarters in and looked back at Lucy. "Anything else?"

She pressed D4. A Twix dropped down. Benji handed it to her and gave her the lowdown on Morbid.

"Last year," he explained, "she was obsessed with plaid skirts, and white button-downs tied under her boobs, and pigtails. It was very Britney circa 1999. Then, apparently, over the summer, she started wearing all black and changed her name to Morbid."

"Weird," Lucy commented as they sat back down.

"And she's not even the weirdest," Benji pointed out. "Let's see, at Beachwood, you've got the classics: your jocks, cheerleaders, band geeks, burnouts . . . then it gets a little tricky. You've also got the crunchy granolas, the Wiccan freaks, and, weirder than the emos, the emo wannabes. You've got your divas, your di*vos*, then your syrup heads—"

Lucy took a wild guess. "Kids who like pancakes?"

Benji shook his head. "Kids who down cough syrup like it's Red Bull." Lucy pushed the Doritos toward him. He popped a chip into his mouth, then dug into the Twix. Lucy had already eaten her half.

"So . . . big plans tonight?" he asked.

She considered thoughtfully. In the two weeks she'd

lived in Malibu, she'd had a total of zero plans. "I don't really have plans," she admitted.

"Well, you know, it's our season opener tonight. Our first home game—" Suddenly, the bell rang. Study hall was over. "If you want to come, there's a party after at Ryan's. . . ."

Lucy gulped. "Wait. *Ryan* Ryan?" As in, CUTE Ryan from English class?

Benji continued. "Yeah, there're always parties after games. Usually just the cheerleaders and football players, but we can invite people. You could even bring some of your friends. You know, whatever . . ."

*Some of her friends?* Unless Annie could make it from Toledo, she didn't know who she'd ask.

"I only joined the team this year," Benji explained. "So I don't really fit in with that whole football crowd yet. . . ."

Lucy had the feeling that even if Benji were on the team for a million years, he still wouldn't fit in with that crowd.

"Here, just call me if you're coming," Benji said, grabbing her cell phone. He quickly programmed his number in and then called his own phone so he'd have her number as well.

"That'd be great." Lucy smiled. The bell rang again, and together, they rushed out of the cafeteria doors.

"We could meet after the game. I could drive you over there and then drive you home," he said hurriedly, as they were swallowed up by a sea of students.

"Yeah," Lucy said excitedly. "That'd be great. The party sounds awesome." And the fact that it was at Ryan's was even more awesome.

As Benji smiled and took off in the opposite direction, Lucy saw Max and Pickle at their lockers. Suddenly, she had an idea. She'd overheard Pickle talking about how much she wanted to go to a football party. Here was a chance to make her dream come true!

"Hey, you guys," Lucy said as she approached them.

Pickle turned around. "Hey, Lucy." She smiled.

"Um . . . I know we don't know each other that well yet . . . so I hope it's not weird, you know, that I'm asking this but—would you want to go to Ryan's party tonight?" she asked tentatively, then turned to Max. "Both of you?"

Pickle and Max's jaws dropped practically in unison.

"Are you serious?" Pickle gasped.

Max looked confused. "I thought those parties were only for football players and cheerleaders." She downed a grape Pixy Stick. Her tongue was chronically purple.

"Yeah," Pickle agreed. "Everyone says it's invite-only."

Lucy nodded. "I know. But Benji just invited me and said I could bring whoever I wanted."

Pickle threw down her backpack in mock annoyance. "Seriously, I'm going to kick that boy's ass. Why didn't he invite *me?*"

Lucy couldn't help but be surprised. "Are you and Benji friends?" she asked.

"*Just* friends," Pickle admitted. "That was kind of the problem." Pickle explained that last year Benji'd had a serious crush on her. "He's such a sweet guy. But kind of the type of guy you're friends with. Not the type of guy you date."

Lucy nodded, sort of getting it. Benji had that chronic "I just want to be friends" vibe. Pickle had probably broken his heart and he was still bummed about it.

"Well, what d'ya say? You guys want to come with?" Lucy asked.

Pickle thought quickly. "Well, Charlie was gonna drive us to the game . . . but maybe she could pick you up too and we could all go to the game together. . . ."

"But Charlie won't want to go to the party," Max interrupted. "No way."

"Why?" Lucy asked. "She knows she's a lock on the team." Tomorrow was the final day of Hell Week, when all the decisions would be made. They all needed to get a good night's sleep.

"It's not because of tryouts," Pickle said, biting her lip. Max nodded knowingly. Lucy wasn't sure what they were talking about. Suddenly, she had an idea.

"I bet Benji would drive us to the party and then home after," she offered. "And seriously, bring as many friends as you want—whoever!"

Pickle clapped her hands together. "Awesome! This is so cool!" She pounced on Lucy and engulfed her in a giant hug. "You're the greatest!"

Lucy beamed, glancing from an elated Pickle to a suddenly worried Max.

"What's wrong?" Pickle asked, noticing too.

Max sighed. "I just need to figure out what to do about my parents. . . ."

Suddenly, the color drained out of Lucy's face. She'd been so excited at the prospect of winning over Pickle and Max that she'd forgotten about one huge obstacle that came in the form of a 6', one-hundred-and-ninety-pound man: *her dad.*

"You are *not* going to a party thrown by someone you don't know and whom I have never even met," her dad said sternly as they were eating dinner in front of the television. Her mom never allowed them to eat anywhere but the kitchen or dining room table. And certainly never in front of the TV. But it was Friday night in the Malone house, and rules were relaxed. Well, some of them.

"Why not?" Lucy whined. She had a precautionary ice bag over each ankle and was propped up on the couch.

Her dad responded matter-of-factly. "Because you're fifteen years old."

"I'm almost sixteen!" she pleaded. "I'll be sixteen in two months! What's the difference?"

"The difference is, you can go to parties like that when you're sixteen. And I talk to the parents first."

Lucy threw down her napkin. One of the ice bags fell to the floor. "It doesn't make any sense! This is, like, globally unfair!" she complained, repeating what she'd heard Max say in the van.

Her dad looked at her oddly. "I don't even know what that means."

Lucy tried to remain calm. She wanted to scream, *It means you're totally ruining my life!* But instead she simply said, "Dad, look. People are counting on me—you really expect me to tell them I can't go because I'm fifteen and ten months?"

"See?" her dad said. "You do get it." Lucy threw her hands in the air, exasperated. "Luce, you can go to the game with your friends tonight and then be home when it's done. How long does a high school game take? A couple of hours?"

Lucy had no idea. She didn't know the first thing about football. All she knew about it was that there was a game tonight . . . and she was supposed to be there.

"But Dad . . ." she protested. She couldn't believe this. She wished her mom were there to talk some sense into him. Like the time when her dad didn't think she was old enough for sleepaway camp. Or the time Billy Miller asked her out on a group date to a movie and her dad said no. Her mom had told her dad that they were going out for a girls' dinner and instead had taken Lucy to the movies to meet Billy and her friends. Sure, her mom stayed and watched the movie too, but from the opposite side of the theater, far enough away that she couldn't tell Lucy and Billy were holding hands. Or maybe she could. Either way, she'd let Lucy go, and that was the point. Her dad was *never* going to let her go . . . anywhere!

"Why do you get to make all the decisions?" Lucy protested. She took a deep breath and mustered her courage. "If Mom were here . . ." She barely got half of the sentence out before her dad grabbed the remote and turned up the volume on *CSI*-something. New York, Miami, Topeka— whatever.

Lucy sighed. She should have known that strategy wouldn't work. Any mention of her mom seemed to make her dad shut down.

"Fine," Lucy said sullenly. She dropped her plate on the coffee table, grabbed her ice bags, and hobbled to her room, slamming her bedroom door for emphasis.

Miserable, she collapsed onto her bed. She couldn't just sit here and do nothing! Pickle and Max were counting on her for this party. She wasn't going to let them down.

An hour later, Lucy stood in a pile of clothes, having taken everything out of boxes. Now her entire wardrobe was scattered around her bedroom. After two emergency phone calls with Annie, she'd come up with a plan.

"Haven't you ever heard of car trouble?" Annie had asked. "I mean, it's not your fault if Benji gets a flat, right?"

"Wrong. My dad's gonna see right through that," Lucy complained. She was a terrible liar.

"Okay, it's simple. After the game, just go to the party. You can get Pickle and Max settled—what's with these names, by the way?—then as soon as they're good, you can sneak out." It was a good idea, but Annie was forgetting one thing.

"Well, how am I supposed to get home?" Lucy challenged.

Annie sighed. "Does California not have cabs?"

Lucy laughed. "Oh, right."

"What would you do without me?" Annie asked. "You'd be so lost."

"No, I'd just ask the cab driver," Lucy joked. She hadn't wanted to admit that she *was* totally lost without her best friend. And that she didn't even care that much about the party, Ryan or no Ryan. What she cared about most was having someone to go to the party *with*.

And now, thanks to Annie, she had the perfect plan; what she needed next was the perfect outfit. Jeans? A skirt? A cute little sundress? Nothing seemed right for her first Friday night out in California.

Suddenly, she heard a honk out front. Charlie and the girls were already there! She quickly threw on a faded pair of jeans and a tight red Urban Outfitters T-shirt that read

LITTLE MISS TROUBLE, and wrapped a long, glittery pink scarf around her neck. Perfect or not, it would have to do.

It was halfway through the fourth quarter (apparently there were four quarters in football), and the home crowd had just erupted in cheers as Beachwood scored against Madison. And now, according to Pickle's play-by-play explanations, Beachwood had closed a big gap.

"We're only trailing by nine!" Pickle yelled. "We can win this!" Cheering wildly next to Lucy, Pickle seemed to personify school spirit and enthusiasm. "Go Beachwood!" she shrieked. "We got this!"

Max and Lucy exchanged amused glances. Charlie, Carla, and a few other girls from the team sat on the bleachers right below them.

"Who's hungry?" Charlie asked. Then she said dryly, "Oh, right—me." Carla laughed and interlaced her arm through Charlie's.

"I could eat," she said. "Something warm. I swear, it's fifteen degrees colder at the beach than in my neighborhood."

As Charlie and Carla headed to the snack stand, Max turned to the girls. "Hey, if we don't make the soccer team, maybe we should go out for cheerleading."

Pickle hit her lightly in the arm. "Don't even think it!" she warned. "We are *so* making the team."

Lucy laughed as the girls' playful argument was drowned

out by the marching band playing in the stands. There was one tuba that sounded so off, Lucy wondered if its owner was actually playing a different song. She tilted her head to get a better look at the cheerleaders who stood on the track that encircled the field, as they gyrated and thrust their hips. Lucy couldn't help but be mildly impressed.

She recognized Regan, the *whatever* girl, leading the charge. A few of the second-string players on the bench seemed more interested in Regan than in the game.

"Regan Holder," Pickle pointed out. "She's a barracuda in lipstick. Avoid her like the plague."

"She's in my English class," Lucy mentioned. "Do you know her?"

"All I know," Pickle whispered as she leaned in close to Lucy, "is that Charlie hates her guts. You can't even spell Regan's name around Charlie without smoke coming out of her ears. . . ." Suddenly, Pickle noticed something on the field. "Interception! Woo-hoo!" she cheered, bouncing up and down.

"What happened with Charlie and Regan?" Lucy asked when the crowd noise had quieted down.

"I don't know the whole deal, because I wasn't at Beachwood yet," Pickle continued, "but I guess they were best friends for, like, ever, and then one day, Regan just kind of dropped Charlie."

Lucy wanted to hear more but stopped talking so she could watch Ryan—gorgeous, even wearing his football helmet—throw a fifteen-yard pass on the field. *Mrs. Lucy Conner*, Lucy thought. It had a certain ring to it.

"Hey." Pickle nudged Lucy in the side. "I think he likes you."

Lucy's eyes widened. "What? Really?" she asked. On the field, Beachwood was going to attempt a thirty-yard field goal to tie the game.

"Yeah," Pickle said. "Look how he's staring." Lucy glanced around, confused. Ryan wasn't even facing in her direction. And suddenly, she figured out what Pickle meant. She was talking about Benji, who was looking right at her.

He gave her an inconspicuous wave. Both Pickle and Lucy happily waved back.

"He doesn't like me," Lucy protested. "He's just being friendly."

Pickle shrugged. "Whatever you say."

At that moment, the whole crowd groaned. Benji and the girls simultaneously turned their attention back toward the field. It was fourth down, and Beachwood's placekicker, Matt, had approached the ball for an attempted field goal at the thirty-five-yard line but had been cut down by a player on the other team.

"That's roughing!" Beachwood's coach screamed, irate. "Roughing the kicker!"

"Fifteen-yard penalty to Madison," the referee announced. "Automatic first down, Beachwood."

"What just happened?" Lucy asked. She knew next to nothing about football.

"Because of the penalty, we move up to Madison's twenty," Pickle explained. "You have to move at least ten yards in four tries, then their team gets the ball. If you do ten yards or more—you get four *new* tries to move again. You're only on your first down," Pickle explained. She paused. "Is any of this making sense?"

Lucy shook her head. "Not really." Luckily, she didn't have to understand pass plays and yard lines. She needed to know throw-ins and corner kicks.

"Coach!" one of the Beachwood players suddenly yelled from the field. "Matt's hurt! He's hurt bad!"

Lucy saw Matt, Beachwood's kicker, lying in a heap, gripping his knee. Coaches rushed the field. The crowd waited breathlessly. The guys on the bench strained to see. The same trainer that worked with the soccer team knelt down beside Matt, trying to assess the injury. He waved toward the sidelines, and within seconds, a medical team ran onto the field with a stretcher. Matt was carefully loaded on. As he was carried off, the crowd respectfully applauded.

"Matt Alexander," the announcer's voice boomed. Again, the crowd cheered. Charlie and Carla returned and took their seats in the stands.

"That sucks," Carla muttered in front of them as she stuffed the rest of a hot dog into her mouth. "Can you even imagine?"

"Dude, if he tore his ACL," Charlie said, dipping a corn chip into warm cheddar cheese, "stick a fork in him. He's done."

Carla shook her head sympathetically. "Poor guy."

"Poor Beachwood, too," Pickle commented. "We don't have another decent kicker. This is bad."

"So what does that mean for the game?" Lucy asked.

"It means Madison's probably going to run out the clock and win."

There was a glimmer of hope when, with two minutes to go, Beachwood's defensive tackle picked up a loose ball and managed to run it back to Madison's twenty-five-yard line. But on the next three plays with three incomplete passes thanks to an aggressive Madison defense, Beachwood needed to go for three points in one last attempt to win the game.

With Matt hurt, the coach had no choice but to put in Benji to go for the field goal. The tension in the stands was palpable. It was the first game of the season. Everyone wanted to win.

Pickle covered her face, unable to even look. "Oh God, here he goes. I can't watch."

Benji jogged out with ten other guys and walked off his steps from the holder. He stood, waiting for the snap. The crowd grew silent. Lucy strained to look over Heather and Jamie's heads. On the call, the ball was snapped back and set up by the holder, as Benji went in for the kick. . . .

Everyone watched as the ball sailed up and up and up . . . and, just as the clock ran out, pinged off the outside of the left goalpost, barely missing the goal, but missing it just the same.

On the sidelines, the coach cursed. "Damn it!" He threw his clipboard onto the grass.

On the field, Benji hung his head. In the stands, Lucy's heart sank. It was over. Beachwood had lost—not only their kicker but the game. The deflated crowd began to disperse. Charlie and Carla headed for the parking lot.

"You guys need a ride?" Charlie asked, then noticed the cheerleaders running for the locker room. "Ugh." Charlie rolled her eyes. "I'm sure they're hurrying to slut it up for some stupid party."

Pickle covered, not wanting to mention that they were hoping to go to the same "stupid party." "Um, that's okay. I think, um . . ." She looked at Max for help, but Max was suddenly engrossed in a Pixy Stick.

Lucy jumped in, saving her. "You have to take Carla all the way home. My dad can pick us up."

"Okay." Charlie shrugged. "See you tomorrow at practice." Pickle waited for Charlie and Carla to leave, then grabbed Lucy's arm.

"Come on, let's go," she said, in a rush to make her way down to Benji on the sidelines. "It's party time!" Lucy and Max followed her to the chain-link fence, which separated the field from the fans, looking for Benji. He was nowhere to be seen.

"I'll find him," Lucy offered. After all, she was the ring-leader of this little plan. She snaked her way through the crowd, searching, but after ten minutes she walked back to Pickle and Max with bad news.

"Well?" Max asked, jumping around to stay warm. Even Southern California got a little cold at night.

"I don't know where he went," Lucy admitted. She pulled out her cell phone to try calling him. But the number just rang and rang. Time passed. The stands and field emptied out.

"Maybe we should wait by the locker room door," Pickle offered. "We could catch him when he comes out."

"Sure," Lucy said. She was open to suggestions. She just felt like an idiot. These girls were waiting and counting on *her*. Where was Benji? It was understandable if he wasn't exactly in the party mood, but would Pickle and Max understand? After all, Lucy had convinced them to come.

After they'd been waiting another twenty minutes with no sign of Benji, Lucy didn't know what to say. "I left him a message that we were coming and needed a ride—I don't know what happened."

"He probably just forgot. I mean, he did blow the game," Max reminded them. "That may be all he's think-ing about."

Pickle sadly agreed. "I'd just never been to one of these parties before. . . ." She trailed off, her voice filled with disappointment.

Lucy looked around, one last time, feeling terrible. "I'm really sorry, you guys."

Pickle looked at her watch. "Tomorrow's the last day of tryouts anyway," she said. "I should just call my mom and have her pick us up," she said matter-of-factly.

Max shrugged. "Yeah, whatever. That's fine."

Pickle turned to Lucy. "Are you okay to get home? Because my mom could probably drive you. . . ."

Lucy shook her head. She didn't want them going out of their way for her. Not after she'd screwed up so monumentally. "Oh no, that's okay. I can just call my dad."

"Okay, well, we'll see you tomorrow then," Pickle said, giving Lucy a small wave. "Don't feel bad about tonight. You know . . . it happens."

Lucy looked down at her shoes and nodded. "Thanks."

Pickle and Max took off toward the front of the school. Lucy stood on the sidewalk, her heart heavy. Here she had been this big talker about getting them into this big party, and she couldn't even get a ride there. Now she felt like a big loser. She opened her cell phone and dialed.

"Hey dad," she said, "the game's over. Could you come pick me up?"

"I thought your friends were bringing you home. What happened?"

"Dad!" she snapped. "I've lived here, what? Two-point-two seconds? I don't have friends yet."

"Lucy?" her dad asked quietly, clearly surprised at her outburst. "What happened?"

"Nothing. I'm sorry," she sighed. And it was true. Thanks to her, absolutely nothing had happened.

It was close to midnight when a *tap, tap, tap* noise woke Lucy up. At first she'd thought it was rain, but then she remembered that it hardly ever rained in Southern California, and when it did, she'd have to worry about her house getting caught in a mudslide and careening into the Pacific Ocean.

She sat up, startled, and opened her phone, using the faint light it provided to make her way to the window.

*Tap, tap, tap* . . . The noise continued sporadically. Her heart raced. Looking through the glass, she made out a dark figure down below. She was a nanosecond away from screaming for her dad, when her eyes adjusted to the dark. Benji was standing below her windowsill. She opened her window.

"What're you doing down there?" Lucy asked, almost laughing. "You just scared me half to death."

From below, Benji gave a wave. "I got your messages. I'm sorry I took off. The game, you know—"

"No, no, it's fine," she assured him. "Are you okay?"

"I didn't feel much like a party," he explained. "For obvious, you know, publicly humiliating reasons."

She shook her head. "It's okay. I wasn't really allowed

to go anyway."

"Well, I just wanted to explain—I didn't want you to think I wasn't interested." He added quickly, "You know, in hanging out with you."

"Oh no, I didn't take it that way," she reassured him. "I know you're interested. I mean, not *interested* interested. But interested in hanging out."

"Right," he said, "I'm interested in a lot of things, now that . . . you know . . . we're friends." Lucy smiled. She liked the sound of being friends.

"How did you know which window was mine?" she asked.

He pointed at the rainbow-colored wind chime hanging from a hook beside the sill.

Lucy smiled. How sweet of Benji to notice that small detail. He playfully tossed another pebble up at the closed window on the other side of her bedroom. Suddenly there was a loud *crack!*

Lucy's eyes widened as a web-shaped fracture formed in the middle of her window. Her father was sure to have heard the noise. Lucy had no idea what he would do if he found a boy outside their house.

"Oh my God!" she panicked. "Go! Run!"

Benji took off at a full sprint. Lucy heard his car start and peel out of their driveway. She hopped back in bed, pulling the covers over her head. Within a minute, her bedroom door opened.

"Luce?" her dad asked, concerned. "You okay, kid?"

"Huh?" Lucy groaned, as if she'd been fast asleep.

"Nothing," he said. "I just . . . thought I'd heard something."

Lucy muttered something incoherent and rolled over, acting as out of it as she possibly could . . . until her dad shut the door. Then she pulled the covers off and crept back to the window, staring at the spot where Benji had been. Her face broke into a wide smile and she spent the rest of the night lying in bed, unable to sleep, just thinking of how fun it was to have a friend who would bother coming all the way over in the middle of the night just to make sure she was okay.

She could at least say it to herself: It felt really, *really* cool.

**five**

Halfway through Saturday's scrimmage, Lucy was seriously hurting. Getting little sleep was definitely taking its toll. Charlie cheered her on.

"Come on, Luce," she said encouragingly. "You got this. Stay on the ball."

Lucy pressed hard, knowing this was her last chance to make a good impression on Martie, who had become more serious as the week continued, knowing she had tough decisions to make.

Lucy won the other team's throw in and trapped the ball between her feet.

"Nice," Martie shouted from the sidelines. "Way to go to it, Luce." Lucy could hear the faint sounds of praise but couldn't let them distract her. She looked for a midfielder to receive her pass. Everyone was guarded.

"Get open," Lucy shouted, searching for a teammate. Her team had the dubious distinction of once again wearing the not-so-flattering, not-so-hygienic red pinnies. Hot.

"Got me! Got me back," Pickle yelled to Lucy from the center of the backfield. Lucy had the ball, and Charlie was fast approaching. Lucy tried to use her body to shield the ball from Charlie, who was relentless in pursuing it. She stole it before Lucy could pass it back to Pickle.

"Stay on her, Luce," Pickle shouted. As sweeper, Pickle was considered the coach of the defenders, constantly shouting out instructions, informing the backfield of what was happening. As Charlie played the ball down the line, Lucy cut across the angle toward the goal, trying to keep Charlie from having a clean shot.

"Switch," Carla shouted to Charlie. Carla and Charlie were both on the opposing team, and the two communicated quickly and effortlessly. They knew each other so well they could practically speak in code. In a clean, swift motion, Charlie drilled the ball to the other side of the field. Pickle jumped up for a header but wasn't quite tall enough. The ball sailed over her. Carla stopped the ball with her knee and easily trapped it at her feet as Charlie made a beeline for the goal.

"Step up, red," Pickle shouted to her teammates, attempting to get Charlie offside, but Lucy barely heard. She was too distracted by her own frustration over the bad pass.

Carla passed the ball to Charlie, who banged it into the corner of the net. Their team was up, three to one.

"Lucy, you could have blocked that shot," Martie scolded. "You gotta stay even with Pickle. That should have been offside."

Lucy looked down at the grass and nodded. The goal

was all her fault. She knew she should never be behind the sweeper. A dumb move like that could mean the difference between winning and losing a game. It could even mean the difference in making it onto this team. Lucy took a deep breath, trying to regain her composure. Pickle ran up, giving her an encouraging slap on the back.

"Keep your head in it, Luce," she said, trying to psych her up. "You got this."

Lucy jogged to her position on the right side of Pickle and told herself the same thing. *Come on,* she thought to herself. *You've got this.*

As the whistle blew, Lucy became more determined than ever to shake off the bad play and show Martie what she was capable of. She just had to. After everything she'd been through, she couldn't fall apart under pressure now. She told herself to keep her head in it, that it was the last practice before the cut. She ran hard on the next fifty-fifty and won the ball.

After tryouts and congratulatory hugs over simply sur- viving Hell Week, all the girls dispersed. Lucy was about to speed-dial her dad when Benji pulled up to the field. He smiled and waved from the driver's seat.

"You got plans?" he called out.

Lucy shook her head no. Benji reached across and opened his passenger-side door. "Well, you do now. Get in."

Within minutes, Benji and Lucy were winding up a

canyon road.

"Where're we going?" Lucy asked.

"It's a surprise," Benji said. "Wait—do you hate surprises?"

Lucy considered. "Well, it depends. I don't like to be, like, caught off guard . . . but I like surprises. Does that make sense?"

"Not at all," Benji said; then he laughed. "Or totally." He turned up Green Day on the radio. Lucy relaxed against the headrest.

"So what's your deal?" he asked. "Actually, wait—don't tell me. I have a knack for reading people."

"Reading people what?" she bantered. "Magazine articles? Newspapers?"

He frowned at her playfully. "Let's see," he considered thoughtfully. "You're a straight-A student. You have an older brother and sister. And your first concert ever was Britney Spears."

"You got one of those things right," Lucy smiled. "I'm an only child. And I got a B last year . . ." She paused. "In sex ed."

Benji cracked up. "I don't know which is more appalling. The B in sex ed or the Britney Spears concert." He turned down the radio a bit. "Okay, your turn. You try reading me."

"Oh God." Lucy blushed. "I don't know. I can't tell that much about people from first impressions."

"First?" Benji gasped. "This is at least our fourth or fifth, I'd say."

"I'm not that good at fifth impressions either," Lucy admitted.

"That's fine," Benji said, turning the car off the road. "Because we're here."

Lucy looked around and realized they were high, high up in the Hollywood Hills. From their parking spot, they could see the entire city.

"What is this?" Lucy asked, as they both got out of his car.

"That is the Valley," Benji explained. "It's even more impressive at night. Have you heard of Mulholland Drive?"

"Is that where we are?" Lucy giggled excitedly. "Oh wow. Annie would freak!"

"Who's Annie?" Benji asked.

Lucy smiled, happy to tell her new friend about her old one. "Annie is my very best friend in the world. . . ."

For the next two hours, Benji and Lucy sat on the hood of his car, telling each other stories about their families and friends and lives, as they looked down at the vast city below. Lucy chatted on, comfortable in a way she hadn't been in a long while.

She had been nervous, so nervous, about the move to L.A., but at that moment, at least for a little while, she thought that everything just might be okay.

•   •   •

"Where have you been?" Lucy's dad asked, panicked, as Lucy walked in the front door, a little after four in the afternoon. "Practice ended at noon!"

Lucy was caught off guard. "Didn't you get my message?" she asked. "I left you a voice mail saying I was with Benji."

"That'd be all well and good," her dad responded, "if I had *any* idea who Benji was!"

*Whoops.* Lucy realized she hadn't really mentioned him. "He's just a friend. From school."

Her dad folded his arms across his chest. "A boyfriend?"

"No!" Lucy recoiled. "I mean, yes. He's a boy. And he's a friend. But he's not a boyfriend!"

"Because you're not old enough to date," he reminded her for the thousandth time. She tried to resist the urge to roll her eyes. Little did he know, she'd already kissed two and a half boys.

"Fine, Dad," she sighed.

"And you have to be more responsible than this, Lucy," he scolded her. "This isn't Toledo."

Lucy looked at him as though he were crazy. Did he really think he had to remind her of that? "Yeah, Dad," she said resignedly. "I know."

He laid down the law. "From now on, I need to know where you are and who you're with at all times."

Lucy grabbed her soccer bag. "Fine. Then you better

up my cell phone minutes, because when I make this team, I plan on going a lot of places." Triumphant, she headed to her room to call Annie and tell her all about Benji and Mulholland Drive.

Monday, at school, Lucy wondered if it were possible for "butterflies" to escalate from a nervous feeling in the pit of her stomach to a chronic condition resulting in her stomach actually turning inside out. Because that's how she felt as she got out of her dad's car and made her way into the school, into the gymnasium, and down the staircase toward the athletic offices. The pit in her stomach felt as wide and as deep as the Grand Canyon; her palms felt sweaty and her tongue felt as though it took up 90 percent of the space in her mouth—which made it hard to swallow. Could a person have an actual allergic reaction to the posting of the soccer list? Because it felt as though she were having one.

As she walked down the hall, a swarm of girls huddled around the sheet of paper that would determine her athletic future. Some girls hugged, others cried, and in the center of it all was Pickle, frozen. With her hair in two little poof balls on her head, she looked particularly young and vulnerable as she stared at the list, wide-eyed. Suddenly, Carla embraced Pickle from behind, lifting her slight body off the ground and spinning her around. Pickle wrapped her arms around Carla's neck and buried her head in her shoulder, tears streaming down her face.

Lucy's jaw dropped in disbelief. *What?* How on earth could Pickle not have made it? She'd worked so hard all summer—she'd been one of the strongest defenders, and she was the most positive, optimistic, encouraging player on the team. Honestly, without Pickle, Lucy wasn't sure she even wanted to play soccer for Beachwood.

She moved toward Pickle, stopping behind Carla and Charlie, who were huddled around her. Over their shoulders, she caught sight of the list. "Nicole Lawson" was the third name from the top. Pickle had, in fact, made it. Lucy turned back to Pickle and saw that she was smiling. Her tears were tears of joy.

"Go Pickle," Lucy said as she patted her new friend's back.

She returned to the list. But as she read through the names, her face fell.

# six

She scanned the list again. Where was "Lucy Malone"?

Surely, there had been a mistake. Martie had practically recruited her. She had convinced her to try out. She wouldn't do that only to leave her off the list. On the bench was one thing, but not even on the team? Lucy read and reread the names. Hers was nowhere to be found.

Suddenly, she felt a hand pat her shoulder. It was Charlie.

"I'm sorry, Lucy," she said softly. "I guess it just wasn't your time."

Lucy's eyes welled up. These were the times she wanted—no, needed—her mom. She blinked back tears.

"Yeah," she answered. "I guess not."

Pickle wrapped her arms around Lucy, her own tears now turning to sad ones. "I can't believe it," she whispered. "You should *so* be on this team."

Lucy shrugged. "Maybe next year, right?"

Pickle smiled, instantly going into cheerleader mode. "Exactly. Next year. You'll do it for sure!"

Lucy tried to keep up a brave face. The truth was, without soccer, without this team, she couldn't imagine making it to next year. As the girls around her celebrated and congratulated each other, Lucy felt lonelier and less a part of anything than she ever had in her entire life.

"Can I talk to you?" Martie asked Lucy, as Lucy hurriedly gathered her books to move on to her next class. So far it had been a pretty crappy morning, and Lucy was willing to bet at least a month's allowance that talking to Martie wasn't going to make it any better. In fact, Martie was the last person Lucy wanted anything to do with.

Lucy had spent the better part of her fifty-minute English class with her arms folded across her chest, giving Martie the evil eye. Not even Ryan lending her a pen could cheer her up. As she listened to Martie drone on about the first few chapters of *Madame Bovary*, she still couldn't believe that the teacher would recruit her and get her hopes up only to cut her.

"I really have to get to bio," Lucy mumbled. She just wanted to disappear. Wasn't there a locker she could hide in? Or a Dumpster?

Martie pressed her lips together. It was obvious she felt terrible. "Look, you're a very talented kicker—we both know that. It's just that some of your other skills could use a little more . . . development."

Lucy had to restrain herself from rolling her eyes.

*Development?* she wanted to scream at Martie. *How am I going to develop if I'm not even playing? By magic? By osmosis, whatever that is?*

Martie kept on. "Like your speed and handling of the ball—you could use a little more work on those." Lucy nodded blankly. She didn't want to hear about handling the ball. She could barely handle this conversation.

"We recruit girls from all over L.A. County. Making this team is extremely difficult. Even the girls who get cut are still head and shoulders above most other high school players."

Lucy's shoulders hunched forward as she stared at her slip-on Converse sneakers, the cool kind without laces. This wasn't making her feel any better. She didn't care about heads or shoulders or other high school players. She cared about her friends back in Toledo. She cared about her old bedroom. She cared about having her name on that list.

"Lucy. You were hands down the best kicker on that field—the best female kicker I've ever seen." She took a deep breath and clasped her hands together. "That's why I have an idea."

The bell rang. It meant Lucy was officially late for bio. "I should go. . . ."

"Don't worry," Martie said quickly. "I'll write you a pass. I wanted to talk to you about something else. It's about the football team."

Lucy's eyebrows furrowed. She wrinkled her forehead.

What did football have to do with anything?

"The field goal kicker, Matt, went down with an injury—"

"I know," Lucy interrupted. "I saw. He tore his ACL or something." She had no idea where Martie was going with this. "What does that have to do with me?"

"They're having a special tryout," Martie explained. "And I think you should."

"Should what?" asked Lucy.

"Try out," Martie said simply.

Lucy's jaw dropped. "Try out for the boys' football team? Are you kidding me?"

"Think about it. You have a strong leg; your aim is perfect; you can kick the ball, what, thirty yards easy. That's enough for most field goals."

*Field goal? Football?* Lucy couldn't believe what Martie was proposing.

"I'm a soccer player," Lucy pointed out. "Not a football player."

Martie gave her the facts. "Did you know that in the NFL, eight of the top ten kickers were soccer players before they became football players?"

"Uh-huh . . ." Lucy said, skeptically.

"And that coaches have actually adapted how they have their kickers kick the football, so that they kick with the instep, like soccer players, rather than with the toe of their shoe?"

"How many of the kickers in the NFL are girls?" Lucy asked. "I'm guessing none, because a girl can't be on a boys' football team. It doesn't make any sense." This was the craziest idea she'd heard since her dad said they were moving across the country.

Martie shrugged. "A lot of things don't make sense the first time you hear them. You know, like twice-baked potatoes or jumbo shrimp."

"Huh?" Lucy had no idea what Martie was talking about.

"Never mind," Martie said quickly. "Just know that girls all over the country are doing this. Even in college."

"They are?" Lucy considered, shocked that she was entertaining this thought for even a second.

"Think about it," Martie urged. "Please. Tryouts are tomorrow after school. Promise me you'll sleep on it."

Lucy sighed. She wasn't sure why Martie even cared. She'd left her off the soccer team, which seemed like such an easy, logical fit; now she was trying to force her onto the boys' team?

"Look," Lucy began, "you don't have to feel guilty—"

Martie interrupted. "It's not about guilt. It's about putting you where you belong."

*Where I belong,* Lucy thought. *Try back home, in Toledo, with Annie and everyone else—certainly not on a boys' football team!* Lucy couldn't think of anywhere she'd fit in less. Maybe a men's prison? Or a convent. . . .

"I know it's hard," Martie continued. "New friends, a new school . . . but sometimes where you think you'll fit in the least is where you may fit in the most. Really, Lucy, you never know what you can do until you do it." Lucy gave her a look, not believing her.

"Trust me." Martie smiled. "You can make it." She handed Lucy a late pass.

Lucy grabbed the slip of paper and headed for the door. Martie was making it impossible for her to say no.

"I'm sorry, kid," Lucy's dad said as he engulfed her in a hug. "I know how much you wanted this."

Lucy nodded as she leaned against his chest, taking a deep breath. She inhaled the familiar combination of men's Speed Stick, Tide, and cologne, and blinked back tears, trying not to think about everything she was going to miss. The practices, the games, the team dinners, the bus rides, the locker room jokes—she'd be missing out on all of it.

"I have a lot of homework to do," Lucy said softly and headed for her room.

An hour later, after she had waded through most of her geometry proofs and conjugated at least twenty Spanish verbs, she heard the doorbell ring. Lucy looked up, surprised. The sound of girls' voices echoed in the foyer. Considering her dad barely knew his coworkers yet, Lucy couldn't imagine who would be visiting them—at dinnertime, no less. Girl Scouts selling cookies? Teen Jehovah's

Witnesses? She tentatively opened her bedroom door and peered out. Down the long hallway, she saw her dad taking coats and welcoming Pickle, Charlie, and Max into the house.

Lucy rushed out. "What's going on?" she asked, concerned.

Pickle handed Lucy's dad her green army jacket and turned to Lucy. "Your dad invited us for dinner!"

Lucy's eyes widened to the size of saucers. "He did?" She looked at her dad, panicked. He put a hand on her shoulder.

"Don't worry," he reassured her. "I'm not cooking." He looked to the girls. "Everyone like pepperoni?" Charlie, Max, and Pickle nodded as Lucy's dad grabbed his keys. "Great," he said, opening the door. "I'll be back in twenty." He shut the door behind him, leaving a stunned Lucy in his wake.

"What—what're you guys, like . . . you know, doing here?" she stammered.

"I called to see how you were doing," Pickle explained, "and your dad said you could use some cheering up."

Lucy tried to hide her look of horror. She knew her dad's heart was in the right place, but these girls barely knew her. They'd only hung out outside soccer once, and that had ended in disaster when Lucy's party plans fell through. Now they were in her house. And it wasn't even her house!

"This place is sweet," Max said admiringly as she walked into the living room.

"It's just a rental," Lucy explained sheepishly. "It's not really ours."

"We sold our house and rent too now," Max said. "My dad says it makes more sense in this market, whatever that means."

"Fascinating," Charlie said dryly. "So, should we tell her why we're really here?"

Lucy stared at the girls, confused. Max turned to Charlie. "Operation Cheer Up. We just told her."

"We're not just here to cheer Lucy up," Charlie responded, nudging Pickle.

"Okay," Pickle admitted. "There's another reason we came over."

Max seemed totally in the dark. "Free pizza?"

Charlie shook her head and laughed slightly. "Uh . . . no." Then she considered. "Is he getting thin crust?"

Pickle looked at Charlie and Max, exasperated. "You guys! We're not here to talk about pizza."

"Can we talk about chips?" Max asked. "Because I'm starving." She headed to the kitchen in search of a snack.

Pickle turned to Lucy. "We're here to talk about football."

Lucy exhaled loudly. Suddenly, it all made sense. She understood exactly what was going on. "Martie put you up to this."

"She didn't put us up to anything," Pickle quickly interjected. "She just told us about football tryouts. And we think you should do it."

"Do what?" Max said as she came back into the living room holding a bag of tortilla chips.

"Lucy's going to try out to be Beachwood's new place-kicker," Charlie said as she collapsed onto the couch and put her feet up on the coffee table.

"Really?" Max asked.

"No," Lucy argued. "I only told Martie I'd think about it. And I have."

The girls waited for Lucy's answer. Finally, Pickle broke the silence. "Well, don't keep us hanging—what're you gonna do?"

"Nothing," Lucy said. "I'm not trying out. I can't be a girl on a boys' team. It's just . . . crazy."

"She's right," Max agreed. "It's crazy. And I bet smelly, too. Boys stink."

"But some of those football boys are ridiculously cute," Pickle pointed out.

"It's not about cute boys," Charlie said adamantly, then nodded to Max. "Hey, you wanna share those chips?" Mouth full, Max reluctantly passed the bag over. Charlie turned back to Lucy, continuing. "It's about showing what you can do."

"She's right," Pickle agreed. "No one has a leg like you, Luce. And forget soccer! If you make this team, you have a chance to do what no one else has ever done at Beachwood. There're only a handful of girls who've done it *anywhere*. You have a chance to really stand out and be a star!"

Lucy sighed. She never wanted to stand out. She wanted to fit in. "I don't know . . ." she said hesitantly.

"Seriously," Pickle prodded, "if you did this, it'd be incredible. *Legendary*. You'd go down in the annals of history."

"Ew." Max cringed. "Don't say anal."

Pickle threw a pillow at her. "I didn't!"

As Max and Pickle began to argue about the difference, Charlie looked Lucy in the eyes.

"Lucy," she said, her voice serious and slow, "if you do this, you'll be like, the toughest, most hard-core athlete in the school."

Pickle nodded. "You'll be our hero."

Lucy's stomach filled with butterflies. This was a big decision. *Huge*, in fact. She didn't want to disappoint the girls. They seemed so excited about the idea. Would it kill her just to try? But before she could answer, the front door burst open. Her dad was holding two large pizzas.

"Who's hungry?" he asked.

"Me!" Max jumped up happily. "I'm starving!"

Lucy's dad took a few slices for himself and let the girls go eat in Lucy's bedroom. As they headed in with napkins, soda, and pizza, Lucy made sure they weren't looking and ran back to give her dad a hug.

"Thanks," she said, "for doing this for me." And then she hurried to snag some pizza before Max inhaled all of it.

The next day, school felt endless. Lucy spent every period staring at the clock above each classroom door, torn. She hadn't said anything about football tryouts to anyone besides the girls—not her dad; not Annie, when they talked for two hours on the phone last night; not even Benji, who'd stuffed a note in her locker saying that he was sorry she hadn't made the team and asking if she wanted to go see the new Will Ferrell movie this weekend. She hadn't yet run into him to tell him that she'd already seen it with her dad, although she'd considered not telling him and just seeing it again. But the truth was, she was too preoccupied with her immediate future to worry about her weekend plans. And even though Martie had delicately asked if she'd made a decision, she'd avoided answering. She just didn't know what to say or do. She knew she didn't belong on a boys' team. But the workout clothes stuffed in her locker said something different. She'd grabbed them at the last minute, right before she'd left the house this morning.

*Sometimes where you think you'll fit in the least is where you'll fit in the most.* Martie's words had played in her head like a broken record all night. And she couldn't shake the enthusiasm of Charlie and the girls.

Lucy tapped her foot on the floor beneath her desk, full of nervous energy. It was a crazy idea. *Beyond* crazy.

She'd be certifiable to even think she'd have a chance to make it against the other boys trying out for the position. Her friends back home would think she'd lost her mind, that the constant California sun had gone to her head.

But then there was Martie's voice again: *You never know what you can do until you do it.*

The bell rang. School was over. Lucy stared out the window at the athletic fields, where she could see guys already gathering for practice, Benji among them.

She knew there was a 99 percent chance she would regret it. It would be the craziest thing she'd ever done . . . but she couldn't help but want to try.

As Lucy approached the football field, a few players were warming up their legs to kick. The rest of the team was stretching as a group on the grass, wearing their full football pads, their helmets strewn on the ground beside them, looking as intimidating as ever. Near the bench, she saw Benji pull a football out of the mesh bag and jog onto the field. He stopped abruptly when she caught his eye.

"Lucy." He smiled, running over. "What're you doing here?"

Lucy looked around nervously. The other players noticed that a girl had set foot on their field.

"Cheerleaders are over there," a red-faced, overweight junior nicknamed Tank yelled out. Lucy looked over her shoulder, where she could see Regan leading a group of girls in some "how-funky-is-your-chicken" cheer.

"Uh . . . thanks," she said quickly to Tank. It was easier than stammering out an explanation.

She turned back to Benji. "Uh, Martie—you know, Miss Reese—she thought it'd be a good idea . . . since I didn't make the soccer team and all."

Benji looked at her, confused. "She thought *what* would be a good idea?"

"You know, me trying out. She said you guys need a field goal kicker or whatever it's called. Since that guy went down."

"Oh . . ." he said, surprised.

"What's wrong?" Lucy panicked. "You think it's a horrible idea?"

"It's not that," he answered slowly. "It's just . . . I'm kind of . . . I'm trying out for that position."

Lucy was shocked. "Wait—I thought you were a punter?"

"I am," he answered shortly. "But I want to be place-kicker—I want to go for the points. You know, PATs and field goals, kickoffs . . ."

Lucy hoped he couldn't tell by the look on her face that she had no idea what he was talking about.

"Oh . . . okay," she responded. "Well, who knows? Maybe you'll become the field goal person and then I could take your place as the punter or something. I can punt pretty far. I started off as a goalie when I was little and—"

"Benji!" A man Lucy recognized as the coach—Coach Offredi—bellowed. "Let's go!"

Benji turned back to Lucy, not quite sure what to say. "Well, good luck." He jogged to join the other potential kickers. Lucy stared self-consciously at her shoes. She'd just worn her soccer cleats because she hadn't been sure what kind of shoes football players wore. Maybe that had been a mistake. Maybe this whole thing had.

"Hey!" Coach Offredi shouted. Lucy jerked her head up to look at him. Her body instantly tensed. *Hey?*

"It's . . . um . . . my name—it's Lucy," she stammered. "That's my name. Lucy."

Coach Offredi approached. "I don't care what your name is," he told her gruffly. "You're standing on my field."

"I'm here to try out." Lucy gulped, trying to keep her voice from shaking. She could feel everyone's eyes on her. Even Benji's. "Martie said she already mentioned it to you. . . . I'm here to try out. For the kicker position."

The coach chuckled as he looked down at his clipboard. He was in his late fifties, with a little bit of a pot belly and a big handlebar walrus mustache. Lucy wondered if he was anybody's dad or grandpa and then instantly felt sorry for them.

"So lemme get this straight. You were cut from *girls'* soccer, and now *Miss* Reese thinks we could find a spot for you here . . . on the varsity football team. Doesn't make much sense to me."

Lucy couldn't really argue. It didn't make much sense to her either. And standing here, in front of this jerk, surrounded by guys who were looking at her as if she had the plague, every fiber of her being wanted to back down, to slink away, to call Annie and tell her what a monumental mistake she'd just made . . . but something in her just clicked. She knew Martie was right. She could kick farther than any girl in this school—maybe than some of the boys, too.

"Look, Martie said there were tryouts, and she said I'm allowed to try out, so . . ." She trailed off, not sure what else to say. She shoved her hands deep into her pockets and shrugged her shoulders up toward her ears. Sure, she wasn't exactly the epitome of confidence, but this was the best she could do.

Suddenly, she heard a voice. "We talked about this, Coach . . . and we agreed." Lucy spun around, coming face-to-face with Martie.

"*Miss* Reese," he said again, emphasizing the "Miss." "No one said she couldn't try," Coach Offredi said, "but no one said she was going to make it either."

Martie smiled. "Oh, she'll make it." Lucy tried to keep a straight face. It felt good to have Martie behind her.

"Go join the others," Coach Offredi said dismissively.

Lucy looked at Martie nervously. Martie gave her a gentle push. "Go on," she said warmly. "You've got this."

## seven

Lucy walked over to where the other kickers were warming up on the sidelines down toward the far goalposts. Martie took a seat in the stands to watch, just as Coach Offredi informed them that they would be waiting until the end of practice to have the PAT and field goal try-out. Lucy had no idea what "PAT" meant, but she nodded along with the other hopefuls, trying to blend in as much as possible.

While the team practiced, under the instruction of another, younger coach, Benji and the other wannabes warmed up their legs, kicking the ball the length of the sideline. As Benji grabbed the ball and set it on a tee, Lucy stood nervously, arms folded in front of her chest. She barely even knew how to kick a football. With a soccer ball it was easy—it was round and every side was the same— but a football had laces, and it seemed oddly shaped in comparison. Lucy grabbed a ball and mimicked the other kickers, setting up a tee on the grass. She glanced around, lost. She had no clue what she was doing. Was this even right?

*Whatever*, she thought. She'd just get this over with so she could show Martie she'd done it. Besides, maybe if Martie saw how committed she was to being a part of a team, she'd reconsider about having Lucy on varsity soccer.

Now that she'd been cut, she couldn't help but feel excluded. Today at lunch, she'd listened to Pickle and Max laugh about something that had happened at practice. Through the giggles, Lucy had been able to make out something about Heather peeing in her pants, but Pickle and Max had never fully explained the story.

Finally, the whistle blew. Practice was over for the team. As the boys headed for the showers, Coach Offredi asked Devon, the backup quarterback, to stay and be the holder. Holder was usually one of Benji's positions, but since he was trying out, Devon didn't mind filling in.

Coach Offredi yelled over to the sidelines. "Okay, *guys*. You're up."

Lucy couldn't help but wince at the emphasis on "guys" as Coach Offredi explained what they were going to do. They'd start at the ten-yard line and attempt to kick a field goal.

Lucy wanted to clarify, *Kick it between those big posty things, right?* But she didn't dare ask.

Coach Offredi continued to explain that if they made the kick three times in a row, they'd advance back another ten yards. The person who kicked the farthest and the most accurately would be named Beachwood varsity's placekicker.

The placekicker from the freshman team, Colin, went first. Lucy could tell he was nervous to be up with the big guys, but the other players obviously knew of him and cheered him on. He had no problem, at ten yards, making the distance. The ball easily sailed between the goalposts and cleared the crossbar. Colin made the kick once, twice, but then the third time, it bounced off the left upright. Flustered, he tried again. And again. Benji and Lucy watched, nervously, as Colin seemed to unravel before their eyes. Finally, after he had tried eight times . . .

"Colin, that's enough," Coach Offredi barked gruffly. "Benji, you're up."

Colin had no choice but to hit the bench. He was out.

Benji stepped up. He rubbed his palms on his pants and took a deep breath, then easily kicked three field goals in four tries. A few of the lingering players gave a cheer as Benji jogged back to the bench. He sat down, triumphant.

Lucy stood up next. Her heart pounded so loudly she was sure everyone could hear. With the exception of warming up, she'd never seriously kicked a football in her life. Playing around with her dad was one thing, but this was something entirely different. And while she'd scored plenty of soccer goals, a field goal was another story. She didn't even know how many points you earned for a field goal—one, three, seven? She wished she'd run this whole trying-out idea by Pickle and Max one more time. Surely they would have stopped her.

She stepped up to the ten-yard line, where Devon knelt with the football. Lucy felt all eyes on her. Even Regan and the cheerleaders had put down their pom-poms to watch.

Lucy stepped back and off to the side, just as she'd seen the boys do. She took a deep breath, then sprang forward, taking two long strides before she drove the toe of her shoe—like she'd seen Colin and Benji do—into the football. Her foot landed high. She kicked a low line drive, end over end, right into the ground.

Couch Offredi chuckled. "That's what I thought."

Lucy's face turned red. She saw Benji give her a slight sympathetic smile from the bench, as if to say, *It's okay— no one really expected you to be able to do it.* She glanced at Martie in the stands.

Martie gestured and shouted. "Kick with the top of your foot," she indicated. "Like soccer. Not with your toe."

"Okay, let's move it back," Coach Offredi ordered.

Lucy didn't budge. Everyone else had had more than one turn. Why was she suddenly the exception?

"Don't I get to go again?" she asked, indignant, hoping no one heard her voice wavering a little. "I mean, everyone else did." She wanted to try to kick with Martie's adjustment. It might make a difference.

Coach Offredi looked at Lucy and gave a long sigh. "Fine. Go ahead."

Devon set up the ball again. Lucy kept her head down but let her eyes rise up and look at the space between the goalposts, the space where the ball was supposed to go.

She took a deep breath.

She took two steps back. And then moved one step to the left to get a better angle from which to kick the ball.

Another deep breath. She could do this. *Right?*

Her eyes looked once again at the space.

She licked her lips. They felt dry. She wondered where her Burt's Bees was. She quickly dismissed that thought. Now was *not* the time to be thinking about lip balm.

Another deep breath. She told herself to focus.

She thought of Martie's words. *Top of your foot. Not your toe. Like soccer.*

Then she lunged forward.

One step . . . another step . . .

Her foot swung back and then forward, hitting the football lower this time.

It flew from under Devon's finger, toppling end over end.

Lucy's head jerked up as it soared closer and closer and closer—above the crossbar and through the goalposts. . . .

It sailed through perfectly!

Lucy's jaw dropped in disbelief. She couldn't believe it! She'd made it! She'd actually kicked a field goal on only her second try!

Excited, she jumped and spun around, giving out a little yell of joy. But all she was greeted with was dead silence. No one even clapped or cheered. Coach Offredi's face was frozen in a look of shock and horror. Devon's mouth hung open like that of a dead fish. Even Benji looked stunned.

Lucy tried to conceal the smirk on her face as she turned back around for her second kick. She couldn't deny it. That had been awesome. Her heart soared. Knowing she'd just done something that no one expected her to do made her feel . . . as if anything were suddenly possible. She pressed her lips together. Now she was ready. She knew what it felt like to do it right. She knew she could do it again.

BAM! And BAM! She kicked two more through. Coach Offredi raised his eyebrows, surprised.

"Okay," he ordered her. "Ten yards back. Let's go to the twenty. Benji, you too."

Lucy looked to Benji. "Good job," she said.

He nodded, impressed. "Yeah, you too, Luce." As he walked by her, he playfully punched her in the arm. "Next time, warn a guy if he's about to get his butt kicked." Lucy smiled as he took his turn at the twenty-yard line.

On his first try, he missed.

The ball easily flew over thirty yards, but his aim was off. Martie *had* pointed out to Lucy that soccer players were even more accurate than football players.

From the bench, Lucy sighed. "Come on," she murmured under her breath. It didn't matter that they were competing for the same position. She still wanted him to make it.

Again he tried. And missed. Again. And again. Finally, it sailed through. But the next time, he missed again. Finally, even Coach Offredi had to concede that it was Lucy's turn.

He looked at her as if the mere sight of her annoyed him. "You're up." Benji sank onto the bench, discouraged.

Lucy stood up and dried her sweaty hands on her shorts—not that she needed dry hands to kick the ball. As she headed to the twenty-yard line, she realized that the closer to the middle of the field she stood, the tinier she felt. It seemed strange being this little girl standing in the middle of such a giant field. Even though it was only one hundred yards long, it felt more like one hundred miles. She glanced around nervously, and to her surprise noticed that a small crowd had gathered on the opposite side of the field. Pickle, Charlie, Max, Carla, and a few of the other girls from the team had joined Martie. Lucy smiled at the sight of them all together.

"Let's go, Luce," Pickle yelled. "You can do this!"

"I can do this," Lucy murmured to herself. She nodded to Devon that she was ready. He knelt down to hold the ball, as she told herself to do what she'd done a few minutes ago. Well, not what she did on the first kick, obviously . . . but what she'd done on the other three.

She took a deep breath, then easily knocked the ball through the goalposts one . . . two . . . then three more times! Lucy's heart soared. The other players stared in disbelief. She'd known she had a good sense of where to send the ball from soccer—she could always be counted on for corner kicks—but this was pretty incredible. She beamed.

She was doing it! She was kicking field goals! And not only kicking them, but making them! She tried to conceal her smile but couldn't. The corners of her mouth couldn't help but turn up, until she saw Coach Offredi.

His arms were folded across his chest as he shook his head. This obviously hadn't been what he wanted to see. He couldn't hide the shock on his face. Even some of the players who had come up from the locker room to watch looked stunned. Benji's jaw dropped. Even Devon shook his head, amazed.

"Back to the thirty," Coach Offredi snapped, without giving her an inch. He was obviously fed up with having to indulge the idea of a girl on a football team. He wanted to prove she didn't belong.

Lucy stepped back ten more yards as Devon knelt down once again. His eyes darted over to the guys on the sidelines, watching. Lucy took another deep breath, trying to calm her rapidly beating heart. This time it was her turn to go first.

She stepped back . . . one . . . two paces. Then she lunged

forward, taking two strides, and just as her foot was about to collide with the ball—WHOOSH! She completely missed it and stumbled back, having to keep herself from falling backwards. As she struggled to keep her balance, the guys snickered. Devon had a sadistic smile on his face. Shocked, Lucy knew in an instant what had happened.

He'd purposefully sabotaged her kick.

She felt just like the cartoon Charlie Brown when the cartoon Lucy would whisk the football out of the way as Charlie Brown tried to kick it. She would have laughed at the irony if she hadn't been so pissed.

"You moved the ball," she said accusingly to Devon.

He was instantly defensive. "No, I didn't."

"Yeah, you did!" Lucy exclaimed. "Right before my foot hit."

Coach Offredi stepped in. "You making excuses now?"

Lucy felt a growing lump in her chest and was determined not to cry. That would only give them another reason to keep her off the team. She wanted to scream, *Yeah, it's not as easy when someone moves the freaking ball!* She tried to stay calm. Getting upset wasn't going to help. She knew that from soccer.

"I need a sec," she said as she walked to the sidelines. Coach Offredi tried to contain his smile.

Pickle ran over, followed by Charlie and Carla. "Lucy, you're doing awesome. Now keep your head in it."

"You saw what just happened!" Lucy said. "You saw what that guy just did!"

"Yeah, he pulled a Lucy on you," Charlie said dryly. "I'm cringing at the irony." Martie walked over. Max bounded up beside her, joining them.

"Lucy, you look awesome out there," Max encouraged.

"You really do," Carla agreed. "So stick with it! You've got this!"

Martie put an arm around Lucy. "You're the best kicker out there. Now finish this, hon."

Lucy's heart swelled. That was what her mom had always called her. Hon.

"Okay," she said, determined. "I'm ready."

Wordlessly, she jogged back onto the field, ready to kick again. Coach Offredi's posture deflated. There was no way anyone was stopping her now.

"Come on, Luce," the girls yelled. "Do it!"

Devon set up the ball again. Lucy shot him a dirty look. If he moved the ball again, she planned to conveniently kick him in the head . . . or somewhere worse.

Another deep breath.

Benji stood up to get a better look.

The cheerleaders crowded in. It was so quiet that Lucy imagined even traffic on the road behind her stopped for a minute. She popped forward, and this time, her foot hit the center of the football perfectly. It sailed up . . . up . . . a perfect end-over-end . . . five . . . ten . . . fifteen yards. It was right on target, heading for the metal posts . . . twenty yards . . . and it took a turn toward the left post. . . .

"No," Lucy whispered. As if it could hear her plea, the ball sailed through, just grazing the post, but still—*good!*

From the sidelines, the cheerleaders exploded! She'd done it! Lucy had done it. She'd kicked a forty-yard field goal! Farther than any other guy on the team.

Coach Offredi turned his back, upset, and looked down at the ground. He appeared momentarily distracted by a patch of dirt.

Lucy ignored his not-so-subtle reaction and proceeded to kick two more times. She made them both! She couldn't wipe the smile off her face as she grinned from ear to ear.

Coach Offredi shook his head. "That'll be it," he muttered. "Hit the showers."

Lucy looked at him, surprised. That was it. No "good job" or "awesome kick" or "you made the team." Just "hit the showers."

Devon looked at him, panicked. "Well, who's supposed to show up to kick at practice tomorrow? We've got a game on Friday—"

"I'll make a decision when I decide," Coach Offredi barked. "Now hit the showers."

Devon slunk off, clearly worried. The other guys followed. Lucy walked to the bench to grab her athletic bag and book bag.

"Hey," a boy's voice called. Lucy turned. It was Ryan.

"Nice job out there. I didn't know a girl could kick like that."

Lucy shrugged. "Lots of girls can—it's just no one ever asks them."

Ryan nodded. "Good point. And, you know, good luck." He turned and jogged to catch up with the other guys. Lucy watched him go, a broad smile spreading across her face. Then she hurried to join the girls on the sidelines.

They grabbed her and without a word of explanation ushered her into Charlie's car.

"Where are we going?" Lucy asked, laughing.

"To celebrate," Pickle informed her as she pulled the car door shut and cranked the radio.

"But I haven't even made the team yet," Lucy pointed out.

Charlie peeled out of the school driveway. "Oh, don't worry. You will."

Thirty minutes later, Lucy was suffering from a full-out sugar coma. The girls had taken her to Ben & Jerry's, where, between the five of them—Lucy, Pickle, Max, Charlie, and Carla—they had scarfed down an entire Vermonster.

"A what?" Lucy had asked when Pickle ordered.

"A Vermonster," Pickle explained. It was a tub of thirty-two flavors of ice cream, bananas, hot fudge, caramel, whipped cream, nuts, and all the toppings. Lucy seriously doubted she'd be eating dinner tonight.

Max collapsed back into her chair and rubbed her belly. "I look pregnant," she lamented. "At least, like, six months."

Pickle stuck out her belly. "I look nine months pregnant!"

"I just feel sick," Charlie groaned. "I could seriously puke."

Lucy's eyes widened. "Oh God, really?" she gasped. Some people were scared of spiders or drowning—she was scared of throwing up. It didn't matter whether she was the one doing it or whether someone else was the culprit; the whole idea of it terrified her.

"Someone's going to need to roll me out of here," Carla said. "Thank God we don't have practice tomorrow."

Pickle nudged Lucy in the side. "But you might."

Lucy smiled. She'd momentarily forgotten about football tryouts but suddenly, football was back at the forefront of her mind.

If she did have practice tomorrow, she'd be ready for it. *Yeah,* she thought with a private smile. *Bring it on.*

That night, as Lucy boiled the hot water for another dinner of mac and cheese, the phone rang. She wasn't the least bit hungry, but she couldn't exactly tell her dad she'd pigged out on thirty-two scoops of ice cream before dinner.

"Probably one of your friends," her dad said, not looking up from the work he was doing at the dining room table.

"My friends call my cell," she reminded him as she hurriedly dumped the macaroni into the pot and grabbed the cordless off the wall. And by friends, she meant Annie. Although since the girls from the soccer team had cheered for her at tryouts and taken her out for ice cream, Lucy couldn't help but think she might have a few more incoming calls than usual. All the girls had programmed her cell number into their phones at Ben & Jerry's.

"Hello?" she said into the phone, as she headed back over to the stove to stir the noodles and add a little salt, just the way her mom had taught her.

Coach Offredi was on the other end of the line. "*Ms. Malone?*"

*Ms. Malone?* That was her mom. Or, as her mom would say, that was her grandma.

"This is Lucy," she responded nervously. She wasn't sure if Coach Offredi calling her at home was a good sign or bad one.

"I just wanted to tell you . . ." He took a long pause, as if the words were hard to get out. "You . . . uh . . . yeah, you made the team."

"I did?" she gasped.

"Mm-hmmm," he responded, his voice tight. "You'll be our first-string placekicker this year. Congratulations."

Lucy was so surprised she dropped the wooden spoon directly into the pot. Quickly, she grabbed tongs to fish it out.

"I . . . really?" she stammered, in complete disbelief.

Her dad looked up from his work. "Is that Coach Reese?" he asked. Since Hell Week, Martie's name had become a fixture around the house.

Lucy shook her head no and turned her back toward her dad for privacy. She listened as Coach Offredi told her to be there tomorrow before school for weights. *Weights?* Lucy had never lifted anything heavier than three-pounders.

"Okay." She gulped. "I will." She paused, feeling obligated to say something nice. "Um . . . thanks." Coach Offredi muttered something on the other end.

Lucy cringed as she hung up the phone. It was obvious the guy hated her. She turned the water down to a low simmer and placed the metal lid on the pot.

Her dad looked at her expectantly.

"Well?" He waited.

Lucy smiled and gave a cute shrug. "I, um . . . I made the team."

Her dad beamed. "Luce, that's great! I knew Coach Reese would come to her senses."

"Not the soccer team, Dad," she explained. "The football team. The *boys'* football team. Can you believe it?"

It took a minute for her father to process this information. "Wait—you tried out for football?" he asked, unable to wrap his head around the concept. "When?"

"Today, after school," Lucy admitted. She hadn't told him because she hadn't definitely planned on trying out.

But from the look of betrayal on his face, it was obvious this had been a mistake.

"How could you have kept this from me?" he asked, clearly upset.

Lucy recoiled, surprised at his reaction. "It's just football, Dad. It's not like I have a crystal meth addiction or an illegitimate child or something."

Her dad gave her a look that quickly shut her up. The timer on the oven went off. Lucy turned the burner off and searched in the drawers for pot holders. She was still learning where everything was.

"Dinner's almost ready," she said, as she slipped the pot holder mittens over each hand and grabbed the handles on either side of the pot, dumping the water and noodles into a colander in the sink. She loved the feeling of the steam hitting her face. It was like getting a facial—not that she'd ever actually *had* one before.

"We'll eat after you call the coach back," he responded firmly.

Lucy gave him a funny look. "Call back? Why? I'm gonna see him tomorrow. . . ."

Her dad folded his arms across his chest. "No, you're not . . . because you're not playing."

Lucy sighed. Not this again. What was with all this forbidding and arguing? Her dad had never been like this back home. First Ryan's party, now this . . .

"Don't tell me," Lucy replied, exasperated. She ripped

open the packet of cheese powder and dumped it over the noodles. "I can't play football until I'm sixteen, too?"

"You can't play football *period*," he snapped.

"But why?" Lucy cried. This morning, she hadn't even wanted to play football, but now, after going through the tryouts and making the cut, she had something to prove—to the coach, to the other players, to Benji, to her dad . . . to herself. "Why can't I play? I made the team, fair and square!"

"Because I am your father, and I said so!"

"Dad, come on," she begged. "Remember how we used to play in the backyard at home?" When she was seven, her dad had given her a Nerf football for Christmas, and for three days straight they'd practiced different running patterns and passes. Of course, she'd quickly lost interest when a Barbie Dream House had shown up from Grandma. Hello, Ken and Barbie. Goodbye, Nerf.

"I'll drop you off early tomorrow," he said matter-of-factly. "You're going to tell Coach . . . Coach whoever . . . that you're not playing."

"But Dad—" Lucy protested.

"But nothing. I *don't* want you playing. I *don't* want you getting hurt."

Lucy couldn't believe it. "Who died and made you boss?" she spat, then realized what she'd said. They both knew who'd died.

"Go to your room," her dad said sternly.

"Dad . . . wait . . . I'm sorry—"

"GO!" he ordered.

Lucy tearfully thrust the bowl of macaroni and cheese at him. "Fine."

As she slammed her bedroom door and collapsed on her bed, she thought back to being in the hospital with her mom. She thought back to sitting by her mom's bedside, talking to her, telling her about some stupid thing she and Annie had done in school, or how she'd done on some test that didn't matter—not really—or what disgusting meal her dad had attempted to cook for dinner. And then she'd told her she couldn't leave her, that she had to wake up, that she couldn't be in this world without her. . . .

And then her dad had come in and told her that he'd made a decision.

Now, today, Lucy was certain of one thing. There would be no more letting her dad make the decisions. He'd controlled her fate for long enough. She was sick of it! She'd made this team, and no matter what anyone said, she was playing football.

Period.

## eight

The smell of stale sweat hit Lucy like a ton of bricks as she pushed the weight room doors open. It was six-thirty in the morning, and the players who didn't have eighth period free to lift had to do their weight workouts twice a week before school. Lucy was definitely not a morning person, and the idea of getting up before the sun rose was not exactly her cup of tea. Of course, she didn't drink tea, she drank coffee . . . so whatever. It wasn't really her cup of anything.

At least getting a ride hadn't been a problem, since her dad had already offered to drop her off early so she could tell Coach Offredi that she was quitting the team. Which, for the record, she wasn't. Although her dad didn't know it.

As soon as she'd hopped out of her dad's car, she'd run into the girls' bathroom and changed out of her white knee-length peasant skirt and ribbed orange tank top into her workout clothes. Wearing baggy shorts and a white sleeveless tee, with her hair pulled up into a messy bun on the top of her head, she'd hoped to blend in as much as possible. But as soon as she walked into the weight room—

into a sea of biceps and testosterone—she knew she'd be out of place no matter what she wore.

All heads swiveled toward her as the door opened. Chalk dust filled the air. The squeak of the machines came to a grinding halt as the guys gawked at their new *female* teammate. It was amazing, the difference boobs could make—even relatively little ones. It was like they were looking at an alien from Mars.

Across the room, Benji stopped his leg presses. Ryan was mid-pull-up. He continued, unfazed by her entrance. Lucy was grateful. She stared at him, momentarily transfixed. Being that cute should have been illegal in all fifty states.

Coach Offredi stepped in front of Lucy and turned to the guys. "What? You boys never seen a girl before? Let's go!" Then he turned to Lucy. "You're late."

Lucy inhaled quickly and then explained. "I know. I'm sorry. I had to change—"

"I don't want to hear excuses. I want you here on time. You want to be on this team? You show up with the team." She felt as though she'd been slapped across the face. Public humiliation was never fun, but especially not before 8 A.M.

"Go join Benji," Coach Offredi said dismissively. "He'll show you what to do." Lucy rolled her eyes. *What was* with *this guy?* Music blared from a radio that looked so old, it might have been Coach Offredi's when he was in high school. Obediently, she wove around the guys, making her way over to Benji. Ryan hopped off the pull-up bar, landing right in front of her. She stopped abruptly.

"Oh, hi," she said quickly. God, he could even make sweaty pit stains look hot.

"Hey," Ryan said as he moved around her, headed to the bench press. "So, you made it," he said, hitting her on the arm.

"Oh yeah," she responded. "I just had to change—that's why I was late."

Ryan laughed. "I meant the team. You made the team."

Lucy's eyes widened. "Oh, right," she realized. "Right, right. Yeah. I made it. The team." She shifted uncomfortably, staring down at her gray New Balances.

"Lucy, you ready?" Benji asked, interrupting the moment. Lucy spun back around. Benji was standing at the leg press, smiling, waiting for her.

"See ya," she told Ryan. She hurried over and Benji engulfed her in a huge hug.

"Congratulations," he said proudly. "Obviously, you made the team."

"I know," she admitted bashfully. "I hope—I know you wanted to be the placekicker—"

"Hey, hey," Benji reassured her. "I'm glad we'll get more time together. I just can't believe I was beat by a girl—"

"Wait a minute," Lucy said, punching him in the arm. "When you say it that way, it sounds like a bad thing—like a huge insult to girls."

"Insult?" Benji gasped. "It was a compliment. There's no one I'd rather be beaten by."

Lucy smiled, then nodded toward the leg press. "So . . . what do I do?"

"It's called a leg press," he teased. "What you do is you use your legs, put them right there, to press the weight."

"Oh, really?" Lucy asked sarcastically. "I couldn't have figured that out."

"You two!" Coach Offredi snapped. "Enough talking." He tossed a thick binder in Lucy's general direction. It landed near the leg press machine with a thud. "Playbook," he explained. "I suggest you learn what's in there."

Lucy picked up the binder. Her arms sagged under the weight. She gulped and looked at Benji, holding up the book. "Well . . . maybe I could just leg-press this."

By the time Lucy had showered and made her way to first period, word about her making the team had already spread. As soon as Pickle saw Lucy, she bounded over.

"You have *got* to be kidding me!" she said with a huge smile on her face. "You made the team? The boys' football team? Martie just told me. She's so excited!"

Lucy giggled. "I know. It's crazy."

"Everyone's talking about it," Pickle bragged. "We're all so proud of you! We have to celebrate!"

"Oh God," Lucy groaned playfully. "I can't take another Vermonster."

Pickle laughed. "When are you free? Today? Tonight?"

Lucy considered. "Well, definitely not after school today." She smiled, then told Pickle, "My first practice."

Pickle smiled. "Then tonight it is."

At the end of the school day, Lucy stood in the girls' locker room, completely alone. Coach Offredi had reluctantly given her pads and a helmet to change into. Getting dressed for football practice was more work than getting ready for prom—not that Lucy had ever been to one, but she could imagine.

There was the helmet with a face mask—because she was a kicker, Lucy's face mask had just a single bar across it, while linemen wore something that looked more like a cage.

There were two jerseys—a blue and gold away one and a white home one, each with the number 2 on the back and front. Apparently in the pros, quarterbacks and kickers had to be numbers between 1 and 19; Coach Offredi had implemented the same policy on their team.

There were football cleats that fit Lucy's feet like a glove ... although she had been told by Coach that kickers often used a football cleat on their plant foot and a soccer cleat on their kicking foot. Most comfortable in soccer cleats, Lucy planned to do the same.

Then there were the pads: shoulder pads, thigh pads, elbow pads, hip pads, and knee pads—there was even a butt pad! And although Lucy had eventually sorted it all out, it hadn't been easy to tell which pad was supposed to cover which body part.

But when she slipped on her jersey, she noticed it didn't quite cover *all* body parts. Lucy gasped. Two giant holes had been cut out of the chest, where her boobs were supposed to be. She stared at her reflection, horrified. She couldn't go out onto the field like this, with her sports bra showing through . . . or could she?

Lucy shook her head defiantly. Someone had obviously sabotaged her uniform. Someone who wanted to keep her down in the locker room, too embarrassed to show her face. Well, she'd show 'em her sports bra instead.

She put on her helmet and tucked up her hair.

She couldn't go as far as to say she looked like one of the guys. In fact, with her bra showing through, she looked more like a girl than ever.

She sighed. It was now or never. She figured she had come this far. It might as well be now.

She told herself to be tough, to be strong. She couldn't let them get to her. That was what they wanted—to drive her away. Besides, what would Pickle and Charlie and all the girls think of her if she let some stupid holes in her jersey force her to quit? Not much, probably.

She looked at her reflection again, steeling herself for what she was about to go do. It was time to start playing football.

If Lucy had thought soccer Hell Week was torture, it was nothing compared to her first official football practice with the team.

"What happened?" Coach Offredi barked as he took one look at Lucy's cut-up jersey.

"Oh," Lucy said, acting surprised. "It wasn't supposed to come like this?"

A few of the guys stifled a snicker or two. Coach Offredi folded his arms across his chest.

"Run a lap," he said. And before Lucy could protest, he added, "NOW!" As Lucy took off running, she heard him ask an assistant coach to get her another jersey.

By the time she returned, she was out of breath and a new jersey was waiting for her on the bench. She quickly pulled off her old jersey and changed. *Who cares,* she thought. *Why be modest? They've already seen my bra. . . .*

And once she was fully dressed and covered, things went from bad to worse.

It wasn't just the fact that Coach Offredi treated her as though she had the plague, or that a few of the guys kept knocking her thigh pads intentionally—it was that she simply had no idea what she was doing. And she hadn't exactly had time to read the playbook between geometry and U.S. history. Luckily, she was paired up with Benji.

After warm-ups, when the rest of the team moved onto sled drills or pass plays, depending on their position, Lucy and Benji walked over to the sideline to warm up their legs and alternate taking kicks. The truth was, since you never knew what could happen on the field, Lucy and Benji had to be prepared to take over for each other at a moment's notice. Just as Benji had to be ready to kick point after touchdowns, field goals, or kickoffs, Lucy had to be ready to punt on the fourth down.

"Deep punts first," Coach Offredi instructed as he walked off to work with the rushers, the group of guys who would try to block the opponent's kicks. "Then take some shorter, low ones."

"Low ones?" Lucy asked, confused.

Benji explained. "It's basically a low line drive, closer to the ground. It'll bounce around when it lands, be hard to settle. You can punt a squib or kickoff that way." Lucy squinted, staring at Benji. *Uh, translation please?*

"Why would you do that?" she asked, feeling over-whelmed by how little she actually knew about a sport she was supposed to play.

"You know, like, if the weather is bad," Benji offered. "Or if you have a really tight lead with only minutes to go, or their return man is really fast. You might want to kick off that way to do an onside kick. . . ."

*A* what *kick?* Lucy nodded fiercely, as if it all made perfect sense—even though it hardly made any at all.

Benji stared at her a moment longer than was necessary.

"Uh . . . what?" she said.

"Do you have plans tonight?" Benji asked. "Because if you do, cancel them."

"Okay, why?" She felt bad canceling on Pickle, who'd been so enthusiastic and sweet.

"Because tonight," Benji explained, "I'm giving you a crash course in all things football."

The sun was just setting over the ocean, and it was that special time of night when the sky deepens to dark blue, but it's still light enough to see.

"No, no," Benji said, recovering the football. "Try again." He and Lucy had stayed after practice for a one-on-one tutorial. They were working on kickoffs, since that was part of Lucy's job.

"I don't get it," Lucy said, frustrated. "Shouldn't I be just trying to kick as far as possible?"

"Sometimes," Benji explained. "But sometimes not. Not if we want to do an onside kick. You need a short kick with a predictable bounce. That way we can gain possession."

Lucy giggled.

"What?" Benji asked.

Lucy shrugged, not wanting to say.

Benji pressed. "What?"

"You're funny when you're all . . . footbally and serious," Lucy admitted.

"Footbally?" He laughed. "Is that a word?"

Lucy laughed too. "It should be!"

Benji set the ball on the tee. "Okay, once more, before it gets dark. You gotta get this before Friday. . . ."

Lucy nodded. Benji was right. Friday was fast approaching, and she'd be expected to perform.

"Remember," he instructed, "start low. We're looking for a high bounce right before it hits ten yards."

"Then you catch it?" Lucy asked.

"Recover it," he corrected her.

She acted as though she'd just said a bad word and put her hand to her lips. "Oh, sorry," she joked. "*Recover.*"

"Okay, smarty. Kick the ball." She smiled and lined up behind the tee. She took a deep breath. *Low*, she told herself. *Ten yards only.*

She lunged forward and gave the ball more of a hard tap then a solid kick. It started low, then bounced end over end . . . three, four, five, six, seven, eight yards. At the ninth, it bounced high and soared to ten, where Benji pounced on the ball and grounded it. He jumped up, ecstatic.

"You did it!" he yelled. "That was perfect!"

"It was?" she asked, then realized. "It was!!!"

Excited, he ran over and picked her up. He spun her around. Her hair came partially out of its ponytail as the field and stands and goalposts whirled by. He finally set her down.

"That was awesome, Lucy!" he said, breathless.

She smiled. "Thank God. Because I'm starving." They headed to the bench. "Good," he said. "What sounds good?

Pizza or In-N-Out?"

"What?" she asked. Was he taking her to dinner now?

He picked up the playbook sitting on the bench, shook it at her, and broke the bad news. "Our night's not done. You still have a lot to learn."

Thirty minutes later, a huge pepperoni pizza sat in front of them as Benji quizzed her.

"What's a sack?" he asked.

Lucy feigned thought, then smiled brightly. "I know this one. A sack is something you carry your groceries in."

Benji gave her a look of mock annoyance. "Funny. A sack is when the quarterback is tackled behind the line of scrimmage."

Lucy nodded. "And the line of scrimmage is . . . ?"

"Lucy!" Benji said, exasperated.

"I'm kidding," she said. "Line of scrimmage is the starting line for each play and is where the ball is set."

"Okay, good." The waitress walked by. Benji looked up. "Can we get two more Cokes?" he asked. The waitress nodded.

"Now, punts—you should know the different kinds, just in case," he instructed. "There's a directional punt, a coffin corner kick, a pooch punt—"

"Pooch punt?" Lucy laughed.

"Hey, don't shoot the messenger. I didn't name these things."

Lucy took a bite of pizza and swallowed. "Before we talk about coffins and pooches and whatever else, I think I need the basics."

"The basics?" Benji asked.

"Yeah, like who are all the people on the field and what do they do?"

The waitress dropped the Cokes off. "Can I get you anything else?" she asked. "Coffee? Dessert?"

Benji looked from Lucy to the waitress. "Coffee, definitely. I think we're gonna be here awhile." As the waitress left to get the menus, Benji started to explain. "So, there are eleven guys on the field at a time. . . ."

Lucy *ahem*ed loudly.

"Sorry." He corrected himself. "Eleven *people* . . ." And as he continued, Lucy vowed that she was going to focus and listen intently to every word he said until she fully understood football—even if it took all night.

And it pretty much did. She'd called her dad, telling him her study session was running late. He said to be home by nine. But even after Benji dropped her off, she called him before she went to bed, and they stayed on the phone until one in the morning, talking about two-point conversions and hang time and first downs.

By practice the next day, Lucy might not have been fluent in football, but if football were Spanish, she would have at least been able to say, "Hello, my name is Lucy";

"How are you?"; and "Where is the bathroom?" Benji had been an enormous help. Of course, she had told her dad they were studying for bio lab, not going over football plays. But it *was* studying, so it only qualified as half a fib.

"Okay, deep punts first," Benji reminded her. "I'll start." He continued to explain. "Usually we'd practice with the snapper, but he's also the center, so we'll just hold our own balls for now." Lucy giggled. If the soccer girls had been here, they'd have been having a field day with that one. *Hold our own balls.*

Benji continued. "So, remember what we went over last night? This is the opposite: you want to kick the ball far and high, with at least four seconds of hang time in the air. That'll make the chances of returning the punt a lot less. The farther you kick it, the farther back you pin the other team. That way Beachwood gets downfield to cover the return. Got it?" Lucy giggled.

Benji blushed. "I'm all footbally again, right?"

She nodded, then turned to follow Benji's instructions and give herself and him some distance from each other.

Once Lucy was a safe distance away, like half the football field, Benji took two steps and dropped the ball toward his right foot, which was the foot he apparently kicked with. His foot hit the ball right in the center, and the ball flew into the air at least forty yards, toward Lucy. She lunged toward it, almost catching it after the first bounce, but it slipped through her fingers. So catching wasn't her strong suit. Whatever. This wasn't baseball.

Now it was her turn. She mimicked what she had seen Benji do. Two steps . . . drop the ball down and . . . The ball hit the side of her foot and flew more sideways than forwards. Coach Offredi looked at his clipboard and made a note. Lucy bit her lip nervously.

"It's okay," Benji encouraged. "Remember? That's called a shank when the ball does that. Try to strike the ball right in the center. Here, try it again." He threw the ball back to her. This time, she followed his instructions; the ball sailed higher and farther. Punting was easier than going for a field goal. It required less precision.

"Good job, Luce," Benji cheered. Lucy smiled broadly—until Tank called over to her.

"If that's what you're going to do Friday night against Curtis, I'd say we're all screwed."

"Hey." Benji was quick to defend her. "She's just getting the hang of it. It's only her second practice." It was technically her third if you counted her extra work with Benji, but no one besides the two of them knew about that.

"That's one too many if you ask me," Tank muttered. The other guys laughed.

Benji put a hand on Lucy's shoulder. "Just focus on the ball. Don't worry about them." Lucy nodded. She wasn't going to let Tank get to her. She'd heard his real name was Robbie. Some punk named Robbie wasn't going to intimidate her, even if he *was* the size of a Mack truck.

She tried again and was much improved. After a few more kicks, she headed to the bench to grab some water. A senior with thick glasses approached her.

"You're Lucy Malone, right?" he asked, pad and pencil in hand.

"Um, yeah," Lucy answered self-consciously, as she took off her helmet and pushed her hair behind her ear.

"I'm Wesley," he said. "I write for the *Sand Dollar*." Lucy quickly put two and two together. The *Sand Dollar* could only be the school paper. "We wanted to do an article on you, to come out in tomorrow's edition."

Lucy noticed Coach Offredi looking over at her. "Um . . . I don't really think—"

"A good story always helps get people in the seats," Wesley interrupted. "Tomorrow's game against Curtis is a big one. Team could use all the fans it can get."

Lucy hesitated. "I don't know if writing something about me would really help. . . ."

"Well, it wouldn't be solely about you," he explained. "It would be about the whole team."

Lucy considered for a minute, then tentatively agreed. "If you really think it's a good idea."

"Absolutely. You know what they say—any press is good press."

Lucy bit her lip and shrugged. "Okay, well then, I guess . . . ask away."

Wesley followed Lucy back onto the field, asking her questions and taking down her every word.

"Have you always been interested in football?" *No.*

"When did you start playing?" *Um . . . two days ago?*

"What's the most fun about being on this team?" *Definitely staring at Ryan's butt in tight pants.*

Okay, so she didn't actually say any of those things. She answered the questions as simply as possible, talking about how she had just moved from Toledo, how she'd been a soccer player all her life, blah blah blah.

Then one question stopped her in her tracks.

"So, how are your new teammates treating you?" Lucy thought about that. With the exception of Benji and Ryan, they pretty much acted like she was a social pariah. And she had the cut-out jersey to prove it. It was definitely going to take longer than five minutes to explain that.

Lucy tried her best. Then Coach Offredi blew the whistle. "Sorry," Lucy apologized to Wesley. "Gotta go." She and the rest of the guys quickly began their ritual warm-up: running fast in place, dropping down to hammer out ten to twenty push-ups, popping back up for jumping jacks and then back down for push-ups, flipping over for sit-ups, getting back up to run, dropping back down for mountain climbers. . . . Since Lucy was new to the routine, it was tough to follow. She watched Benji and thought she was keeping up okay. When they finished, Coach Offredi called them over.

"Okay, bring it in, bring it in," he said. "Offense, let's work through some pass patterns; line up Split T first, then Two Tight Ends. I want to see some buttonhook passes— Cope, you listening?" A scruffy-looking junior, Cope, who was momentarily distracted by the cheerleaders, jerked his head back around.

"Yeah, I'm listening," he assured Coach Offredi.

"Good, because this is for you. Your timing last week cost us at least two first downs."

Cope hung his head, ashamed. Lucy had absolutely no idea what they were talking about. And what kind of name was Cope?

As Coach Offredi continued, Lucy was surprised to see that the emo girl, Morbid, had joined Wesley. She raised up a Nikon camera and began snapping rapid-fire pictures. Lucy didn't know quite what to make of it. She'd figured that in her spare time, Morbid wrote depressing poetry or filled vials with her own blood to wear around her neck. Who knew she was a photographer, too?

Lucy chuckled to herself. It *was* always important to have a hobby.

She supposed she should act natural as the *click, click, click* of Morbid's camera drifted toward her. But nothing about being singled out and photographed felt natural.

And the stares of the guys on the team were making her uncomfortable.

When Lucy, Benji, a cute freckled redhead named Caleb, and the rest of the Point After Touchdown team broke off to practice their drills, Morbid followed. Finally, when Coach Offredi called them in for plays with the rest of the team, he put his foot down.

"No more pictures," Coach Offredi snapped to Morbid. "PAT team, on the field! Defense, line up against them." Lucy took a deep breath. This was her last chance to kick before tomorrow's game—to prove to herself that she could handle this tomorrow, under the lights.

Wesley waved to Lucy as he and Morbid packed up to leave. Lucy gave a slight nod and took her place on the field.

She lined up for a field goal kick as the defensive team took their place a few yards away. She hadn't yet kicked from a snap. The key, Benji had told her, was working out the timing. She raised her arm as a signal that she was ready.

Coach Offredi's whistle blew.

From seven yards downfield, Caleb snapped the ball back to Benji. Benji had trouble putting it down as it slipped in his hand. One second passed, then another. . . . The defensive line was closing in, a solid wall of muscle aiming to run her down.

Lucy tried to kick anyway, but as her foot barely grazed

the ball, BAM! She was pummeled to the ground. Her head whacked against the dirt with a deafening thud.

"What the hell—" she mumbled, dazed. She could feel her head still rattling inside her helmet. It felt like her organs had been scrambled inside her body.

Benji ran over. "Luce, you okay?" he asked, his voice filled with concern.

"That was roughing, Adam," Coach Offredi warned one of the linebackers, his voice much more calm than the situation warranted.

*Roughing?* Lucy wanted to scream. *Try attacking, for no good reason!*

"Cute." Tank laughed, nudging Devon. "Benji's worried about his girlfriend." Benji looked down at his shoes as Adam tried to explain himself.

"I couldn't stop, Coach," he lied. "What's that equation? Momentum plus force . . . ?"

". . . equals girls shouldn't be on the team," Nick chimed in, finishing Adam's thought.

"Hey." Tank shrugged. "If she can't take a hit, she should get off the field."

The other guys laughed as Lucy lay there, motionless, the wind knocked out of her. If she'd been able to breathe, she might have thought of a witty retort. But all she could do was gasp for air. She'd never taken a hit that hard before. Not in soccer, not anywhere. Her eyes welled up with tears. She didn't feel like crying, but clearly, her eyes had a mind of their own. A few blurry faces above her stared down at her. Suddenly, Coach Offredi's walrus mustache came into focus above her face.

"Hey? You crying?" he asked, louder than he really needed to. "Are those tears?"

Lucy sniffed. "No." She sat up.

"There's no crying in football," he reminded her. Lucy wanted to roll her eyes but she hurt too much to even do that. Who was this guy? Tom Hanks in *A League of Their Own*? She remembered renting that movie with her mom. Did Coach Offredi really need to steal other people's lines?

"You're here to kick," he reminded her. "Not cry." Lucy felt like melting into the grass. *Thanks for the news flash,* she thought. Although at this point, she wasn't sure *what* she was there for.

The coach turned to Benji. "And you call that a set? What, d'ya have grease on your hands? When the ball's snapped, you put it down or you sit on the bench. Your choice."

Benji nodded obediently. Lucy felt worse for him than she did for herself. Well, almost.

Coach Offredi blew the whistle. "Let's go. Bull in the Ring. Tank and Caleb, you're up first.

Lucy rolled over, groaning. *God.* This practice was far from over and already her entire body was black and blue. How was she going to hide that from her dad? Say she'd been beaten with a floor hockey stick in gym class? And what was "Bull in the Ring," anyway?

Lucy stood up and turned to Kevin. "What're we doing?" she asked curiously. Well, only semi-curiously. A part of her didn't really care. She just wanted a warm shower, an ice pack, her big comfy bed—and maybe a plane ticket home to Toledo.

Kevin nodded toward the circle. "Whoever has the ball has to run to the other side. The guy in the middle has to stop him.

Ryan tossed Tank the ball. Tank tucked it in to his right side and faced off against Caleb, who was about half his size. Tank smiled sadistically; Caleb gulped. They squared off against each other. The whistle blew. Tank and Caleb ran straight into each other. Lucy cringed at the sound of their helmets crunching as Tank plowed right through the smaller guy, knocking Caleb to the ground. The whistle blew again. Tank had made it to the other side. He'd won that round.

Not that it was exactly a fair matchup, Lucy thought. Running into Tank was like crashing into a brick wall—a brick wall who could scarf down five double-doubles from In-N-Out Burger in one sitting.

Coach Offredi picked two other players. "Devon, Ryan," he ordered. Tank tossed the ball back to Ryan. Lucy wished she'd been paired with him. If she was going to end up on the ground anyway, it'd be better to end up there with Ryan on top of her.

She watched as Ryan beat Devon, then Max beat Kevin, then Nick beat Little Jimmy *and* Big Jimmy . . . and then Coach Offredi looked in her direction.

"Benji, Lucy—you're up." Lucy's eyes widened to the size of doughnuts. Benji looked like he'd just been punched in the gut.

"What?" he asked, the panic in his voice rising. A bunch of the guys around the perimeter of the circle began to laugh.

"You know the rules, Benji. Girls go together," Tank called out mockingly.

Benji glared at him. "Shut up."

Tank closed in on him, ready to fight. "What'd you say, punk?"

"Nothing," Benji answered, obviously intimidated.

Tank smiled, pleased with himself. "That's what I thought."

"You two," Coach Offredi insisted. "Benji, into the ring." He tossed Lucy the ball. It slipped through her fingers and onto the ground. Embarrassed, she grabbed it up quickly, then tucked the football into her right side, just as she'd seen Tank do.

Benji stood across from her, looking as miserable as she did. This was the last place either of them wanted to be, squaring off against each other in front of everyone. The whistle blew.

Lucy lunged forward, using all the momentum and

strength she could muster as she slammed her body into Benji's. Her hit caught him off guard because, clearly, he had decided to take it easy on her, just as she'd decided to go all out. He stumbled back and she hit him again, knocking him off balance and to the ground. Lucy made it to the other end of the circle.

"No way!" Kevin laughed.

Next to him, Caleb snarfed the water he was drinking. "Dude, now I don't feel so bad. . . ."

Lucy ran out of the circle, triumphant, casually tossing the ball back to Coach Offredi.

Tank was doubled over, gasping for breath. "Oh, man. That girl just kicked your ass!"

Ryan shook his head, impressed. "Nice hit, Malone." Lucy smiled shyly. Who knew her last name could sound so sexy?

Benji ripped off his helmet, shaking his head. Lucy could tell he was embarrassed. His face was bright red.

"I was going easy on you," he mumbled to Lucy.

All the guys started to groan. "You making excuses now?" "Give it a rest, Mason." "Wuss!"

Lucy didn't know what to say. "I'm sorry. I didn't know. . . ."

Benji tried to reassure her. "It's okay. I mean, I wanted you to look good in front of the team. I just didn't want to look quite so . . . bad."

Lucy felt a lump form in her throat. Benji had been

so great to her—had spent so much time teaching her. "Benji—" she started to say.

He stepped back. The guys were watching. "I'll call ya later, okay?" he said quickly as he hurried off. By the time everyone gathered their equipment and went to hit the showers, Benji was long gone.

## nine

Twenty minutes later, as Lucy emerged from the girls' locker room, the last of the cheerleaders were clearing off the sidelines, and the football team was heading for their cars. It wasn't dark yet, but the streetlights had already come on. She walked across the field. Her dad would be picking her up any minute, and was bound to ask how her biology project was coming along. She was already anticipating lying to him, and the thought made her sick. It would be so much easier if she could just tell him what she was doing.

It was times like this when she missed her mom—her partner in crime, always helping to convince her dad to lighten up a little and not be so strict.

Her mind wandered as she crossed toward the parking lot, remembering how her mom's hands looked and the smell of her spaghetti sauce on the stove and—

Suddenly, she was jarred out of her memories. Someone was grabbing her from behind, pinning down her arms, engulfing her in a bear hug. Panicked, she let out a frightened yelp.

"Let go of me," she screamed. But she was helpless. Paralyzed. A bunch of guys circled around her and she recognized them instantly. They were her teammates, now in their regular T-shirts and jeans. And they were laughing, as if this was some funny prank.

"Get her arms." Tank laughed.

"And her legs," Kevin reminded them.

Nick and Adam whipped out a roll of industrial-size duct tape as they dragged her over to the goalposts, carrying her like a sack of potatoes. She couldn't tell how many guys were there—fifteen, twenty—it felt like half the team. She could hear both Jimmys laughing. Together, the guys hoisted Lucy up to the top of the singular post and pressed her firmly against it.

She heard the ripping sound of the tape and felt it wrap around her body, again and again, securing her to the goalpost right above the blue pads. The guys were cracking up as they tugged at her a little, to make sure she was on there tight; then they took off running. The whole sneak attack had taken less than two minutes.

"Wait!" Lucy called after them, practically in tears. "Wait! You can't leave me here!"

As she watched the guys run for the parking lot, she made out a few more faces. She recognized Aidan, Devon, and Carl. . . . There was Daniel, Cope . . . and then there was Ryan. Lucy felt as though she'd been slapped. Ryan? She couldn't believe it.

She looked over, crushed, and to her surprise, realized that Benji was right beside her. He'd been taped to a goalpost too.

"Benji?" she asked, shocked.

Benji looked as pathetic and helpless as she did. "Guess I don't need to call you later, huh?"

Lucy wasn't sure how much time had passed. It felt like hours, but maybe it had only been minutes. She and Benji were both too upset to speak. The tape was digging into her skin, cutting off her circulation. Eyes wet with tears, she hung there, stunned that her own teammates could be so cruel and so mean. She could make out the bricks of the building and the blades of grass on the field, but just barely. Everything was beginning to blur together. She wondered if she was going to pass out.

Suddenly, in the distance, she saw someone. A girl.

"Help!" Lucy yelled. When the girl didn't turn, she screeched, "Please help me!"

Mercifully, the girl turned at the sound of her voice and caught sight of Lucy hanging from the goalposts. Breaking into a sprint, the girl ran over, horrified. As she ran closer, Lucy saw it was Regan Holder. The *whatever* girl from her English class. The cheerleader.

"Oh my God," Regan gasped, clapping her hand over her mouth. "What happened to you?" Lucy couldn't even look Regan in the eye. Another person witnessing this—

especially someone as perfect and popular as Regan—was almost too much humiliation to bear.

"The guys—they taped me up here," she explained, her voice wavering a little. "Both of us."

Benji tried to comfort her. "Luce, it's okay. They were just . . . being guys."

"How comforting," Lucy mumbled.

Regan reached up and grabbed a piece of tape. With a giant rip, she began stripping it off, piece by piece, until Lucy fell in a heap onto the ground. Regan did the same thing for Benji.

"Are you okay?" she asked them both, genuinely concerned. "I mean, I've seen them do some stupid things before, but this is seriously twisted."

Lucy could barely speak.

"Here, come on," Regan said, helping her up. "Do you have a ride home?"

Benji said he had his car.

"I should call my dad," Lucy said. Her dad had probably shown up and not seen her waiting. "He's probably worried sick by now. I don't even know what I'm going to tell him. . . ."

"You could tell him I'm bringing you home," Regan offered.

"Oh, I can give her a ride," Benji said quickly.

"I don't mind," Regan insisted.

Benji reluctantly agreed and gave a little half-wave to

both girls. "See you tomorrow then," he said. "And Regan . . . um, thanks."

Lucy and Regan walked in silence to Regan's BMW and got in. They drove silently for a mile or so. Lucy could still feel the stickiness from the tape on her legs and arms. She wasn't sure what to say, but she figured she should probably say something.

"My dad—I didn't exactly tell him I was playing football," she began, then corrected herself. "Well, I told him I was playing. He said I couldn't, and I did it anyway."

Regan glanced over at Lucy from the corner of her eye. "Huh," she said. Lucy failed to detect any judgment in Regan's voice.

"He's going to kill me," Lucy continued. "I don't know why I even wanted to play stupid football anyway—this is all Martie's fault."

"Ugh," Regan groaned. "Martie drives me crazy. It's like she's trying to be thirty or something."

Lucy remembered the soccer girls talking about Martie's birthday one day before practice. "Um, I think she *is* thirty."

"Whatever," Regan interrupted, changing the subject back to football. "Those guys are serious jerks. All of them. People at this school can be such a-holes."

Lucy didn't mention that she'd heard Regan had been exactly that to Charlie. This wasn't the time to bring that up, she figured.

"Oh, take a right here," she said, remembering she was supposed to be the one who knew where they were going.

"So what're you going to do?" Regan asked. "About the team? Isn't tomorrow supposed to be your first game?"

Lucy nodded. It was *the* first game, but it wouldn't be hers. "I'm quitting," she said simply. Obviously, that was the only option. Tomorrow she would march into Coach Offredi's office and tell him and his ugly walrus mustache to shove it. She was almost looking forward to it. They could lose every game for the rest of the season for all she cared.

But before she could deal with Coach Offredi, she had to deal with her dad.

When Regan pulled her car into Lucy's driveway, almost careening into the garage, the front door flew open. Lucy's dad rushed out, worried sick.

"Lucy!" he yelled. She could see the look of relief on his face, even in the dark.

"Thanks so much for the ride," Lucy said quickly to Regan. She grabbed her bag from the backseat.

Regan smiled politely. "Sure." Then she added, "I know it's hard to, you know, come to a new place and make friends. So if there's anything I can do . . ."

"How about talk to my dad for me?" Lucy joked as she jumped out of the car. She quickly rushed up to her dad, without a clue as to what she was actually going to say.

• • •

Fifteen minutes later, after hearing her dad rant about how he had checked everywhere at the school (well, not quite everywhere) and how he'd been "this close" to calling the police, she still hadn't come up with an explanation.

"We agreed to meet at six," he said, then finally asked the question she'd been dreading. "Where were you?"

Lucy's head spun. What could she say? She debated just telling him the truth. But why? It wasn't like she was going back to the team. Not if this was how her teammates were going to treat her.

All that would happen was that her dad would be pissed. Pissed that she'd defied him and joined the team. She would not only get a big "I told you so" about why she didn't belong on the boys' football team, and she'd probably be grounded for all eternity. If she thought her social life was nonexistent now, imagine what it would be if she couldn't leave the rental house.

No, "the truth" wasn't an option.

What she needed was a good excuse. She'd already used the class project, but he'd checked all the classrooms and the library, so that wasn't going to hold up. She could say she'd taken off with friends, but that would seem irresponsible and would probably get her grounded as well. And why hadn't she picked up her cell phone when he'd called (according to the "missed call" log, seventeen times), leaving four panicked messages?

Playing
WITH THE
Boys

Then suddenly she had an idea.

"I was locked in the women's bathroom," she lied, hoping desperately that he would buy it. Frankly, it wasn't that hard to believe. She was clumsy. And it had happened before. Just in the past year alone she'd been trapped in ladies' rooms three times: once on the plane to L.A., once at a Mexican restaurant, and once at Annie's cousin's apartment, where she'd had to climb out the window on the second floor to the fire escape!

"What?" he said. "Locked in the bathroom?"

"Yeah." She nodded vigorously.

"For all that time?" he asked. "Why didn't you crawl out under the stall?"

Hmm. Good question. She thought fast.

"Well, it wasn't that kind of bathroom. You know, with the stalls. It was the one-person kind. So it was the main door that locked. I'd slammed it really hard. And no one knew I was in there because it was downstairs, by the boiler room."

"The boiler room?" he asked. "What were you doing there?"

Oh God. This was the problem with lying. It always required more lies.

"Um, I was upset. About not making the soccer team. And about having to tell Coach Offredi that I couldn't play football. And, um . . . people . . . other kids . . . they were making fun of me. You know, because of my clothes and

Midwestern accent and . . . you know . . . it's just hard. I don't really fit in. . . ."

Her father's face softened. "So you went down there to kind of hide out?" he guessed.

Sure. That sounded good. Right. Hide out.

"Exactly," she said. "I just . . . didn't want to be teased by everyone."

Her dad thought for a minute. "Here's the thing, kid," he said warmly. "You can't let other people keep you from living your life, from doing what you want. You're not always going to fit in someplace, especially someplace new, and people, especially kids, can be jerks."

If she hadn't been so freaked out, she would have smiled at her dad's encouragement.

"Seriously," he insisted. "They can be. But the answer isn't running away. It's not letting the jerks win. You stay and you face them and you show them that you aren't backing down. . . ."

Lucy stared at her dad, taking in every word. He had no idea how appropriate his advice was—how scared she'd been tonight. She could feel her eyes welling up with tears.

Her dad looked at her, worried. "Hon? What is it?" He pulled her chair close to him. "Lucy? What's wrong?"

She shook her head, unable to answer. *Try everything.* She missed her mom. She missed trading clothes with Annie for school. She missed being on a team where her teammates actually liked her—or at least didn't try to cut off her circulation with duct tape. She missed having a dad she could talk to about things, instead of hiding things from him.

But instead she just said, "I don't know." She tried to compose herself. "It's fine," she quickly added. "I'm okay." Over the years, she'd become good at putting on a brave face.

Her dad put a firm hand on her shoulder. "I know this is tough, Luce. But so are you, okay? Just remember that. You're tougher than you look. You know your mother dropped you on your head at least . . ."

". . . five times," Lucy and her dad said simultaneously. Lucy smiled. Her mom loved to say she had the toughest head in the Midwest. Maybe now she had the toughest head in California, too. Both her dad and mom were right. She *was* tough. Tougher than Coach Offredi or any of those stupid boys were giving her credit for. She wasn't going to be intimidated by their stupid hazing or pranks. And it was abundantly clear that she wasn't ever going to be one of the guys. She was a *girl*. A determined girl who was a member of the boys' football team. From here on out, she was going to act like it. Her dad, without even knowing it, had made her see that.

"Thanks, Dad." She smiled, giving him a tight hug back. "That really helped."

He tousled her hair, pleased, having no idea that his little speech had just convinced her to do the last thing he would have wanted. She was going back to the team.

## ten

The following morning, as Lucy grabbed her bag for school, she made a startling discovery. Pom-poms.

Rifling through it, she realized that she must have accidentally grabbed Regan's bag while hurrying out of the car the night before. That meant Regan had her backpack, which she desperately needed. But it also meant something else—the perfect excuse she needed to keep her dad from knowing what she was up to.

"You *what?*" he gasped as they drove to school. That was what? Big lie number two? Or was it three? She was losing track.

"I joined the cheerleading squad!" Lucy explained. She couldn't even believe she was uttering the words. She held up Regan's pom-poms, pretending they were her own. "See?"

"Between last night and this morning you joined?" he questioned, as if this were impossible . . . which, in fact, it kind of was.

"Um, well," Lucy stammered. Here came lie number

four. "No. I joined yesterday. I just didn't get to tell you about it. I'd been thinking about it, ever since the whole football thing didn't work out. Regan—she's the girl who drove me home. . . . Anyway, she said they needed a few more girls, so . . ." She trailed off, barely even knowing what she was saying. Was her dad actually buying this crap?

"Aren't you the one who said cheerleaders aren't real athletes?"

Lucy nervously tugged at the sleeves of her sweatshirt. "Did I say that?" she wondered innocently. "I don't think so." Not only had she said it, she remembered exactly where she'd been *when* she'd said it. At Hillcrest's homecoming game. She was sure she was so transparent he'd be able to see right through her.

"It's just, I love . . . you know . . . school spirit. And clapping."

Her dad raised his eyebrows but didn't question her. "Well, I'm just happy you're getting so involved. Maybe this will help you feel like you're fitting in."

Lucy kept a fake smile plastered to her face. Fitting in was apparently not what she did best. However, lying? It turned out she was pretty good at that.

And actually, this plan was perfect. The cheerleaders and the football players had identical practice and game schedules. It was the ideal cover, until . . .

"So what time's the game?" her dad asked enthusiastically.

Lucy's eyes widened. "What?"

"The game tonight. What time? It'd be fun to see you out there. You know, with your pom-poms and school spirit."

Lucy gulped. *Oh no.*

"It's just—it's my first game . . . and I don't even know all the details. I mean, I just don't think I'm ready to have you see me yet—I haven't even had one practice with the team, and if I totally suck, well—"

Her dad interrupted, putting her out of her misery. "Fine, fine. I won't come. I don't want to make you any more nervous than you already are."

Lucy breathed a sigh of relief. Crisis averted . . . for now. Her dad signaled and pulled into the school driveway.

"The next one," her dad promised. "I'll be there."

Lucy nodded. She'd just have to deal with that when the time came.


Her heart raced as she headed down to Coach Offredi's office. This would be her first time facing the team since last night's hazing incident. She knew they'd probably expected her to quit. And she'd been just about to do it, too. But now, at the thought of showing them how wrong they'd been about her, her pulse pounded. She couldn't wait to see the looks on their faces when she walked in the door. Suckers.

She peeked in and found most of the team already

there, sitting on folding chairs that had been dragged in and placed around the TV. Coach Offredi hadn't yet arrived. Everyone wore his football jersey. A few players were looking down, reading something, as Caleb read aloud.

"'Sophomore standout Lucy Malone is garnering lots of attention for being the first female player on the Beachwood football team in history. . . .'"

Lucy quickly realized they all had copies of the latest edition of the *Sand Dollar*. The article! It had come out just as Wesley had promised.

"'Delicate and thin, she doesn't look as strong as she actually is. In only her second practice, she was able to hold her own in a drill against her male opponent. . . .'"

In the back of the room, Benji cringed. Lucy bit her lip nervously, then told herself to stand tall. She wasn't going to be bullied into quitting something that she knew she was better at than anyone in the school. No more showing weakness, no more letting these boys think they'd gotten the best of her. From now on, she wasn't going to be ashamed to make her presence known. The irony was that now, standing in the back of the room, no one had even noticed she was there.

"'It's just great to be a part of this team,'" Caleb read in a high-pitched voice, mimicking her as he read her quote. "'You can't walk into a group of people that have this established bond and expect to just fit in. But these guys definitely have my respect and I hope I can earn theirs. . . .'"

He dropped his voice down, realizing it wasn't funny. He finished reading slowly. "'They're a really . . . great group of guys.'" Caleb looked up guiltily.

Tank scoffed. "What? We are!" Everyone laughed.

"It's not funny," Lucy said loudly from the back of the room. The sound of her own voice surprised even her. Benji looked over at her.

"Lucy—" he started to say.

"No!" she interrupted. "You guys—you're all jerks. You're jerks to me, to Benji . . . We're supposed to be teammates, and you're more interested in taping people to goalposts than in even giving them a chance."

"We haze everyone," Devon remarked defensively. "What's your problem? It's initiation."

"What's *your* problem?" Lucy demanded. "It's not about initiation, or Benji wouldn't have been up there too!"

Benji stepped up and put his hand on her arm. "Don't, Lucy. It's okay—"

"It's not okay!" she protested. "There's no reason to have anything against us! We haven't done anything."

"Yeah, you did." Cope nodded. "You joined our team."

She felt a lump forming in her throat. She swallowed it down, determined not to let her emotions get the best of her. At least not right here.

"Well, news flash," she said, her voice not even wavering. "It's not *your* team anymore. It's ours."

"What was that?" Coach Offredi asked as he burst in the door. "Is there some kind of problem here?"

The room was silent as the rest of the team stared at Lucy, their eyes pleading with her, begging her not to tell Coach Offredi about the goalpost incident.

"It's—it's nothing," Lucy stammered. The boys let out a collective sigh of relief.

"All right then," he barked. "Let's do this."

Lucy slid into the closest empty seat. The moment was over. But she had done it. She'd stood up for herself, and even though her heart was racing, a wave of calm started to wash over her. Her days of being intimidated were over.

"Curtis," Coach Offredi said loudly, referring to the school they were playing tonight. "They've got a strong offense and an even stronger defense. . . ."

He rolled tape of the opposing team, going over their plays in order, so that Beachwood would know what to expect. "We need to secure the gaps, charge straight ahead, and get some penetration across that line of scrimmage. . . . We're gonna need to knock 'em off their game."

As Lucy listened to Coach Offredi's instruction, it suddenly hit her. She was actually going to be playing in a real football game tonight! Forget touch football with her cousins on Thanksgiving. Tonight she was going to be on the field, under the light—with all eyes on her.

Coach Offredi snapped her out of her thoughts.

"Malone! You part of this team or not?" he asked bluntly.

"Yes, I am," she said proudly, without an ounce of hesitation in her voice.

"Then get your jersey on," he responded. "This team wears their jerseys to school on game day."

Lucy glanced down at her tank top and jeans. No one had mentioned the jersey rule. Must have slipped their minds while they were covering her with duct tape.

When Coach Offredi dismissed the team, Lucy darted out of the room to do what he asked. If she wanted to fit in, she was going to have to look the part.

Moments later, Pickle and Charlie found her in the girls' locker room. Lucy had just changed into her football jersey, which was definitely a huge fashion "don't." Yes, she wanted to be part of the team, but she didn't want to wear a circus tent!

"I don't know," Pickle considered as she tilted her head and looked at Lucy. "It's so baggy."

Lucy shrugged. "Normally it has shoulder pads and stuff under it," she explained, tugging self-consciously at the billowing material.

Charlie cringed. "Yeah, that's not good." Max burst in, armed with, as usual, Pixy Stix.

"What's everyone doing?" she asked. She took in Lucy's reflection in the mirror. "It never occurred to me—skinny jeans and a football jersey. It's . . . a look, I guess. . . ."

Suddenly, Pickle had an idea. "Take off your pants!"

"What?" Lucy laughed.

"Wow," Charlie said dryly. "You're forward."

"Actually, I'm a defender," corrected Pickle, referring to her own position on the soccer field. "*You're* a forward."

"Ha, ha," Charlie said, semi-amused by Pickle's lame soccer joke.

"Now seriously . . ." Pickle turned back to Lucy. "Drop 'em. I'll put on your jeans and you wear my skirt." Pickle was wearing a cute faded denim skirt that was worn out perfectly, with cute gold leggings underneath.

Quickly, the girls traded. Luckily, they were close to the same size. Lucy was just a little taller, so the miniskirt hit her a little higher on the thigh; Pickle, who was a little curvier than Lucy, sucked in her stomach to button Lucy's jeans.

"Okay," Pickle instructed, wiggling around inside the jeans a little, as they conformed to her body and actually fit. "Let's fix this." She spun Lucy around, grabbing the back of her jersey, gathering all the excess material and tying it into a big knot in the center of Lucy's back. Lucy's white tank top poked out underneath, keeping her belly covered. The gold in the jersey was complimented by the gold in the leggings. The outfit was . . .

"Perfect!" Pickle exclaimed.

Lucy admired her reflection in the mirror. "It's totally cute," she said, a hint of hesitation in her voice, "but I don't know. . . . I look so—"

"So *what?*" Max asked. "You look like the cutest football player Beachwood's ever had."

"I'm supposed to be trying to fit in, you guys. Do you really think dressing like this will help?"

Pickle grabbed Lucy by the shoulders. "That's what your problem is, Luce," she admonished. "Stop trying. You're not one of the guys."

"Obviously," Max concurred. "You have boobs."

Lucy looked down at her less-than-impressive chest. "With these? I practically *could* be one of the guys."

Charlie stepped in. "Lucy, listen to me," she advised. "I'm going to make your life a whole lot better. Don't be afraid to be a girl. You're good at it. You'll get further just being who you are than worrying about who you think they want you to be. It took me about sixteen years to figure that out for myself."

Lucy nodded, grateful for Charlie's advice. She glanced at her own reflection and reminded herself of her decision last night. She wasn't one of the guys. They'd made that perfectly clear. She was a girl; she might as well look and act like one.

"Okay," Lucy agreed, wanting to please her friends. "I'll wear it."

"Good." Pickle gave Lucy's shirt a final tug.

But suddenly Lucy remembered something she had to do.

"I'll meet you in the gym," she told Pickle. "I've gotta find Regan before class."

"Regan?" Charlie asked. Pickle shot a nervous glance at her.

"Yeah," Lucy quickly explained. "We accidentally switched bags last night, when she gave me a ride home."

Charlie looked horrified. "She drove you home?"

Lucy looked at Pickle. Had she said something wrong? Pickle was no help. Lucy tried to play it off.

"Yeah, I mean, it was that or walk." She shrugged.

Charlie rolled her eyes. "I'd have picked walking. Stay away from her, Lucy. Trust me. She is bad news."

"Uh, okay." Lucy forced a smile and grabbed Regan's backpack, in a hurry to get out of there. She didn't want to admit to Charlie that Regan had been totally sweet to her last night. And she *definitely* didn't want to mention that she was kind of looking forward to thanking Regan for the lift.

She darted out of the locker room and found Regan getting a latte at the campus mini-Starbucks.

"I said *no* sugar, *no* foam," Regan sighed as she handed the defective latte back to the frustrated barista.

"Regan," Lucy said, as she approached, "I think I accidentally took your backpack—"

Regan grabbed it back. "Oh, thank God! I left my favorite thong in there."

Lucy cringed. *Thong?* Ew.

Regan quickly reassured her. "Don't worry. It was clean." Then she apologized. "Sorry. TMI."

"TMI?" Lucy asked blankly.

Regan spelled it out. "Too. Much. Information. You'll get a lot of that around here." She handed Lucy her own backpack.

"Thanks," Lucy said, taking it.

Charlie walked by, heading to class. Lucy spotted her first and quickly dropped down on the ground to hide behind a trash can.

Regan peered down at her. "What're you doing?"

Lucy thought quickly. She shut one eye. "Oh, my contact—it's gotta be around here somewhere." She didn't actually wear contacts, but Annie did. Lucy had spent a couple of hours on her living room carpet one afternoon in search of her best friend's tiny transparent lens. It seemed like as good an excuse as any to be on the floor.

When she was sure the coast was clear, Lucy popped back up.

"Did you find it?" Regan asked.

Lucy blinked her eye a couple of times. "Oh, I guess it's still in there after all." Regan looked at her as if she were crazy. Lucy smiled nervously. Regan nodded at Lucy's outfit.

"So I guess you didn't quit? You know, the team? The jersey kind of gave it away."

Lucy looked down. "Oh, right." It was her turn to explain. "I told my dad I'd joined cheerleading. . . ."

"Oh? So my pom-poms came in handy?" Regan asked,

grabbing her new no-sugar, no-foam latte.

"Yeah, totally." Lucy smiled.

Regan lifted her coffee in a "cheers" gesture. "Glad I could help, then."

The second bell rang. Lucy turned. "I'd better get to gym."

Regan grabbed her arm, stopping her. "Hey, what're you doing after the game? Do you have, like, plans?"

Lucy shrugged. She'd been so focused *on* the game, it hadn't even occurred to her that life continued *after* it.

*Pickle and Charlie might want to do something,* she thought. But they hadn't mentioned anything yet.

"I don't really have any, like, plans . . ." she said, trailing off.

"Because I think Kendall's having a party. You know Kendall, right?"

Lucy didn't. And Regan was shocked. "Hello? Senior captain? Cheerleading?"

"Oh, right." Lucy nodded.

Regan gushed, "Her parents are in Cabo, and someone from football or cheerleading always throws something after the home games. It's just for us. You know, invite only. We try to keep it small, to keep the field hockey sluts away."

Lucy chuckled. *Field hockey sluts?*

"Anyway, if you want to meet up in the locker room after, we could go together," Regan offered.

"Really?" Lucy asked, beaming. This was incredible. Regan was one of the most popular girls in school! She knew Charlie hated Regan for whatever had happened between them last year, but maybe it had been a giant misunderstanding—because as far as she could tell, Regan was sweet and friendly. Not to mention beyond cool. And now she was inviting her to a *football party?* At a *senior cheerleader's house?*

"That sounds amazing," Lucy said. "I'll definitely be there."

By midday, as Lucy walked down the hall in her jersey, she couldn't believe how many people had stopped to talk to her.

"Good luck," some guy called out as he walked past her.

"Kick butt out there," a girl cheered as she was leaving the bathroom. It was as if having this jersey on made her part of something and made her belong. She imagined how it would be on Monday if she played well. Instead of walking tentatively through the corridors of Beachwood, she'd be strutting confidently with her head held high. She'd walk by Ryan and Devon and Cope, and they'd swarm her as if they'd been waiting for her, rushing to tell her how awesome she was Friday night.

Senior girls would walk by, noticing that she was surrounded by every hot football player in school. They'd come over to see what the commotion was, and when they realized Lucy was at the center of it, they'd invite her to the next big party they were having.

Ryan would say, "Not so fast," implying that she might not be free next Friday. Then he'd ask her out. In front of everyone. And she'd say yes, of course. Then he'd swoop her up into his arms and spin her around, like Benji had done on the football field, and she'd be so close to him that she'd be able to smell his cologne or deodorant or whatever it was about him that smelled so good.

Or . . . she would blow it. Blow the kickoff, blow the field goal, blow the game. And everything would stay pretty much like it was. No one except Benji would talk to her. Maybe Ryan would give her the time of day—like if she actually asked what time it was. Or maybe not. Maybe after tonight, no one would want to have anything to do with her.

As the day continued, the pressure mounted. Kids kept wishing Lucy well. Even Morbid resisted growling at her in gym class. And Martie made a special announcement in English, reminding everyone to come to the game tonight. In a rare move, she was even letting the soccer team finish practice half an hour early so they'd have time to shower, eat dinner, and get to the game.

Late, Lucy flung open the school doors, heading toward the parking lot. Coach Offredi had told them to meet there at three o'clock sharp. It was five minutes after.

Suddenly, Tank yelled, from a bus window, "On the bus, people! Let's go to the Sizzler!" But "Sizzler" came out more like "Sizzle-HER." Lucy reasoned that Tank must have been dropped on his head as a baby even more than she had.

Within minutes, the entire team was piled onto two different school buses to make their way to West L.A. to hit Sizzler for their pregame meal. Lucy looked around for a seat on the bus. Benji was sitting by himself. He was about to wave Lucy over when Ryan looked up and noticed her.

"Here, Malone. I have room," he offered. Lucy slid onto the bench next to Ryan. She was still mad at him for being part of the prank on her, but she couldn't help but notice as she sat that their legs were only inches apart. She thought she could smell Orbitz gum on his breath. Her heart raced despite her effort to control it. The loud bus engine roared as it started up, and with a lurch they headed out of the parking lot.

"So, this is a tradition," Ryan explained. "Pregame meal. It's basic carbo-loading at its worst." Lucy gave a polite, obligatory smile. She wasn't going to let him off the hook that easily.

"Come on, Lucy," Ryan cajoled. When she didn't respond, he leaned in. "Look, you were right. We're total jerks," he admitted. "I was there last night. I was part of that stuff. I mean, there's all the locker room teasing we always do—you know, guy stuff. . . ."

"Guy stuff?" Lucy asked skeptically.

Ryan tried to explain. "You know, we stick athletic tape to the really hairy guys. . . . Tank pees in peoples' shampoo bottles. . . . People turn off the lights while everyone's in the shower and you're grappling around and inevitably someone ends up in the middle of the room, covered in baby powder, usually Cope—"

Lucy interrupted him. "Just 'cause you do something all the time doesn't make it right, ya know?"

Ryan did. "No, I know. Think of it like we were treating you like one of the guys."

"Funny," she commented, amazed at how bold she was being. "You treat me like one of the guys when you're taping me to the goalpost, but not during actual practice."

"Look, I'm sorry," he continued. "You got it much harder than anyone. And you didn't deserve it. I don't have a problem with you being on the team—"

"But the other guys do," Lucy said dryly. She looked around. A few guys in the back were trying to give a sophomore an ultimate wedgie.

"They're idiots," Ryan insisted. "Listen, I think what you're doing is cool. I have a little sister—she's in seventh— and I was telling her that you were on the team. She thought it was the coolest thing. She's always been into football because of me, and last night at dinner, she was saying maybe when she was in high school, she'd try out."

Lucy smiled. That made her feel good.

"Besides," Ryan admitted, leaning in, "I like to win. And you're the best kicker we've got, so I don't care if you're a guy, a girl, a moose, whatever. . . ."

Lucy gave him a funny look. "A moose?"

"Okay." He smiled. "I'd care if you were a moose. Look how close we're sitting. People would talk. Mooses would talk. . . ."

"Is it mooses?" Lucy asked thoughtfully.

"Maybe it's meese," Ryan considered. "Like goose and geese?"

They both laughed as the bus turned into the Sizzler parking lot. Ryan gestured for her to lean in, as if he had a secret to tell her.

"A piece of advice: Eat the breadsticks," he instructed. "That's the key to winning the game. At least five breadsticks."

Lucy smiled. "I'll take your word for it." The team piled off the bus and into the restaurant, taking over as if they owned the place. She tried to find Benji, but he'd already made his way to the opposite end of a long table. Some of the guys grabbed booths. Ryan sat down in a seat.

"Here," he said, indicating a chair for her. It was sweet. He was suddenly looking out for her.

But just as she sat down, someone kicked the chair out from under her. She slammed down on the floor. Tank, Adam, and Nick nearly snarfed their Cokes laughing.

As Lucy pushed herself onto the chair, red-faced and

humiliated, Ryan looked ready to pummel all three of them. He rammed the table so that it banged into them, spilling their Cokes.

"Hey!" Adam yelled. "Watch it!"

"Why don't you guys pick on someone your own size?" Ryan seethed.

"Tank can't," Nick pointed out. "No one's his size." Everyone laughed, except Lucy, who stared at her water, mortified.

The waiter set down breadsticks, interrupting the awkward moment. Ryan slowly counted five out and placed them on her plate.

"For tonight," he reminded her. "You'll need it."

## eleven

There were forty-five minutes until game time when Lucy barreled into the girls' locker room to get dressed. She hadn't wanted to disappoint Ryan, but eating five breadsticks was completely out of the question. She'd placed three of them in her napkin and slid them into her purse. Now, she threw them into the trash as she rounded the corner to the last row of lockers. She stopped suddenly.

Her locker, the third one from the end, was covered with streamers and balloons and cutouts of little tiny footballs.

"Surprise!" a bunch of voices screamed in unison. The soccer girls poured out of the athletic office. Pickle was holding a big banner that read: IF SOMEONE TELLS YOU YOU KICK LIKE A GIRL, SAY, "THANKS!"

Lucy gasped in disbelief. She couldn't believe it. Charlie, Carla, Jamie, Erica, Heather, Karen, Ruthie, Max—they were all here to cheer her on.

Max threw her arms around Lucy's neck. "Go for it out there," she said.

Pickle patted her on the back. "Just pretend the ball is CW's face." Pickle and Lucy had taken to referring to Coach Offredi and his handlebar mustache in code. *CW* stood for "Coach Walrus."

The girls cheered as Lucy pulled on her knee-length white pants and secured her pads before pulling on her jersey. Charlie handed Lucy her helmet.

"Here," Charlie said. "Do it up." It was the same thing the soccer girls often said before practice.

"And afterwards, we're taking you out to celebrate." Pickle smiled.

Focused, Lucy grabbed her helmet and placed it on her head, snapping the straps together beneath her chin. She felt powerful and invincible, as if nothing could stop her, as if she was ready for battle! On her way out of the locker room, all the soccer girls hit her on the helmet, psyching her up.

"You got this, Luce!" they cheered. "Go show them what you can do!"

She crossed the hall and tentatively pushed her way into the boys' locker room. Coach Walrus—er, Offredi—had instructed her to come in as soon as she was ready. He was already mid-speech. Lucy lingered in the doorway, but Benji sweetly grabbed her hand and pulled her in.

"Come on," he said. "It's okay." Lucy stepped in and listened raptly to Coach Offredi.

"I want everyone to do their job out there tonight. Play

as a team. Be the hitters, not the ones who get hit. You walk onto that field tonight, you represent Beachwood. And what happens on the field stays on the field. Now let's do this!" Whoops and cheers went up from the group. The team roared and in a mass exodus trotted to the door, each hitting, tapping, or smacking the school crest for luck on his way out. Lucy had to jump to reach, but her fingertips managed to graze it. She was fired up and ready for this game.

"Let's go!" Coach Offredi yelled. "Tonight, we're one unit, one team!"

"One unit!" the guys chanted back. "One team!" Then, running as a pack toward the field together, they burst through a huge WILDCATS paper banner the cheerleaders were holding.

Lucy kept her head down, staying tight on Benji's heels as she jogged onto the field. She'd be too overwhelmed if she looked up. She just hoped one thing: that tonight, for once, she had luck on her side.

"Ryan Conner," the announcer said over the sound system. Ryan jogged out from the sidelines and took his place on the field. The cheerleaders went wild. The Beachwood part of the crowd erupted. As the senior star quarterback, he was clearly a sentimental fan favorite.

"Benji Mason," the announcer blared. Benji jogged out.

The announcer continued all the way down the Beachwood roster until . . .

"And making her football debut . . . newcomer Lucy Malone!" he yelled. The crowd clapped politely, but in the stands, people whispered, "Did he say *Lucy*? A girl? On the boys' team?"

Lucy jogged out confidently. *That's right! A girl on the boys' team!* The soccer girls and Martie cheered wildly.

"Go Lucy!" Pickle screamed.

"Girls rule!" Max yelled.

"Let's go, chickie," Carla called out.

"Do it up, Luce," Martie shouted, clapping her hands.

From the sidelines, Regan excitedly waved her pom-poms. "Yay, Lucy!" she screamed.

Lucy kept her gaze forward, slowly jogging to the end of the growing line of Beachwood players. As she ran past them, she felt as if everything was in slow motion, as if she were in a dream. Ryan reached out and, in a gesture of camaraderie, grabbed her face mask and butted helmets with her in front of everyone. Lucy felt as though she were soaring; she was floating on cloud nine . . . and ten . . . and eleven!

*"Oh, say, can you see, by the dawn's early light . . ."*

"The Star-Spangled Banner" was warbled out by an a cappella quartet. Standing on the field with her right hand over her heart, Lucy could feel the adrenaline coursing through her veins.

*"O'er the land of the free . . . and the home of the brave."*

That's what she was tonight. Free and brave. Tonight

for the first time, a girl was going to play football under these lights. She might have looked slight and slender, like she was a fragile doll that could easily break, but she wasn't. If this week hadn't broken her, nothing would. She was fired up. She was ready.

"Bring it in tight," Coach Offredi called out. "All right. You've worked hard. You've practiced. You've conditioned. You're ready. Fly around out there. Hit people and have fun." The guys slapped each other's shoulder pads and helmets, their adrenaline pumping. No one except Benji tapped Lucy to psych her up. She appreciated it.

"You and I," Benji reminded her. "We're a team tonight. It's us against everyone, okay?"

Lucy nodded fiercely. "Yeah. Us against everyone," she agreed.

"Hands in," Ryan ordered the team. Everyone put a hand in the center. Lucy was last to reach in. Ryan put a hand on top of hers. She felt tingles through her entire body. "Together on three," he instructed. "One . . . two . . . three . . ."

"TOGETHER!" the team yelled.

Ryan and Tank, the team captains, took the field for the coin toss. Tank called heads. It was tails. Curtis decided to take the ball first, which meant Lucy would kick off. She tried not to panic, but she just wanted to scream, "Oh my God, am I really supposed to be doing this?" What if she blew it? What if she topped it? Or squibbed it off the side of her foot? Or worse? What was worse? She didn't even know yet, but she was sure the possibilities were endless.

She looked up into the stands where the soccer girls were jumping up and down so excitedly that the bleachers seemed to be shaking in anticipation of what she was going to do. Lucy wished circumstances were different and that her dad was here to see her.

At least she knew her mom was with her—in her heart.

Coach Offredi grabbed her shoulders. "Now listen to me, kid," he said. Lucy inhaled quickly. That was what her dad called her. "This is what you wanted, your chance to prove something. So you go out there and get it done. I wanna see that ball land on their twenty—or better yet, their fifteen. You put 'em as far back as they can be. Go, kid, go!" He hit Lucy on the back too hard. The momentum practically catapulted her onto the field.

She jogged out with the kickoff coverage unit—the craziest guys on Special Teams. She hadn't known it before but Special Teams incorporated all the different kicking teams: the kickoff unit, the kick receiver unit, the punting unit, the PAT unit—basically, there were a lot of units. And these were the guys with the least field time but the most to prove. It was all or nothing for them, and they were prepared to go all out. The rule was that no one could run past the thirty-yard line until the ball was kicked, but the Beachwood team didn't like to start running from a dead stop as soon as the kicker hit the ball . . . which was why they lined up on their own fifteen-yard line. This was the play Coach Offredi called Rolling Thunder.

"I wanna hear a storm coming!" he yelled from the sidelines. "A storm!"

Lucy wondered if he'd settle for a drizzle. She set the ball on the tee at the thirty-yard line and backed up five yards to get a running start as well. If a person didn't know better, they'd think she looked like any other player out there—like she belonged.

Coach Offredi called to her, "Let's do it now. Go deep with this!" Lucy stood in the center of the field with five guys lined up to her right and five guys lined up to her left. They spread out behind her, spanning the width of the field. Lucy raised her arm. She was ready . . . or as ready as she was ever going to be.

The whistle blew. Lucy dropped her arm to signal the guys. They started running, gaining speed and momentum. Lucy popped forward, joining them, and BAM! She kicked the ball deep into Curtis's territory. Curtis's wide receiver gathered in the high, end-over-end kick on his own ten-yard line—even further than Coach Offredi had hoped. Lucy trailed the play, praying the Curtis return man didn't make it through the wedge of Beachwood defenders. Tank, leading the charge, brought the ball carrier down, hard, at the Curtis twenty-two-yard line.

On the sidelines, Beachwood cheered. Lucy jogged to the bench.

"Nice kick," Coach Offredi yelled from the sidelines. "Now let's keep it going, let's keep it going! We're in this now. Defense, make sure we play hard and fast. Smash 'em to bits! Tank, I wanna see a sack! Gimme a sack!"

On the initial series of plays, Beachwood's defense was strong. Tank applied pressure on Curtis's quarterback, who was young and skittish. After two hurried incomplete passes and being forced out of bounds after a gain of only five yards on the third down, Curtis was forced to punt to Beachwood.

On the sidelines, Lucy cheered as Sascha, Beachwood's punt retriever, took the kick on the Beachwood thirty and sidestepped an onrushing Curtis defender to find an open hole. He juked, darting one way and then quickly back the other way, and broke away down the right sideline, advancing an impressive thirty yards to the Curtis forty, before being knocked out of bounds. The Beachwood bench erupted in cheers, while on the field, the guys pounded Sascha's helmet excitedly. The band played and the cheerleaders bounced up and down as if their lives depended on it.

With every pass and every gained yard for Beachwood, Lucy's nervous energy increased as a potential field goal or PAT attempt loomed even larger. Her casual foot tap had morphed into her entire leg shaking uncontrollably.

She kept telling herself, *I can do this. I can do this.* But could she? Now? When it counted most?

Ryan threw a perfect spiral pass to Kevin on a down-and-out pattern. Kevin caught it almost effortlessly in the corner of Curtis's end zone. TOUCHDOWN! Lucy knew what that meant. She gulped. *Her* turn.

"PAT unit," Coach Offredi ordered. "We're goin' for one." He grabbed Lucy by the shoulders. "This is all you, kid. Let's go."

*Thanks, CW,* Lucy thought. *Way to take off the pressure.* But the truth was, no one could take off the pressure. This *was* all her. She glanced down the field at the goalpost. The space between the uprights looked so much narrower than it had seemed in practice. She was so nervous that not even looking at Benji helped.

The PAT unit ran onto the field, settling at the three-yard line. Lucy ran out behind Benji, knowing they each had a job to do. Caleb would snap the ball back seven yards, where Benji was waiting at the ten. Then all she'd have to do was kick.

Lucy stepped off her paces. So much adrenaline was pumping through her, she felt as though she could explode. Caleb and the line moved into position, looking for the signal from Benji. The crowd quieted down. Lucy waited, holding her breath. Benji put his hands out in front of his body, in a position to catch the ball. The flash of Benji's hands signaled Caleb to snap the ball back, straight into Benji's grasp. This time, Benji caught it perfectly, and in one smooth motion he brought the tip of the football to the ground. He deftly spun the laces away from Lucy's foot, a split second before Lucy nailed it. BAM!

It sailed up, up, and directly between the goalposts. They'd done it! Hell, *she'd* done it! She'd actually kicked a PAT! The score was 7-0! The Beachwood section of the bleachers roared.

As Lucy jogged back over onto the sidelines, she could feel the hands of a few of her teammates patting her on the back and hitting her helmet.

In the bleachers, the soccer girls chanted, "Lu-cy! Lu-cy! Lu-cy!"

Regan cheered from the sidelines. "Nice, Luce!"

Lucy smiled broadly. She felt as if her body could barely contain her happiness.

Taking a seat on the bench, she took off her helmet and shook out her hair. Inside, her helmet was damp with sweat. This would definitely qualify as a bad hair day, but she didn't care, because she had done it. She had scored! A hand gripped her shoulder, giving it a little squeeze. She looked up to see Coach Offredi. He wasn't even looking at her, just giving that small gesture of wordless praise. Happily, she exhaled. Had she proven herself? Was he actually proud of her?

The rest of the game felt like a giant blur, like a dream she didn't want to end. Leading 7-0 at the half, Beachwood ran for two more touchdowns in the third quarter. Lucy nailed both PAT attempts, and Beachwood held off a strong fourth-quarter rally by Curtis to win 21-13.

As the team rushed into the locker room, the excitement in the air was palpable.

"Way to get it done tonight." Coach Offredi grinned. Even his mustache looked happier. "You should all be proud."

Lucy lingered in the doorway. After all, it was the boys' locker room.

Ryan pushed her in. "Malone, you're on the team. Get in here. No one's naked." He placed a hand on her back, ushering her in. Benji noticed.

A shirtless Tank howled in the background, pleased with himself. "Well, almost no one." Ryan smiled, his hand resting on the small of her back. "You did great tonight." Lucy prayed his hand would linger there for a few more seconds.

Coach Offredi clapped his hands loudly and Ryan moved to take a seat on the bench. "Great passing game, great defense—that was a hell of an effort out there tonight, men."

Lucy grimaced. *Men?*

Coach Offredi *ahem*ed and corrected himself. "I mean, people." A small smile crept across Lucy's face.

The coach grabbed a football off the ground, from next to his feet. The guys cheered. Lucy glanced around anxiously, not knowing what to expect.

"And the MVP ball goes to . . ." Coach Offredi paused

dramatically. The room settled down and grew quiet. "Who else?" He tossed the ball to Ryan, who caught it in his lap. He held it up in celebration.

"To our season," Ryan said. "To victory." The entire team, including Lucy, cheered wildly.

## twelve

The hot water felt like liquid heaven as it rushed over Lucy's entire body. Wearing flip-flops and a bikini (no way she was getting naked), she scrubbed all the sweat, dirt, and anxiety off her. The girls' locker room shower wasn't as great as the one at home—which was marble, and had a rain nozzle—but it felt just as good. Better, in fact. She turned off the faucet and grabbed the towel she'd thankfully remembered to pack in her athletic bag. Wrapping herself in it, she padded out toward the lockers, leaving a trail of wet, soapy footprints behind her.

The cheerleaders were mid-transformation from their uniforms into party attire. As soon as they saw Lucy, they applauded. Lucy beamed, surprised. Regan turned and smiled.

"You were seriously amazing tonight," she gushed. "Did you notice how Ryan was cheering you on?"

*He was?* Lucy beamed.

"Seriously," she continued. "You kicked farther than any of the boys ever did."

"Yeah," a beautiful brunette agreed. "And you looked

like one of them, too." Lucy stared at the girl, confused at this out-of-the-blue insult.

"Um . . ." Lucy didn't know what to say. She didn't even know this girl.

Regan realized, jumping in. "Oh, Lucy. This is Kendall. She's having the party tonight." Regan quickly turned to Kendall, worried. "I invited Lucy. That's okay, right? I mean, technically she's part of the football team—"

Kendall shrugged as if she could care less. "Whatever." Regan forced a polite smile to Lucy, who was standing in front of all these new girls feeling suddenly self-conscious. She felt as though Kendall could see right through her.

"I'm just going to—um—put some clothes on," Lucy said hurriedly, as she padded on wet feet to her locker. Rifling through her athletic bag, she pulled out a pair of jeans and a long shirt with an empire waist to wear over them. She liked the dress/jeans combo. In fact, she'd seen Regan sport it a few times, so it must have been cool enough for Malibu.

Regan followed her over. "Sorry about that. Kendall can be a little intimidating to new people," she explained. "But she's really great and super popular. If you're friends with her, your life is infinitely easier at this school."

Lucy nodded agreeably. "Okay."

"So you're still gonna come, right?" Regan pressed. "To the party?"

"Let's go, bitches," Kendall called. "Train's rolling out."

Lucy was surprised. First, *bitches*? Second, was Kendall actually talking to her?

"She calls everyone that," Regan explained. "It's a term of endearment."

*I bet,* Lucy thought.

"Hurry up," Regan urged. "Let's go." Lucy grabbed her stuff, excitedly—and then she suddenly remembered something. Pickle had said she and the girls wanted to celebrate after the game too. She'd become so wrapped up with the cheerleaders' attention, she'd totally forgotten. Lucy tried to stay calm, but this was obviously a crisis situation. It was one step away from requiring canned goods, a flashlight, and a transistor radio. Lucy told herself to speak.

"Um . . . I just . . . I actually was supposed to . . . actually, I forgot. . . ." *Okay, get ahold of yourself,* she thought. "Could I just finish getting ready really quick and meet you at your car?"

Annoyed, Kendall called out, "Regan, you're taking too long. I'm getting a ride from Ryan. Just meet me there."

Regan turned to Lucy. "Sure, just hurry." She took off, nipping at Kendall's heels. "K! Wait up! I can take you!" Lucy had a feeling Regan did a lot of following after Kendall.

Lucy quickly stuffed her uniform and wet towel into her bag and fished around for her lip gloss. She'd forgotten deodorant and perfume. Oh well. Lip gloss would have to be enough. She pressed her lips together, then bolted out of the locker room to find her friends. Pickle, Charlie, and Max were gathered in the parking lot. They cheered when they saw Lucy.

"You were awesome out there!" Max beamed, jumping up and down.

Charlie agreed. "So cool, Lucy. Carla said to tell you congrats. She had to go."

"Oh, thanks." Lucy smiled as she approached. Pickle gave her a warm hug.

"So, where to, superstar?" Pickle asked. "It's your celebration dinner, so you decide where."

Lucy gulped. This was where things got complicated.

"I actually already ate dinner," she admitted. "At Sizzler."

Max cringed. "Ew. I didn't know people actually went there."

"Yeah, so I'm not really hungry," Lucy said. "But there's this party—it's kind of for all the football players and stuff. I was thinking maybe we could all go. And you know, maybe celebrate there."

Pickle's face lit up. "A football party? Really? Oh my God—*we* could go?" A wave of relief washed over Lucy. Of course Pickle would be excited to go to a football party.

Lucy smiled. "Yeah, this time I can get us in without Benji. But I think he'll be there too."

Max smiled. "That's cool. I'm down." All three girls looked at Charlie, who shifted uncomfortably in her Converse. "A football party? Are you serious?"

"Lucy!" Regan shouted from across the parking lot. "Are you coming or what?"

A look of horror spread across Charlie's face. "Did Regan Holder invite you?" she asked pointedly.

"Regan? No," Lucy lied. "She just said she'd drive me. Since, ya know, I'm on the team and all."

Charlie shook her head. "Well, I'm not. And either way, I wouldn't be caught dead at a party with her." She turned to Lucy. "And if you want your high school experience to be the least bit pleasant, you shouldn't either."

Pickle stepped in. "Look, Regan didn't invite her. It's a football party and she's on the football team. No one here is friends with Regan Holder, that's for sure."

Charlie looked skeptical. Lucy looked down at her shoes. She wasn't *friends* with Regan, but she had certainly been *friendly*.

Pickle put an arm around Lucy. "She's cool," Pickle said, referring to Lucy. "It's obvious—she's one of us."

Suddenly, Lucy panicked. "You know what?" she said. "Let's just forget the party and go to dinner. I barely even ate at Sizzler. I stuck, like, three breadsticks in my purse." Lucy headed toward Charlie's car but Pickle didn't budge. "Pickle," Lucy asked, "what's wrong?"

Pickle shifted uncomfortably in her shoes and looked down at the ground.

"I really want to go to the party," Pickle admitted softly. "Charlie, I'm sorry."

"I kinda do too," Max agreed. "Sorry, Charlie."

"Fine." Charlie shrugged, clearly stung. "Have fun celebrating." She hopped in her car and took off. Lucy felt both responsible for the spat and helpless to fix it.

"She'll be okay," Pickle said comfortingly, trying to be positive.

"But how are we going to get there?" Max asked. "She was our ride."

Just then, Charlie peeled out, nearly running over Regan, who was standing in the middle of the school's driveway.

"Hello?" Regan shouted at the back of Charlie's car. "Driver's ed? Look into it!"

Lucy considered. "Let me see if Regan will give us all a ride. . . ." She ran over to ask Regan, "Can we squeeze two more in?"

Regan raised her eyebrows as she scanned Pickle and Max up and down. A handful of cheerleaders were already piled in the back.

Regan hopped in the driver's seat. "Sure," she answered. "If they don't mind the trunk."

Fifteen minutes later, after a long and winding drive, Regan pulled up a narrow driveway and parked her SUV on the grass behind the dozens of other cars already lined up in haphazard rows. Lucy, crammed in the back with a few other cheerleaders, glanced at Pickle and Max, smashed in the way back, behind the last seat. It wasn't *exactly* the trunk, but it wasn't far from it.

Regan's SUV lurched to a stop and all the girls piled out. Lucy opened the hatch. Pickle and Max spilled out onto the wet grass.

"Oh my God, I think my life flashed before my eyes," Max said breathlessly.

"Good thing it wasn't the nachos from the game," Pickle groaned. "I thought I was going to be sick. Regan's driving? Whoa."

"Maybe they'll have some ginger ale or something," Lucy offered, hoping that would settle Pickle's stomach.

"Yeah, maybe," Pickle said, recomposing.

But Lucy quickly realized that ginger ale was not on the list of beverages provided. Forget the basement parties they'd had back in Ohio, where they would pass around a lone beer stolen out of Annie's garage; this was the real deal.

Lucy took in the sight. Kendall's place wasn't a house—it was a mansion. Outside, the yard was sprawling, perched high on a cliff overlooking the ocean, and the infinity pool was full of little fountains and caves where the water seemed to disappear right over the edge. And inside was even better. With a step-down living room and gigantic kitchen, this house was built for parties. And Kendall was perfectly cast in the role of cute hostess, showing everyone to the provisions. "So there's beer pong in the game room, there's an ice luge on the patio, and the keg's in the kitchen."

Max looked around, stunned. Clearly, she'd never seen a party like this. None of them had. Suddenly, a familiar voice called over to Lucy.

"Malone, you made it!" Ryan said, seeing the girls. He was holding a red plastic cup. Lucy beamed as he headed over. Pickle smiled shyly and politely too.

Max gave a chin nod. "'Sup?"

He put a hand on Lucy's shoulder. "Superstar on the field tonight, huh?" he said proudly to Pickle and Max.

Max stuck out a hand. "I'm Max," she said confidently.

Lucy realized that they didn't all know each other.

"Max is on the soccer team," Lucy explained. "So's Pickle," she said, gesturing to Pickle, who stood nervously frozen beside her.

"Pickle?" Ryan asked, confused.

"Wait—you guys haven't met either?" Lucy realized.

Pickle shook her head. She seemed stunned into silence.

"What kind of name is Pickle?" he asked.

"It's . . . um, it's kind of . . . when I was born, my sister . . . she's older . . ." Pickle stammered. Lucy waited for Pickle to get to the point, but she continued to stammer out a reply. "She couldn't say . . . I mean, it's weird because she could say, you know, much harder words. . . ."

Lucy interrupted. "It's short for Nicole."

Pickle smiled at her, relieved. "Right. Short for Nicole."

"Makes sense." Ryan thought it about it for a minute. "Sort of."

Pickle giggled. Kendall rushed over and threw her arms around Ryan's neck.

"There you are," she gushed. Regan was close behind her, carrying two drinks, one for Kendall and one for herself. Ryan grabbed Kendall's legs, literally sweeping her off her feet so that he was cradling her in his arms. Ryan jerked his body, pretending the arm under her upper back was giving out. Her body lurched toward the ground.

"Don't drop me!" she yelled, holding onto him tighter.

"I got you," Ryan assured her. "No one's dropping you. I'm not Regan." Apparently last year, in what was referred to as the Botched Basket Incident, Regan had been part of a foursome that had dropped Kendall on her tailbone.

"That was a long time ago," Regan said defensively. "And a total accident."

"Ryan!" Kendall screamed. At that moment, Regan wasn't even on her radar.

Finally, Ryan set Kendall back down. "Okay, okay— stop freaking out."

Lucy forced a smile. She couldn't help but wish that she had been the girl that Ryan had picked up and held in his arms.

"Who needs a drink?" Ryan asked, worming his way out of Kendall's grasp.

"I have one somewhere," Kendall sighed, annoyed. "Regan?" Regan quickly handed a drink over to Kendall.

Lucy turned to Pickle. "You wanted a ginger ale, right?"

"Ginger ale?" Kendall scoffed. "What're you, twelve?"

Embarrassed, Pickle shot an annoyed look at Lucy. Then she turned to Ryan. "How 'bout a beer?" she asked.

Max nudged Pickle in the side. They weren't supposed to drink during the season. Well, technically they weren't supposed to drink at all, but from the looks of the party, no one was really adhering to that law.

"Girls?" Ryan asked Max and Lucy. "You want anything?"

"I'm just gonna get a pop," Lucy said.

"Pop?" Kendall laughed. Lucy remembered too late that no one in California said "pop." It was "soda" here.

"Come on," Regan said. "I'll show you where everything is." And together they went in search of soda. Moments later, they were pilfering the fridge for anything nonalcoholic.

"So, you and Kendall are, like, best friends?" Lucy asked innocently.

Regan nodded. "Yeah, totally." She noticed bottles in the fridge. "Ew. Wine coolers? So nineties." She found a Diet Coke and handed it to Lucy. "It's better with rum, but whatevs."

Lucy smiled. "Thanks."

Regan leaned in close. "So . . . I think he likes you."

Lucy's eyes widened. "You think who likes me?"

"Ryan," Regan answered. "He was totally flirting with you."

Lucy tried to keep her jaw from dropping to the floor. Kendall walked in, suddenly interested.

"Who was flirting with Lucy?" she said accusatorily.

Regan clammed up. "No one." Kendall nodded, choosing for this moment to believe her.

"I need a refill," she said, holding out her drink. "You want one, Reeg?"

Regan took Kendall's cup. "Sure. I'll get it."

Kendall put an arm around Lucy's shoulder. "Yeah, you should let Lucy mingle." Then, to Lucy, she said, "I mean, you gotta mingle, unless you want to stay single."

Lucy smiled self-consciously. There was only one guy she wanted to mingle with. She decided to go find him.

Walking into the living room, she didn't see Ryan anywhere. And come to think of it, she hadn't seen Pickle and Max for a while either. She glanced around the room and noticed Benji at the cheese squares.

"Cheese is so much better in little squares than big triangles," Lucy pontificated. "Don't you think?" She gingerly sipped her Diet Coke, without the rum.

"You know what's the worst, though?" Benji asked. "That thin cheese. You know, the flat squares, wrapped individually. The yellow ones? Hate those."

"Me too!" Lucy practically yelled. "And what about that white stuff? On top of the Brie? Are you supposed to actually *eat* that? It's disgusting."

Benji agreed. "I always eat the insides out with a cracker." He thought for a second, then asked, "You know what else I hate?"

"That cottage cheese is called cheese when really it's nothing like cheese?" quipped Lucy.

Benji pointed a finger directly at her. "Yes."

Suddenly, Ryan interrupted, shouting across the room. "Malone! Get over here."

Lucy couldn't believe he was actually calling to her. She quickly ran over. He pulled Lucy into the hallway and put his face close to hers. She wondered what he was going to say. That he wanted to date her? That he thought she was beautiful? That he was crazy in love with her?

Then he broke the bad news. "Your friend—the vegetable one—she's puking in the bathroom."

*The vegetable one?* Lucy's eyes widened when she realized what he was talking about. And that was *not* what she wanted to hear.

"What?" Lucy gasped in horror. Pickle was puking? "Oh my God. What am I, like, supposed to do?"

Ryan shrugged, distracted. "I don't know. That freshman's in there with her." He wasn't being rude, Lucy reasoned: he just didn't want to deal with someone puking any more than she did.

"Okay," she said, deflated. "Thanks for telling me." She slunk past all the laughing cheerleaders and Tank, who dramatically crushed a beer can on his forehead. She made her way down the long hallway toward the bathroom. Her heart raced and her knees felt shaky. This was *so* the opposite of how she wanted to be celebrating her first football game. She pushed open the door, where Pickle was hovering over the toilet. Max held her hair back. She looked up.

"Oh, thank God," Max said seeing Lucy. "Help."

Lucy stood frozen in the doorway. She couldn't explain the panic that was enveloping her. For a strange second, she saw her mother's face, gray and ill, instead of Pickle's. "I don't . . . really . . . I don't know what to do," she stammered. She wanted out. Out of this bathroom. Out of this house.

Pickle's body lurched. Lucy bolted out into the hallway, terrified.

"Oh my God, oh my God," she whispered to herself. This was the reason she didn't drink. Fear.

"Lucy," Max called out. "Get in here." Lucy recomposed. It took every ounce of willpower she had not to burst into tears. She peeked her head in.

"I'll go get help," she offered, looking for any means of escape. Before Max could protest, Lucy ran out of the bathroom and down the hall. She wasn't sure what or who she was looking for, but as soon as she saw Benji, she knew she'd found the answer.

"Benji," she called out desperately. Benji set down his sixth mini-quiche of the night and rushed over.

"What's wrong?" he asked, his voice full of concern.

"It's Pickle," Lucy said, breaking down. "She's in the bathroom. She's sick. Well, not exactly sick, but—"

Benji interrupted. "One too many rum and Cokes? Those are her favorite. And by favorite I mean she drank it that one time last year we stole a bottle of rum from my parents' liquor cabinet."

"Really?" Lucy asked, eager for a brief distraction. She always forgot that Benji and Pickle had actually spent a fair amount of time together last year. "What happened?"

"She passed out before I could get up the nerve to kiss her," he admitted frankly. Lucy clapped her hand over her mouth, stifling a laugh. Benji was so brutally honest. It was endearing enough to make her momentarily forget how completely and utterly freaked out she was.

"Listen, I'm supposed to be home by eleven-thirty. My dad thinks I'm at some postgame cheerleading get-together—" A whoop went up from the kitchen, where half the cheerleading team was egging on Kendall, who was drinking beer from a homemade funnel like a partying professional.

"—which, technically, I guess I am," Lucy continued. "But I have to get home—and get Pickle and Max home, too."

"I could give you guys a ride," Benji offered. Max hurried out, looking for Lucy.

"Hello?" Max said to Lucy, exasperated. "Thanks for bailing!"

"I'm not bailing," Lucy shot back defensively. "I'm finding you guys a ride home." Okay, she was bailing.

"Wait. *You guys?*" Benji asked. "Are you not coming with us?"

Lucy gulped. The truth was that she needed a ride, but she wouldn't get in the car with a potential puker for all the money in the world. She wouldn't, even if getting in meant she could move back to Ohio.

Benji shook his head. "So you want me to bring Pickle and Max home . . . and you're not even coming?"

Lucy sighed. Well, when he put it *that* way, it sounded particularly bad. Max walked back toward the bathroom and instructed Benji:

"You get the car; I'll get Pickle." But Benji didn't budge. He stood staring at Lucy.

"No, no," Lucy relented. "I'm coming. I . . . I . . . really appreciate you, you know, driving us."

Max reappeared, using her body to prop up an unsteady Pickle, who looked like she'd been run over by a Mack truck.

"You guys go on to the car," Lucy said. "I'm going to thank Kendall for all of us." Before anyone could protest or ask for help, Lucy ran off to find Kendall or anyone who wasn't on the verge of explosive vomiting.

"You're leaving?" Regan gasped, spilling half of her

rum and Coke on Lucy's silver flip-flops. Lucy could feel the Coke fizzing on the tops of her toes.

"Yeah," Lucy said, disappointed. "Pickle—she's in bad shape, so . . . I should help get her home—"

Regan snorted. "Benji and that frosh can get her there. You're staying." Regan called out to Kendall. "Lucy's staying, right?"

"Whatever," Kendall slurred back. Lucy nervously glanced over her shoulder in time to see Benji and Max drag Pickle out of Kendall's front door.

"I really can't," Lucy said. "I need a ride home anyway."

"One of us can give you one," Regan assured her. "I'm barely even sipping this." Then she leaned in, enticing Lucy. "Besides, I'm driving Ryan home, too." Lucy's heart fluttered. She could actually be squished in the backseat with Ryan. Maybe it'd be so crowded she'd have to sit on his lap. And she wouldn't have to deal with Pickle.

She felt guilty, like a bad friend, but she *had* gotten them into this party after all. And that had to at least count for something. Didn't it?

When Lucy woke up the next morning, she felt terrible. She guessed not as terrible as Pickle probably did—but she felt terrible just the same. The ride with Ryan had been anything but eventful. He'd sat in the front while Lucy was sandwiched between Tank and Kevin in the backseat.

Sascha, Aidan, and Caleb were also crammed back there, so it was cozy, to say the least. She supposed she couldn't complain that she hadn't had any team bonding time.

Regan had dropped Lucy off last, so she'd gotten home at twelve forty-five, which had led to a fight with her dad. . . .

"But Dad! What was I supposed to do? Call you and wake you up?" she'd asked. He'd said she was supposed to do *exactly* that. A firm eleven o'clock curfew had instantaneously been put in place.

She rolled over and turned on her phone. Her multiple late-night texts to Pickle, Max, and Benji had all gone unanswered. And they continued to be unanswered . . . Saturday afternoon, Saturday night, all day Sunday. By the time Sunday night rolled around and her IMs had been ignored, her e-mails received with no response, and her voice mail messages left unanswered, Lucy knew she was screwed. They were officially mad at her.

"Mason, come on," Coach Offredi bellowed at Benji, as the team lifted weights before school. "You really going to let a girl press more weight than you? I've already gotten an earful from your old man. What would he say about that?"

Benji was struggling to complete his third set of ten leg presses. Discouraged, Benji let the weight collapse back down with a crashing thud. Lucy had just finished her leg extensions and glanced over from her drop-downs. She wasn't sure that what she was doing was actually called a drop-down, but it was where she took weight and, with straight legs and a straight back, dropped it down to her toes and back up, so that's what she called the exercise in her head. Drop-downs.

Coach Offredi turned to Lucy. "Lucy, get over there and show him how it's done." A look of panic crossed Lucy's face. She knew Coach Offredi wasn't actually being nice to her. He was just using her to humiliate Benji. She reluctantly set her weight back on the rack. At least he was using her name rather than calling her "little girl," like he had been. That was an improvement, wasn't it?

She approached the leg press machine, wondering if it was called anything more technical than the leg press machine, where Benji was huffing and puffing. Lucy tried to act as though Coach Offredi hadn't just ordered her over there.

"Um . . . you done?" she asked brightly. The real question she wanted to ask was, *Are you mad at me for ditching you on Friday night?* Benji looked up at her without actually moving his head in her direction, just his eyes. He reluctantly swung his legs around the floor and hoisted himself up. Wordlessly, he brushed past her. Lucy had her answer. Yes.

When Lucy entered the locker room for gym class, she found Pickle dressing out and tentatively walked over.

"Hey," Lucy said softly, unsure whether Pickle wanted anything to do with her.

Pickle looked up. "Lucy, oh my God." She hurriedly apologized. "I am so sorry about Friday night."

"Sorry?" Lucy gasped. Why was Pickle apologizing? If anyone needed to apologize, it was Lucy—for abandoning her.

"I got so nervous," Pickle explained. "And I don't know. . . . I was still nauseous from the ride and then I just started drinking. I don't really drink, obviously, except that one time with Benji, and before I knew what happened . . . I just hope I didn't embarrass you."

Lucy exhaled, a wave of relief washing over her. "Embarrass me? No! I mean, it happens to everyone." *Didn't it?* Lucy had no idea, but it sounded good and comforting. "So Max and Benji were okay?" she asked. "I was afraid maybe they were mad because I decided to stay. . . ."

Pickle shrugged. "They didn't say anything to me—but of course, even if they had, I wouldn't have known it. I was out of it all weekend. I had to tell my mom I caught some forty-eight-hour bug."

"Did she buy it?" Lucy asked curiously.

Pickle considered. "Hard to tell. Parents are smarter than we think, I think."

Lucy nodded, thinking of her dad. Hopefully, he wasn't smart enough to figure out that she wasn't on the cheerleading team. Because if he was, she could forget her curfew being eleven o'clock at night. It would be three in the afternoon! The bell rang. Lockers slammed as kids hurried to get onto the gym bleachers before Miss Sullivan marked them as late.

"So I didn't ruin my chances of getting invited to another party?" Pickle asked as she quickly tied her shoelaces. Lucy slipped her T-shirt over her head. "Because I didn't even get to talk to Ryan for more than a second. . . ."

*Ryan?* Lucy did a quick double take. "What?" Since when did Pickle want to talk to Ryan?

"Ryan," Pickle whispered. "That's the guy I like. You know, the quarterback?"

Lucy shook her head, caught off guard. "Since when do you like Ryan?"

"Since last year," she admitted. "When I didn't make the soccer team. As soon as I saw the list, I had to hurry to get to class. But I just couldn't do it. I was so upset. So I went out the back door, by the portables, ya know? And he was there, on the steps. And I couldn't stop crying and I told him what happened. And . . . he hugged me. *Ryan.* The most popular guy in school hugged me. I don't think he remembers it. He never recognizes me . . . but he told me that he didn't make the football team his freshman year and to keep trying . . . and that's what I did . . . and now . . ."

Lucy nodded. Now she was on the soccer team.

"You get to see him every day," Pickle said enviously. "You're *so* lucky."

*Lucky, right.* Lucy quickly slipped her sneakers on. She didn't even bother to lace them up. She just wanted to end this conversation. Fast.

"Come on," she said. "We're gonna be late." She hurried across the locker room, pushing the double doors open into the gym. Her shoes squeaked on the gym floor. Pickle hurried to keep up.

"So, do you think you could help me?" Pickle asked, then grabbed her head. "Ooooh, head rush." They sat down on the bleachers.

"Help you what?" Lucy asked, dreading what Pickle was about to say.

"Get to know Ryan," Pickle insisted, smoothing down her hair with her hands and then tucking it behind her ears. Pickle was so adorable, but compared to Ryan, who was a senior, she seemed like such a little girl.

"Um . . ." Lucy hesitated. "I don't know. . . ." She trailed off. How could she tell Pickle she'd help her get to know the boy that she herself liked? But could she say she wouldn't? Pickle had been great to her, and it was obvious she was really into Ryan. What kind of friend would she be if she said no? Miss Sullivan blew the whistle and began dividing them into teams for badminton.

Lucy and Pickle were placed on competing teams.

"So," Pickle insisted, "will you help me?"

Lucy grabbed a racket out of the pile and took a long look at Pickle.

"Of course I will," Lucy finally answered. And then she headed toward her side of the court. If she'd thought she was screwed this weekend, it was nothing compared to how she felt right now. If Pickle wanted help with Ryan, what did that mean for her?

## thirteen

Benji was still on Lucy's mind as she distractedly flipped through the pages of *Madame Bovary* before English class started. She suddenly realized she had forgotten to finish her assignment. Martie usually assigned three chapters over the weekend, but since they were so close to the end of the book, this time Martie had assigned four in order to finish. Lucy hadn't read the last chapter and knew she would be screwed if Martie called on her.

"Wanna know what happens?" Ryan asked, sliding into the desk next to her.

Lucy looked up at the sound of his voice and smiled. "I do," she said wistfully, then quickly reminded herself he was just offering to synopsize the chapter, not asking her to be his lawfully wedded wife.

Ryan shrugged playfully. "Well, ya shoulda read the book then." He laughed. Lucy gave him a look.

"Thanks for nothing then," she said, mock hurt in her voice. She shut her book, giving up. People were coming in and taking their seats. She wasn't going to get any reading done anyway. Charlie entered and headed toward the back of the class.

"Hey," Lucy said quietly, more to Charlie's back than to her front. Charlie didn't give her so much as a smile.

*This is not going well,* Lucy thought to herself. She looked down at *Madame Bovary* and sighed. She knew Charlie was upset about the party, about the other night with Regan. Benji was upset about her enlisting him to deal with Pickle and Max, then abandoning him. She hadn't had time to make things right with Benji during weights or in gym class, and now, with Charlie across the room, she couldn't talk to her before English started . . . but she could at least keep her promise to Pickle.

She turned to Ryan. "So that party was pretty fun, huh? On Friday?"

"I guess." Ryan shrugged. "It's kinda always the same old thing though, ya know? We've been throwing 'em since sophomore year."

"So it must make it more fun when there are new people," she offered. "You know, people you don't know that well . . . but, you know, might want to get to know better."

Ryan furrowed his eyebrows, unsure at what she was getting at. "Uh-huh," he said slowly. She hurried to make her point.

"What . . . I guess what I mean is . . ." she stammered, "it's nice to get to know new people . . . people who are excited to get to know you . . ."

He looked at her blankly. Up in front of the class, Martie pulled out the attendance roster. Lucy acted fast, before her window was gone.

"Like my friend Pickle," she said, trying to sound as casual as possible. "I know she was excited to get to know you—and I thought maybe you might be, you know . . . I don't know . . . interested in her. Maybe."

Ryan paused for a moment. It felt like an eternity. Finally, he spoke. "Is that the vegetable girl?" he asked, then quickly remembered "Wait—the puker?" Lucy's heart sank on behalf of her friend. No girl would want the boy she had a major crush on to refer to her as "the puker."

"Well, she does a lot more than puke," Lucy quickly interjected. "She plays soccer and sings and—well, there's lots of stuff you'd find out if you were interested in getting to know her."

"Okay," Ryan said, confused. "I'll . . . um . . . keep that in mind." Lucy stared at her own knuckles. Were they inflamed because she'd been popping them? She really had to break that habit. She wondered why she was suddenly thinking about her knuckles when this whole Pickle thing *really* wasn't going well.

"Not that you have to get to know her," Lucy said hurriedly. "I mean, just if you wanted to . . . I think she likes you. That's all." Okay, there. She'd said it. Somewhat clearly and coherently. Finally. She'd always known she was awful at public speaking, but now she made a mental note that maybe private speaking wasn't her strong suit either.

Ryan leaned in close to her. His breath smelled minty, like toothpaste. It always did. God, he was probably the kind of guy who brushed twice a day *and* remembered to floss.

"I'm actually kind of interested in someone else," Ryan responded simply. "Not that your friend's not great, I'm sure." He gave a small smile. "There's just someone else I'm into. . . ."

"Okay," Martie called out loudly from the front of the room. "So, let's jump in. What role does fate play in Emma's downfall? Does she have power over her own destiny?"

Lucy sat back in her chair, thinking of herself. *Did she have power over her own destiny? Was she fated to be with Ryan?* She knew she should have been feeling bad for Pickle, but Ryan's words played over and over in her head.

*I'm actually interested in someone else.*

It was the way he said it. The way he leaned in close that made Lucy wonder if that "someone else" was *her.*

"So? What happened?" Pickle asked, startling Lucy at her locker.

"What happened with what?" Lucy asked back innocently. Pickle grabbed her arm. Beside her, Max held out a Pixy Stick.

"Anyone want?" she offered, her mouth full of orange powder.

"Sure," Lucy said, a little too enthusiastically. "I'll take a purple." Anything to keep from having to answer Pickle's question.

"What happened with Ryan?" Pickle pressed adamantly. "Charlie said you were talking to him in English. Did you ask him? About liking me?"

Lucy fidgeted and focused on opening her Pixy Stick. "God, it's just paper, but is this, like, impossible or what?" she asked Max.

Max gave her a funny look and grabbed it back. "You just rip the top off, genius," she said dryly. "Here." She ripped off the top and handed it back. Lucy tipped back the Pixy Stick and took a swig.

"So?" Pickle said, her eyes wide with anticipation.

Lucy gulped down the sugar and grabbed her backpack. "We were talking about *Madame Bovary*," she partially lied. It was only a partial lie because technically they *had* been. It just wasn't *all* they had spoken about.

"So you didn't say anything about me?" Pickle asked.

"Well, we talked for, like, two seconds about the party," Lucy offered. "And he remembered you were sick. . . ."

"Oh, great," Pickle sighed, rolling her eyes. "I'm sure I made a fantastic impression." She let her head fall into her locker with a loud bang. "I'm such an idiot. Damn you, rum and Coke!"

"I think it was Diet," Max corrected.

Lucy placed a comforting hand on her back. "No, no,

I don't think he thought that." Pickle banged her head lightly again.

"Idiot, idiot," she muttered.

"You're going to get permanent brain damage," Max warned, opening another Pixy Stick.

The bell rang. Pickle didn't budge.

"Why did I drink?" she groaned. "Why?"

"Look," Lucy said, trying to give her hope. "He said he was interested in someone. He just didn't tell me who." Lucy didn't know if she was making this better or worse.

Pickle suddenly looked up. "Wait—he did?"

Lucy smiled. "Yeah. So, you know . . . who knows? Maybe it's you!"

Pickle's face brightened. "You think?"

Lucy shrugged. "I think anything's possible." But even as Lucy said the words, she knew she was talking more about herself than about Pickle. She was certain of only two things: Ryan wasn't interested in Pickle, and Lucy wasn't going to be the one to tell her that.

A whistle blew.

"This is for school pride," barked Coach Offredi, who stood on the side of the field in the sweltering heat. It was already October but still as hot as August. In full pads, Lucy was boiling. The inside of her helmet was wet with sweat, and her hair felt, as usual, matted and gross.

The entire team stood at one end of the field. Someone's

dad stood watching from the bleachers. By the way he shouted—at one player in particular—Lucy quickly realized it was Benji's father.

"You'll go on my whistle," Coach Offredi ordered the team. They were doing something called "pride sprints," which were new to Lucy, and from the groans throughout the team when Coach Offredi suggested them, she guessed the drill wasn't a popular one.

The whistle blew.

The team lurched out of the end zone and sprinted toward the twenty-yard line as fast as they could. As soon as they reached it, they ran back into the end zone. Lucy was in the middle of the pack. *That wasn't that bad,* she thought to herself. But then they didn't stop. She suddenly had a horrible feeling in the pit of her stomach that pride drills were similar to suicide sprints in soccer—but involved *way* more clothes and equipment.

With Kevin and the other running backs and receivers in the lead, they quickly turned and headed back out to the thirty-yard line. Lucy struggled to keep up, her feet slipping as she tried to make the turn. She put one hand down to catch herself. She'd never been the fastest runner, but she wasn't used to being this slow. Her pads were really weighing her down!

"Let's go, Lucy," Coach bellowed. She was barely any faster than the two-hundred-and-fifty-pound offensive linemen.

"I'm trying!" Lucy yelled back defiantly. God! She was sick of this guy being on her back all the time. She'd never even done this before. Shouldn't she get some credit for just keeping up? The team headed back to the end zone and then turned to head out to the forty.

Lucy's chest was heaving. Wasn't the perk of being a kicker that she didn't have to run? She prayed that they'd be done when they reached the middle of the field . . . but no. The hell continued.

Now they had to sprint to the yard line on the opposite side—the forty and back (which was really the sixty), then the thirty and back (which was really the seventy)—all the way to the end zone on the other side, which was one hundred yards away. People were starting to slow down. Coach Offredi was yelling on the sidelines.

"This is for the pride of your school! This is for Beachwood! You wanna be on this team? You prove it, right here, right now! LET'S GO!"

"Aaaagh," Tank yelled. Lucy could feel his pain. She felt as though her lungs were on the verge of exploding.

"Hustle up, Benji!" his father barked.

"Last time! All the way!" Coach called out. Now the team had to sprint the length of the whole field and back. "Last one back does a hundred yards more," he threatened. Everyone picked up the pace. No one wanted to be last and be forced to repeat the longest distance.

Near the back of the pack and still thirty yards from

the goal line, Lucy glanced around. A bunch of the guys were passing her in the opposite direction, already heading back toward the finish. She was still gunning for the opposite goalpost, neck and neck with Benji. Only Tank and another linebacker, DeRosa, were behind her. She tried to pump her arms and legs faster. There was no way she was doing this again. She couldn't be last.

She hit the goal line and spun to turn back. Just one hundred more yards to go. She felt sick to her stomach. The heat was sweltering. She heard a loud scream and felt Tank give one last push, his elbows squeezing a space between her and Benji. Now DeRosa was the only one behind them. Lucy turned her head and realized DeRosa was nowhere to be found. Panicked, she looked up ahead. He was already at the forty, heading toward the thirty. He was ahead of Tank! Lucy couldn't believe it. *Were these guys really beating her?* She put her head down, determined. She couldn't lose.

In one last spurt of energy, she surged ahead, past Benji, who was struggling. Sweat poured off her body, but she hit the center of the field. Fifty more yards. Just fifty more yards. She hit the forty, then the thirty . . . and suddenly she realized, she was beating Benji. She was beating Benji! But then something else hit her. If she didn't lose, Benji would. Benji would lose and she'd be responsible. Her legs slowed a little. Just a little. Just enough for Benji to pull up even with her.

Together, they crossed the twenty, then the ten. . . . She could hear cheering and panting.

"Let's go, son!" Benji's dad yelled.

Lucy wished her own dad could be here cheering her on. But even if he had been, she probably wouldn't have been able to hear him. Her heart was beating so loudly—*ba-boom, ba-boom, ba-boom*—it drowned out everything else. Everything seemed to be happening in slow motion.

Something inside her said, *Push harder.* She didn't want to lose with everyone watching. She had been working so hard to earn her teammates' respect. She wasn't going to lose it now.

She lunged forward, moving ahead of Benji. As she crossed into the end zone, her body hit the ground like a sack of potatoes. A sweaty, disgusting, panting sack of potatoes. She dizzily looked up at the blue sky. It spun around her. But she'd done it! She hadn't won, but she hadn't lost. Suddenly, Ryan's face came into focus.

"You all right?" he asked. She couldn't speak. She couldn't move. All she could think about was oxygen . . . lungs . . . water. . . . She hoped she hadn't collapsed in someone's puke. "Blink once for no, twice for yes."

She tried to blink twice but accidentally blinked three times. Ryan laughed, then held out a hand. She grabbed it and in one quick motion, using all one hundred and fifty pounds of his body weight, he pulled her to her feet. Unsteady, she kind of fell into his arms.

"Whoa," Ryan laughed. "Easy there."

Lucy giggled. "Sorry." Benji stared at them both.

"Mason!" Coach Offredi yelled. "You want a personal invitation? Run your last lap!" Once he rejoined the team, Coach Offredi gathered everyone together.

"Who are we?" Coach Offredi yelled, psyching the team up. The guys ferociously clapped their hands together.

"Beachwood!" they all yelled back in unison.

"WHO ARE WE?" Coach Offredi yelled again, even louder.

"BEACHWOOD!" they screamed back. Lucy supposed this was part of the whole spirit/pride thing.

"WHAT DO WE DO?" Lucy considered. *Uh, run so hard we puke?*

"WE WIN!" they answered.

Coach Offredi nodded, satisfied. "Okay, hit the showers."

Exhausted, Lucy headed to grab her stuff. She tentatively approached Benji.

"Sorry about back there," she said. He was still mad at her for sticking him with Pickle at Kendall's party. Beating him in front of his teammates probably hadn't helped matters. But before Benji could get a word out, his dad rushed over, yelling at Coach Offredi.

"Coach!" he bellowed. "What is this crap?" Lucy noticed he was wearing a suit and guessed he must have just come from work. "I don't pay twenty grand a year so a girl can take my kid's spot on the team."

"Dad!" Benji said, horrified. Lucy couldn't believe this was happening. Ryan put an arm around her shoulder.

"Come on," he said. "You don't need to hear this." He ushered Lucy away from Benji's dad. Benji watched them move off.

His dad pointed a finger at him. "What was that out there? I don't want to hear a word out of you." Benji shut up, fast.

Coach Offredi folded his arms in front of his chest. "I don't think you want to do this here," Coach Offredi said to Mr. Mason, raising his eyebrows. "If you want to go down to my office, we can talk."

"Talk about what?" Mr. Mason scoffed. "You bringing this girl onto the team as a publicity stunt? What? You think you're gonna move up to coaching college that way?"

Coach Offredi looked pissed. "We talk in my office. Or we don't talk."

Mr. Mason threw his hands in the air. "Fine, lead the way." As the two men marched off, Lucy looked helplessly at Benji. She'd had no idea he was getting this not only at school but at home, too.

"Benji," she began, "I'm so sorry."

Benji angrily grabbed his stuff. "Forget it, Lucy. Don't worry about it."

But as Lucy changed into her cutoff sweatpants and a tank top, she couldn't help but worry. Suddenly, she heard her voice mail beep. She'd listened to the message and realized it was her dad. And her worry turned to full-out panic!

"Hey, kid," he'd said. "Got done early. Thought I'd come grab you and maybe we could try that Italian place off PCH for dinner. See you in a few."

Panicked, Lucy looked at her watch. Her dad had left the message eight minutes ago. She bolted for the door and up the stairs to the field. She started to run for the parking lot but realized the cheerleaders were still practicing their half-time routine. If her dad showed up, he'd wonder why she wasn't with them. Frantic, she ran over to Regan and breathlessly explained her situation.

"Okay, calm down," Regan said, as the girls grabbed water, preparing to do their routine again. "Just grab some pom-poms and jump in." Kendall sighed nearby. Regan asked her tentatively, "K, is that okay?"

"No offense," Kendall answered, "but I'm supposed to lie for some girl I barely know?"

Suddenly, Ryan and Cope walked by, heading to their cars. Ryan saw Lucy holding two pom-poms and laughed. "Malone," he called out, "don't tell me you just gave up the pigskin for some pom-poms."

Lucy blushed deeply as he walked over. "No, no. My dad—he's coming to get me, and he thinks I'm on the cheerleading squad. . . ."

Ryan's jaw dropped. "You've been lying to him all this time?"

"Well, not so much *lying*," Lucy said innocently. "More like omitting the truth."

Ryan nodded. "You seem so . . . good. Who knew you had it in you?"

Lucy shrugged. "Well, I can be bad when I want to be." Was this flirting? Was that what they were doing? Kendall cleared her throat, obviously annoyed.

"Why don't you two just make out already?" she said dryly. "Okay, are you doing this or not, Lucy?"

Lucy waved a quick goodbye to Ryan and took her place in the back of the formation. Regan stood beside her.

"Just try to follow along," she instructed. Lucy nodded, then glanced toward the parking lot, just knowing her dad would be there any minute.

With Kendall leading, Lucy tried desperately to follow the dance moves. She'd follow to the left, then back to the right—suddenly, the girls were down on the ground, rolling in one direction, then jumping back up and doing a leap! Lucy could barely keep up. All this time she'd thought cheerleading was a cinch, that all you did was stand on the sidelines and cheer for other people who were actually doing stuff—this was hard work! All the girls did simultaneous backflips! Lucy was stunned. *What?* They were amazing!

By the time the routine ended, she had barely been able to do anything, but she was dripping with sweat and

out of breath. She looked up to see her d
with his eyebrows raised.

"Thanks, everyone," Kendall said. "Tha
today. We'll see you tomorrow. And if you b
to practice during lunch, Miss Sullivan said we
gym."

Lucy thanked Regan and tried to act as th
knew these girls and fit right in. *Was her dad buyi.
it?* She wandered over to him. Regan followed, l
toward her own car.

"You ready?" he asked brightly.

"Yeah, totally," she answered. "So, what'd you think

Lucy's dad gulped. "Um . . . you were . . . good. You ju
seemed maybe a little . . . I don't know . . . behind."

Regan interjected. "She joined late. She's just getting
the hang of it."

"Yeah." Lucy nodded. "The hang of it."

## fourteen

The next day, Lucy hurriedly made her way to English, trying to keep all her thoughts in order for her *Madame Bovary* test. What with all her classes, football practice, and lying to her dad about football practice, her head was spinning. It was hard to keep everything straight—including her homework assignments.

Now she stood at her locker, frazzled, trying desperately to remember her locker combination. She could never keep it straight, and if she actually tried to think about the numbers and which direction she was going, rather than just doing it by instinct, she'd never get it open. Finally she heard a click. She sighed with relief.

As she tried to figure out what books and folders she needed, something caught her eye: a folded-up sheet of paper. She grabbed it and opened it. It was a note. She quickly scanned it, reading it to herself.

*Malone—You and me. Under the bleachers. Six o'clock. Don't tell anyone. Just meet me there.—Ryan P.S. You look cute today.*

Lucy's jaw dropped as she read the note. *Bleachers? Six?*

*Cute? What?* She read it again. And again. She could feel the red creeping up her neck and over her face. She was blushing. This couldn't be real. She had to be dreaming. And if she was, she didn't want to wake up.

She folded the note back up, stuffed it into the outside pocket of her backpack, and rushed to class. Forget *Madame Bovary*, forget football practice, forget everything—all she cared about was getting through today and meeting Ryan under the bleachers after practice.

At an exhausting practice that afternoon, Lucy and Ryan hadn't so much as made eye contact, and that was okay with her. Clearly, he was playing it cool.

She remembered Regan's instructions from last night. "Be cool," she'd said. And Lucy was doing her best to do that as she practiced.

The whistle blew. Coach Offredi put his hand on Lucy's shoulder. "You ready to run now?" he asked pointedly.

Lucy looked at him blankly. *Run?* She was the kicker. Her job was to kick, not run.

Coach Offredi sighed. It seemed as though at every practice he had to explain something else. Yesterday it had been that the quarterback doesn't actually say "hike" (he often said "hut"). Today it was trick plays.

"These are plays we use when the moment is right," Coach Offredi told her as Benji waited nearby, seemingly annoyed. He hadn't really spoken to her in days.

"So with trick plays," Coach Offredi continued, "you'll act like you're going to kick, but you'll run the ball instead." Lucy's eyes widened. Run the ball? Like down the field? Full of players? "We don't spend much time practicing these things, because we don't run 'em much," he explained. "But you should be prepared either way. Just in case." He looked to Benji. "You too, Mason."

Lucy nodded obediently. But truthfully, as potentially interesting (and terrifying) as getting to run the ball was, all she wanted to be prepared for was six o'clock, when she could meet Ryan. She glanced at her watch. Only two hours and seven minutes to go.

She'd told her dad that cheerleading practice would be running late again tonight because they were learning cupies and cradle catches (whatever that meant). Surprisingly, her dad had bought it. Lucy was almost sickened by the fact that she'd become such a good liar. Who knew that all it took was a poker face and access to Google to come up with excuse after excuse?

After practice, she confronted Benji.

"Hey," she said, grabbing his arm. "Are you still mad at me? Is this about the party? Because I'm sorry—"

"I don't care about the stupid party," he interrupted.

"Then what is it? Because we've barely even talked—"

"You seem to have plenty of other people to talk to," Benji said, nodding over to where Ryan, Cope, and Sascha were standing. "Must be a perk of being the *star* kicker."

Lucy sighed. Obviously, his dad's words had gotten to him. He was upset that Lucy had, according to Mr. Mason, "stolen his spot."

"Benji," she pleaded. "Please don't be mad at me. It's not fair."

"Life's not fair," he said. "Get used to it." He grabbed his stuff and hit the showers. Lucy couldn't believe he was acting this way. Where was the boy who'd thrown rocks at her window? But the truth was, she didn't have time to worry about him right now. She ran to the locker room to shower and change.

She spent the next half hour doing homework on a bench in the main hallway. Finally, she glanced at her watch. It was five forty-five. She wasn't sure if she should show up "fashionably late," but after showering after football and slipping on her Gap boyfriend trousers and ribbed white tank top, she wasn't sure how fashionable she was anyway.

She closed her book and spiral notepad and headed outside. The air was breezy and cool; her hair was still a little damp from showering after practice. Since she'd forgotten a hair dryer, she'd tried to use the electric hand dryers in the locker room, but instead of dry hair, all she'd gotten was a wrenched neck. Whatever. It was all worth it.

Rounding the corner of the school, she hurried down to the bleachers. Stuffing her hand into her book bag pocket, she grabbed the note and reread it just to clarify. It specifically said *under* the bleachers, not on top.

Following the instructions, she dropped her book bag and headed under the bleachers, although she didn't go too far. She wanted him to be able to see clearly that she was there. She glanced at her watch again. It was five-fifty. She had ten more minutes to kill.

She grabbed her phone and texted Annie.

"Under bleachers waiting for R as in cute QB. ttyl." she typed. "Loooong story. Will tell you later. So excited! Xoxo." She hit send and checked the time again. It was five fifty-five. Only five more minutes to go. She paced back and forth nervously, taking deep breaths, the kind she took in yoga the two times she'd tried it with Annie.

Her phone beeped. She grabbed it. There was one new text. She clicked and opened it. It was from Annie.

"No way," it read. "You are a rock star." Lucy smiled. She loved Annie's enthusiasm, even about people she didn't even know. That was why Annie was her best friend. It was as if she was experiencing everything right there with her. Lucy was about to type a reply when she heard . . .

"Lucy?" a girl's voice asked. Lucy spun around, coming face-to-face with Pickle.

## fifteen

Lucy gasped, surprised.

"Pickle . . . um . . . hi," she stammered. "What're you doing here?"

Pickle shrugged shyly and held up a folded piece of paper. "I'm supposed to meet Ryan. Under the bleachers."

Lucy's face turned white. How was that possible, she thought? *She* was supposed to meet Ryan under the bleachers.

"You are?" Lucy asked, shocked.

"Wait—what're *you* doing here?" Pickle asked, equally as surprised and caught off guard. Lucy couldn't even think quick enough to lie. Not that she would have wanted to lie to Pickle anyway. There was no poker face or search engine good enough to help her get out of this one.

"I . . . um . . ." Not knowing what to say, she held up the similar note. "I got the same thing. From Ryan."

Pickle gasped. "What? Let me see that."

Lucy handed over the note, not knowing what else to do or say. "It said to meet him here. And to not tell anyone."

"I don't get it," Pickle said, squinting as she read the note again, as if she thought the words would somehow change. "It doesn't make any sense. He couldn't have given this note to both of us—"

"No," Lucy supposed. Why would anyone do that? "Unless . . ." she wondered. "Do you think it's possible he didn't write it?"

"Then what?" Pickle said quickly. "Someone else did? Why would anyone write a note pretending to be Ryan?"

Lucy thought hard. She had no idea.

Suddenly, a look of even greater concern crossed Pickle's face. "Wait a minute," she realized, folding her arms across her chest. "Why would you be meeting Ryan here either way?"

"What do you mean?" Lucy said, worried. The tone in Pickle's voice was different than she'd ever heard before. Of course, she'd only known her a few months, but still . . .

"Well, think about it," Pickle reasoned. "Let's just say you got that note in your locker, and let's just say that Ryan likes you. You know I like him, and you said you'd help me get together with him . . . so why would you be here unless . . ." Suddenly, she stopped short, realizing she already knew the answer. Lucy felt her entire body cringe, knowing what Pickle was about to say.

"Unless," she added slowly, "you like Ryan too. And just didn't tell me."

Lucy pursed her lips together. Pickle stared at her,

waiting. Lucy shifted uncomfortably, gazing down at her Converse. This was beyond awkward.

"I'm sorry, Pickle," Lucy said softly. "I like Ryan too. And I didn't tell you because . . . I don't know . . . I didn't want to hurt you."

Pickle threw her hands in the air. "So going behind my back isn't hurting me?"

Tears welled up in Lucy's eyes. "I know, I know. I shouldn't have done that. I just—you asked for my help, and I tried to give it to you."

Suddenly, Charlie showed up, with Carla and Max.

"Hey. I thought I heard yelling. What's going on here?" Charlie asked.

Lucy spun around. *Charlie was here? And Carla? And Max?* A crowd of soccer girls started to form. "Nothing," Lucy said quickly. "Nothing's going on."

"It doesn't look like nothing," Max retorted. She rushed over to Pickle's side. "You okay?" Pickle just stared at Lucy as if no one else was even there.

"I was your friend," Pickle said slowly. "I thought you were mine."

"I am," Lucy said quickly trying to reassure her. "I am, Pickle. Seriously, you have to believe that."

Charlie stepped in. "Pickle, what's going on?"

Pickle finally looked at her. "You know that note I got from Ryan?" Pickle reminded Charlie. "Well, he's not here. But she is."

"I don't get it," Carla said. "Why would Lucy be here?"

"Because it was a trick!" Lucy tried to explain. "Someone was playing a trick on us!"

"Who would do that?" Carla asked, confused.

Suddenly, there was a chorus of giggles and laughs. The soccer girls looked over their shoulders and saw a group huddled by the wall, cracking up.

There was Kendall, covering her mouth, giggling. Next to her was Regan. And behind them, a few football players were gathered. Cope, Adam, Nick, Caleb . . . and— When Lucy saw him, her heart dropped. Ryan. Ryan was standing there. Right next to Benji, of all people. Clearly, they'd all heard the entire fight.

Suddenly, it made perfect sense. This had been a huge setup.

Lucy's face turned a deep shade of red. She stood there, completely speechless, as Kendall smirked in delight.

"You did this?" Lucy asked.

Kendall chuckled. "Everyone knows Pickle had a thing for Ryan. She's liked him since last year. And you came along all moony-eyed—" she broke into laughter—"It was just too easy!" Lucy turned to Regan. "And you helped her?" Regan looked down at her shoes, guiltily.

Charlie shook her head. "I guess Pickle was telling the truth, Lucy." Charlie stared her down. "Regan Holder's clearly not your friend at all."

Lucy felt a wave of humiliation crashing over her, drowning her. She couldn't take the eyes staring at her, the kids laughing at her, amused by her crush on Ryan and her argument with Pickle, as if her feelings were some sort of joke. She grabbed her stuff and ran out from under the bleachers, past the kids, past the school—she just had to get out of there.

Sobbing, she walked down the driveway leading back to the main road. She heard a beep from her phone and tried to wipe the tears away to make out what it was. There was another text from Annie.

"You and Ryan making out yet?" it read.

Lucy threw her phone back into her book bag, upset. She wiped another tear away with the back of her hand. Right now, making out with Ryan was just about the farthest thing from her mind.

The next day was game day, and Lucy knew she should have been nervous. After all, it was only her second game. But how could she be nervous when there were bigger things on the line than winning? Like *everything*.

First of all, she was a total laughingstock. She couldn't bear the thought of facing Ryan, Regan, Kendall, or anyone. Charlie hadn't spoken to her in days, and now Pickle clearly wasn't going to either. Lucy had sent her a lengthy e-mail trying to explain everything last night, but Pickle hadn't responded. She had even blocked Lucy from her buddy list and taken her off her MySpace friends. Same went for Max, who was loyal to Pickle. And Benji—he wanted nothing to do with her either. She wouldn't have been surprised if Martie was pissed. Maybe it would work out in her favor and she wouldn't get called on in class, because God knew she hadn't even cracked open her English homework, not with her entire life falling apart.

Martie began passing back their *Madame Bovary* test as Ryan slid into a seat, late. Lucy couldn't even look at him.

She stared straight ahead, feeling at an all-time low. It was as if she were sitting under a dark cloud of angst. She couldn't imagine being more humiliated.

What she didn't know was that she was still about to suffer the biggest humiliation of all—on the football field.

Her first heartbreak occurred when she looked up in the stands, just after "The Star Spangled Banner," and noticed that Pickle, who was a fixture at every football game, was not there. Neither was Max. Or Charlie. Or Carla. Or Heather. Or anyone else from the girls' soccer team. The very girls who had decorated her locker and waved handmade banners for her last week. Any cheering section she'd had was gone.

And that included the cheerleaders. Clearly, Kendall had obviously had it in for her, and with Regan as her lapdog, doing virtually anything and everything she asked of her, Kendall had succeeded. Lucy didn't know what the story was or why Kendall would want to humiliate Lucy in front of Ryan and everyone else—and the truth was, it didn't matter. All that mattered was that Lucy knew what kind of girls these were. Mean ones. She now understood why Charlie had been so hurt that Lucy had befriended Regan. It was the ultimate slap in the face. Lucy thought of a few people she'd like to slap in the face, but managed to restrain herself. Any aggression she had would be taken out on the football tonight. She'd just picture Kendall's face on one side and Regan's face on the other and enjoy kicking it as hard and far as possible.

With Beachwood losing the coin toss, Lucy had to kick off first. She took the field with her ten defenders who were poised to charge down the field. She set the tee down, more toward the left side of the field than right, because that was what Coach Offredi had instructed her to do. She put up her right hand, signifying that she was ready. The referee blew his whistle. She dropped her hand and kicked a respectable, if a bit short, kick to the Carter twenty-two-yard line. The Carter halfback caught Lucy's kick in full stride and sliced through the leading pack of Beachwood cover men before being brought down by an onrushing safety at Beachwood's forty-five-yard line, while Lucy hovered safely out of harm's way back at the thirty-five-yard line on the opposite sideline. After the play, she jogged back to the bench.

"LET'S GO, DE-FENSE," the cheerleaders sang and clapped in unison.

Lucy couldn't help but steal a glance at Regan, her right foot balancing precariously on the palm of one of her teammates. Lucy thought that if the girl happened to drop her, it might not be the *worst* thing that had ever happened. What was the worst she'd get? A broken arm? Or worse, a broken ego? A concussion? Maybe it would knock some sense into her. Lucy felt sick looking at her, and as she glanced from the cheerleaders to the field, everything looked blurry. It was as if she could no longer see things clearly. And in fact, that was exactly how she felt.

Suddenly, she was jarred back to reality by the crowd's excitement. Stepping in front of a Carter wide receiver, Nick intercepted the ball and streaked down the sidelines with no one between him and the Carter goal line sixty-five yards away! The moment he crossed the line, he raised the ball over his head with both hands, jumped high into the air, and spiked the ball back between his legs. The crowd went wild!

"PAT unit!" Coach Offredi yelled. In a haze, Lucy stood up and jogged onto the field behind Benji and Caleb. She barely remembered kicking the ball between the posts, but the sound of the cheers let her know she'd successfully done it; Beachwood now led, 7-0.

But by two quarters in, Carter had made up some ground. As they left the field for halftime, the scoreboard read BEACHWOOD 7, CARTER 6.

In the locker room at halftime, Coach Offredi yelled out phrases like "Draw blood!" and "Kill!" and "You have twenty-four more minutes to beat the crap out of them!" *Try putting* that *on a T-shirt,* Lucy thought as she tried desperately to focus.

Everyone huddled together. "This is what it's about," Coach Offredi told them. "Time to finish the job. This is where it counts!" He'd been talking so ferociously, he was out of breath. "Now let's go out there and WIN!"

As Beachwood ran onto the field to start the third quarter, Lucy took a seat on the bench. It was Carter's kickoff to start the second half.

On the field, Ryan called out the coded play. "Red 60, Red 60, hut-hut!" On the second "hut," Caleb snapped the ball. Ryan took the snap and dropped back, looking around for an open receiver, as two Carter linebackers blitzed through the line toward him.

"Get rid of it," Coach Offredi screamed from the sidelines. "GET RID OF IT!"

Ryan looked around desperately. Lucy could almost see the wheels turning in his head. Should he just run it himself? But before he could make a choice, both linebackers hit him at almost the same instant. BAM! And BAM! He was sacked.

Coach Offredi threw down his clipboard, pissed. "I TOLD YOU TO GET RID OF IT, CONNER!" he screamed.

God, that man was loud. Lucy wished she could tap him on his walrus shoulder and say sarcastically, "Oh, wait? Did you want him to get *rid* of it?" She guessed that sort of humor wouldn't go over too well, but it was the type of joke she and Annie made to each other all the time. She looked back toward the stands, to the spot where her friends *weren't*. It made her miss Annie all the more.

And suddenly, she saw something. She blinked quickly, hoping she was mistaken. No—this couldn't be happening. It just couldn't.

## sixteen

She spun back around to face the field, putting her head in her hands.

"Oh my God, oh my God," Lucy muttered. "This isn't happening. Please tell me this isn't happening. . . ."

Nervously, Lucy glanced over her shoulder again. Her dad was staring at the cheerleaders, confused. He was obviously looking for her. Little did he know, he simply wasn't looking in the right place. When the cheerleaders set down their pom-poms to take a water break, he approached.

"Oh my God," Lucy gasped, horrified. She cringed through her face mask as she saw Kendall explaining something and pointing toward the Beachwood bench, right in her direction. *Of course, Kendall had no problem selling her out.* Lucy tried to hunker down in front of Benji.

"Hide me," she begged Sascha, who was sitting on the bench next to her.

"What're you doing?" he asked, annoyed. "Lucy, seriously, get up. Coach Offredi is gonna kill you."

"So is my dad," Lucy insisted. She panicked. "I can't let him see me. I have to hide. I have to . . . um . . . yes! I have to pee." She sprang off the bench and sneaked as inconspicuously as possible to the nearest opening in the chain-link fence surrounding the field. Once she was through it, she bolted toward the locker room, unsure whether her dad had seen her make a break for it or not.

Bursting through the doors of the girls' locker room, she ripped off her helmet and frantically paced, not sure what to do. She couldn't go back up there. But she had to. She couldn't leave in the middle of the game. Her teammates were depending on her. But her dad would kill her if he saw her. She tried to think fast. Was there *any* way on the planet that Kendall and Regan hadn't ratted her out? Maybe out of guilt . . . or some sense of loyalty that didn't exist . . . She shook her head, knowing she was a goner. Of course they'd told. Kendall had probably done it with a big smile plastered on her face. Nothing would make her happier than finding yet another way to make Lucy's life hell.

She glanced at her reflection in the mirror. Her hair was matted down. Helmet head definitely wasn't her best look. She put her helmet back on and took a deep breath. She couldn't hide out down here forever. Sooner or later, she was going to have to face her dad. But did it really have to be now?

When she emerged from the locker room , she heard a voice.

"Stop right there, young lady." Young lady? Where was "kid?" She realized it didn't matter. All that mattered was that her dad was standing there. At the top of the stairs. With his arms folded across his chest. And the look on his face wasn't a good one.

"You lied to me," he said. "You've been lying to me for weeks."

Lucy rubbed her lips together. She didn't know what to say. She *had* been lying to him for weeks.

"I know," she admitted. "And I'm sorry."

Her dad shook his head. "Cheerleading," he mumbled to himself. He looked at her. "And I was stupid enough to buy that."

"You weren't stupid," she said protectively. "You just . . . trusted me." She looked down at her mismatched cleats, feeling terrible.

"And you betrayed that, Luce. You do realize how grounded you are? And how serious this is?"

She sighed. "I know." A lecture was coming, but now just wasn't the time. "It is serious, and I know I'm grounded, like, for life and we should . . . you know . . . talk about it. Maybe after the game?"

He interrupted. "I don't give a damn about the game!"

"Well, I do!" she said, defiantly. That was it. She couldn't take it anymore. She'd tried to be nice. She'd tried to be accountable for her actions, but no more. Beachwood was on the field. Without her. This conversation had gone on long enough. "My teammates are up there—and they need me!"

"They need you? They don't need you," he scoffed. "Lucy, this is a *boys'* sport, that *boys* play—you don't belong out there!"

"How would you know? You just forbid me to play! Without even hearing me out—"

"Oh, I heard you—and the answer was no!"

Lucy threw her hands in the air, exasperated. "It's like I have no rights or something. I barely have a say in my own life!"

"That's not true—" her dad started to say.

"Yes, it is!" Lucy exploded, interrupting him. All the emotion she'd been trying to contain for months—for *years*—came pouring out of her. "You just—you decide these things, like, arbitrarily! Without any consideration for what I want. I'm the one who agrees. I'm the one who doesn't argue, who tries to make everyone happy, but it's not fair! When do I get what I want? You decide I can't play football, then that's it, end of discussion, and I'm supposed to tell Coach I'm not playing." Tears formed in Lucy's eyes as she continued to rant. She pushed her hair out of her face.

"You decide we're moving across the country, and next thing I know, I'm packing my whole life into suitcases and leaving all my friends! You decide it's time to pull the plug, and just like that, Mom's gone!"

"Lucy, I—"

"No!" Lucy yelled. She angrily pushed by him and headed toward the field.

He firmly grabbed her arm. "Lucy, we're going home."

She ripped her arm from his grasp. "You can go wherever the hell you want," she spat. "But I'm not coming with you." She ran back to the field, leaving her dad shocked and stunned.

As she approached the sidelines, it quickly became apparent that her dad was only one of her many problems. Her teammates were scurrying around frantically, while Coach Offredi lectured Benji, gesturing wildly. As soon as he saw Lucy, his tack changed.

"What the hell?" he asked, stomping over. "Where the hell have you been?" His walrus mustache was so close to her, she could barely stammer out a response. Even his mustache looked pissed.

"I'm sorry. . . . I just . . . I just . . . it was a . . . um . . ." She had to think of a lie he couldn't get mad about—well, at least any more mad than he already was. His face was so red, Lucy half expected steam to shoot out of his ears as from a boiling teapot.

"It was a girl . . . thing," she said quickly.

"For ten minutes?" he asked incredulously.

"You know, a . . . um . . . feminine issue," Lucy stammered. Coach Offredi's eyes widened. Obviously this wasn't a subject he was particularly comfortable talking about.

"Listen," he said, pointing a fat finger in her face. "I don't care what kind of issue it is—you don't leave the field without telling me. We just got a delay of game called on us."

*Delay of game?* Lucy didn't know what that meant. Except that maybe that . . . the game was delayed?

"They gave us a five-yard penalty because you weren't here!" he barked.

"Well, why didn't you just call a time out?" Lucy retorted.

Coach Offredi put his hands on his hips. He looked more and more walrusy with each passing second. "Are you talking back to me?"

Lucy shook her head no and looked at the field. Five yards didn't seem like such a big deal. "We had a fourth and five on their twenty! But with that down penalty, we're back to their twenty-five, which means, Little Miss Feminine Issue, that you have a forty-two-yard field goal to kick!"

This time it was Lucy's eyes that went as wide as saucers. She had to kick the twenty-five yards on the field . . . plus the ten yards of the end zone, plus the seven-yard set behind the line. She'd never kicked a ball that far in her life. And all because of her stupid five-yard penalty.

"Now get out there!" he ordered, practically shoving her onto the field.

Lucy glanced up at the scoreboard, trying to figure out what she'd missed. Apparently a lot, because Carter was up by two, leading the low-scoring game. If she could score this three-point field goal, they would overtake Carter by a point and would just have to try to hold them off in the fourth quarter and run out the clock.

Lucy lined up behind Caleb and Benji and the rest of the field goal unit. The lights shone down upon her. The crowd seemed to go silent. Her heart felt like it would pound right out of her chest. A sense of being totally overwhelmed flooded over her, almost like a wave. She didn't know if she could kick the ball that far. In fact, right now, with her dad watching, she didn't know if she could kick the ball at all.

She looked up toward the goalposts. They looked a million miles away. But as she looked up and past them, she couldn't help but think of her mom. She tried to imagine what her mom would think of this. She would have laughed at Lucy's pathetic lie to Coach Offredi. . . .

"You *didn't* use the period excuse!" she could picture her mom saying. "That's just wrong," she would laugh. "But good going!" She would have been able to talk to her mom about everything. She would have been able to ask her mom to convince her dad to let her play football; then she wouldn't have had to sneak around and lie. If her mom were here, everything would be different. They would have still been in Ohio, she would have been with all her friends, and she wouldn't have been standing in the middle of a football field with a pissed-off coach and about forty pissed-off teammates staring her down.

She took a deep breath. She could feel her dad watching her.

*Forget about everything,* she told herself. About her dad. About Regan and Kendall. About Pickle, Max, and Charlie. About Ryan. And Benji. God, the list was long. About everything. All she needed to think about was making this field goal. That was all that mattered right now. That was the only thing she could control.

She looked in front of her, at the backs of nine blockers, Caleb among them, ready to snap the ball to Benji, who was already kneeling down. He gave the silent signal.

Caleb snapped the ball back. Within two seconds, Benji had it solidly in his hands. He placed the ball on the ground for Lucy. His left index finger held it in place. Lucy lunged, her foot striking the ball a moment later . . . and the ball sailed up and up . . . passing over the heads of Beachwood's blockers and the outstretched hands of the Carter defenders, heading toward the goalposts. Lucy, her teammates, the fans, even her dad watched breathlessly . . . as the ball fell just two yards short of the crossbar.

She gasped, stunned.

She hadn't made it.

The hope of three points was now gone. And Carter still maintained their lead. On the sidelines, Coach Offredi threw his clipboard to the ground. One of the junior coaches scurried to pick it up and place it back in his hands, as he huddled the Beachwood defense together, screaming at them to go out there and kill.

"Don't let them gain a yard," he yelled. "You have

twelve more minutes to beat the crap outta them! Let's do this now! You get an interception, you cause a fumble, you get the ball back! Don't let them into that end zone!"

But with Lucy's missed field goal, Beachwood was fast losing momentum, and a pass down the sidelines into a Curtis receiver's hands might as well have sealed Beachwood's fate. Curtis scored again. Moments later, they made their PAT. They were up by ten.

Lucy sat sullenly on the bench, desperately wishing this game would just be over so she could be put out of her misery. There was a ray of hope when Beachwood got onto Curtis's ten-yard line and Ryan nailed a pass to Nick, who drove and slid into the end zone. TOUCHDOWN!

*Thank God,* Lucy thought to herself. She jogged onto the field and kicked a field goal. This one easily sailed in. Now she had to kick off to Carter. She jogged and picked up the tee off the sidelines. Coach Offredi grabbed her face mask.

"Now's your time, little girl," he said, "to make up for what you did out there. You lost us five yards; then you missed the field goal. You make up for it right now!" He let go of her mask. "I want you to set the ball to the left," he instructed. "They only have one kick returner, and we'll force him to come down the side." Lucy wondered if someday coaches would be saying "and we'll force *her* to come down the side." Probably not any time soon if she continued to screw up like she had tonight.

Coach Offredi pulled everyone into the huddle to explain their strategy. "Funnel the coverage to the left, understand? You close that gap. Lucy, all the way to the end zone. Let's go. Hands in."

Everyone's hands went into the center, including Lucy's. She didn't even notice that Ryan was only one hand separated from her. She didn't even care.

"Break!" they yelled simultaneously.

Lucy ran back onto the field, determined. She wanted to make it up to the team. She knew she'd screwed up. *Everyone* knew. Her dad was watching. She wanted him to see what she could do. To show him why she should be playing football. She set the tee down and placed the ball on top of it. She took a deep breath and raised her hand. The ref blew the whistle.

Lucy's foot hit the ball squarely in the lower center of the ball, sending it just where Coach Offredi had ordered— down the left side of the field. Her teammates ran down-field toward Carter's end zone to cover the kick as the ball hung in the air, traveling far and deep to the left and into Carter's backfield. Carter's returner caught it at the eighteen-yard line and looked for an opening as Beachwood tried to close any gaps on the left side. He ducked behind his blockers, who held off an aggressive Beachwood. He juked to the left, then cut back to the right, shot through a small gap between two Beachwood defenders, and sprinted down the center of the field.

Lucy, standing on the field a little bit shy of the fifty-yard line, was suddenly terrified. The Carter ball carrier careened toward her, skirting around one Beachwood defender after another, gaining yard after yard after yard. She couldn't believe what she was seeing. She was the last line of defense—the only person who would be able to stop him!

A million thoughts raced through Lucy's head. Was she supposed to actually attempt to tackle this guy? She'd never tackled anyone in her life! Forget breaking a nail—what if she broke something worse? She quickly knew she didn't have a choice. She'd already blown the field goal. She wasn't letting this guy into the end zone. If she was the last line of defense, she was going to defend! She raced toward him.

The Carter player cut over the sideline. Lucy took a step that way, but he cut back the other way. She followed and felt her ankle twist just seconds before she threw her body weight into him. CRUNCH! They collided and both went down, hard, at Beachwood's own twenty-five-yard line. The crowd went wild. Her teammates rushed over. The Carter player pushed himself up. Lucy lay on the ground, motionless. She wasn't getting up.

## seventeen

Coach Offredi and the team's trainer rushed onto the field. Lucy could hear their voices above her but couldn't open her eyes.

"Lucy!" Coach Offredi called out. "Lucy, can you hear me?"

Lucy wanted to tell him that she could, but getting the words out felt impossible, as if her mouth were cemented shut.

But suddenly, she heard another voice.

"Kid," a panicked voice cried. "Kid, come back to us." Lucy would have known that voice anywhere. It was her dad's.

She couldn't answer. She couldn't move.

It felt like two bricks were sitting on her eyelids. It took all the strength she could muster to open her eyes. She pressed them open. Her dad came fuzzily into view.

"Dad?" she whispered, her voice barely audible. "I'm okay, I'm okay," she assured him.

Her vision was blurry, but still, she could make out the look of relief on her dad's face.

"Can you stand?" Coach Offredi asked. Lucy nodded weakly. The coaches started to help her up until Lucy let out a cry of pain.

"My ankle," she gasped. "It's my ankle."

"Can you put any weight on it?" Coach Offredi asked.

Lucy shook her head. She didn't think so. In an instant, Coach Offredi scooped her up in his arms.

As he carried Lucy off the field to wild applause, Lucy didn't know which was more shocking: the fact that she had tackled someone, or the fact that Coach Offredi was protectively holding her in his arms.

The next hour was a blur to Lucy, as trainers checked her ankle, then sent her to the hospital for x-rays, her dad by her side all the while. And it wasn't until after the x-rays came back and the doctor explained that Lucy's ankle wasn't broken, it was just a severe sprain, and that she had a slight concussion, that she and her dad finally spoke.

They were in the car, heading home. Lucy's crutches were crammed awkwardly in the passenger seat with her, and she was still wearing her football uniform.

"Lucy," he said slowly.

This was it, she thought. Now it was coming. The lecture. But instead he said . . .

"There was nothing we could have done. She wasn't living any more with tubes coming out of her and a machine breathing for her—she wouldn't have wanted to live like that. That's not a life, kid."

Lucy inhaled quickly, caught off guard. That hadn't been what she was expecting her dad to say. She looked down at her hands. He waited a long time . . . until she finally said something.

"It's just . . . you didn't ask," Lucy said softly. "You just *decided*. Like I had no say. What would you have done if I'd said no? If I'd said I didn't want you to shut down everything?"

Her dad thought for a moment. "I don't know," he said, at a loss. "Maybe that's why I didn't ask."

Lucy took in this admission. It made sense. He didn't give her a choice because he didn't want her to have one. She looked down at her ankle and thought about her mom. *What would her mom have told her to do in this situation?* The words came to her.

"Then ask me now," Lucy said, determined. "Ask me what I want."

Her dad sighed. He touched his hand to his forehead and rubbed it, as if his head hurt. "What do you want?"

"To play football," she answered, quickly. "That's what I want."

He looked at her. "You're on crutches, kid. Your ankle—"

"Will heal," she interrupted. "And then I can play."

They pulled into the driveway. He turned off the ignition. "No, you can't," he responded sternly.

"Dad, just listen," she begged. "Being out there? On that field? I feel like I can do anything. I feel strong and brave and tough . . . and it's pretty much the only place I feel that way. I need that. And I don't want to give it up."

"You can talk to the coach tomorrow," he said.

"About what?" she asked, confused at what he was implying.

"You're going to tell him you're sorry, but you're quitting the team." He shook his head. "I'm sorry, Luce. I'm not going to sit on the sidelines and watch you get hurt. I lost your mother and I'm not going to lose you too." He tried to put a hand on her shoulder but she just wiggled away. "Can I help you get out of the car?"

In a swift, angry motion, Lucy grabbed her crutches, not caring what they banged into. "No," she snapped. "I don't need your help. I'll do it myself."

And with that, she clumsily made her way into the house.

So it was official. Everything had changed. Now that she was injured and forbidden by her dad for the *second* time to play football, Lucy could describe tenth grade in two ways: B.T. and A.T. Before the tackle and after the tackle. Because the tackle changed everything.

Well, okay, maybe not *everything*. Regan and Kendall were still monumental witches to the one hundredth degree. Pickle, Max, and Charlie still didn't speak to her at all. Ryan was still friendly despite knowing she had a huge crush on him. And her dad was still crazily overprotective. So the only thing that had really changed was her relationship with Benji. But the change had been significant.

First, Benji had been named Beachwood's new first-string placekicker. Lucy hadn't been there for the announcement, obviously, but she'd heard it through the proverbial grapevine. She could only imagine how happy Benji's father was that Lucy was off the team. She and Benji hadn't actually spoken until he approached her the Tuesday A.T.

"Does it hurt?" Benji asked. She'd been sitting out in gym class, watching everyone play touch football, of all things, while she lamely did sit-ups on the grass.

Lucy stopped at forty-two sit-ups. "Yeah," she gasped, out of breath. "My abs kill."

"I meant your ankle," he admitted.

Lucy looked at the crutches strewn beside her. "Oh, right." She smiled. "Not too bad. That's what Vicodin is for." Benji took a seat on the ground next to her . . .

. . . and from that moment on, he barely left her side. He sat with her at lunch. He helped her with her books, since she was on crutches. He even took her to the movies and made sure no one sat in front of them so that she could elevate her leg. Truthfully, it was the best time she'd had in Los Angeles, except for maybe those Hell Week van rides with the soccer girls. Some nights they stayed on the phone until two in the morning. Her dad even let Benji hang out in the bedroom, confident that nothing would happen between them.

"Who's this?" Benji asked one day, looking at the pictures taped to her wall.

"Oh, that's Annie," she replied. "My best friend from home."

"This isn't home yet?" Benji asked.

Lucy shrugged. "Not really." But she couldn't deny that the more time she spent with Benji, the more it started to feel home-ish. She loved having him to hang out with—but she couldn't ignore the simple fact that if she were still on the team, Benji wouldn't be giving her the time of day either. It made her sad to think that they were only friends now that he'd been given her position.

"So you're not upset?" he asked, as they downloaded songs off iTunes. "That I'm placekicker?"

"Upset?" Lucy asked, incredulously, as if the very thought were preposterous. "Why would I be upset? You deserve to be placekicker—especially after how hard you've worked. Your dad must be happy."

"Yeah, he is," Benji said. And as he went on to explain the moment that Coach Offredi told him, Lucy had to admit to herself that maybe she was a *little* upset. But it wasn't about his kicking—it was about their friendship. She didn't want it to be based on who was taking the field for a stupid extra point! Not that she planned to tell him that . . . and risk pissing off the one friend she had left!

"Seriously, Benj," she said sincerely. "I'm happy for you. You really worked hard for this." It was true. Benji often stayed after practice to work one-on-one with the assistant kicking coach, trying to develop his aim and accuracy. He hadn't become better overnight. Little by little, he became better every day. Maybe he wasn't as good as she was, but still, he was clearly better than he had been.

"So you'll come?" Benji asked. "To my first game?"

Lucy forced a smile and clicked on a new Killers song. "Of course! I wouldn't miss it. Even if I have to sit in the lame bleachers . . ." And the bleachers were exactly where Lucy sat—for two Friday nights in a row.

Finally, on the third Friday, Lucy received good news at her weekly checkup. The physical therapy she'd been doing had paid off. She could ditch her crutches at last. Her specialist, Dr. Cane, was impressed with her fast recovery.

"You're still icing?" he asked as he wrapped her ankle with an Ace bandage.

"Three times a day," Lucy said. "It's really working, huh?" She stood up and put full weight on her foot.

Dr. Cane examined her stance. "Any pain?"

Lucy shook her head no. It probably helped that her ankle was tightly wrapped but she actually felt great. "It's good," she assured him.

"So—when's homecoming?" he asked.

Lucy was caught off guard by the question. "Um . . ."

She paused, trying to think. "Next week. The game's on Friday and the dance is on Saturday."

"My son went to Beachwood," Dr. Cane explained. "My wife and I still go to watch them kick Oakwood's butts." Oakwood was one of Beachwood's biggest rivals. Maybe the fact that their names were similar made them more competitive. "Well, if you keep up the PT, Lucy, you may be able to kick by then."

*What?* Lucy couldn't believe it. "Really?" Was there a chance she could actually finish out the season? The thought of going back to the team made her heart leap. Even though the guys hadn't made her feel particularly welcome, she found herself missing them. She'd become used to the jokes and ribbing and even the smell of sweaty, disgusting boy. But then she was snapped back to reality.

"Even if my ankle gets better," Lucy remembered glumly, "my dad won't let me play."

"Afraid of your getting hurt?" Dr. Cane asked. "Not surprised. *Overprotective* and *fathers* are two words that go hand in hand—especially when it comes to their girls." Lucy laughed the kind of laugh that wasn't because something was funny; it was because something was true. "Do you want me to talk to him?" Dr. Cane offered. "Tell him how important this game against Oakwood is?"

"That's okay," she said. She appreciated the offer, but knowing her dad, it wouldn't do any good.

"How about this? Do your exercises," he said encouragingly, "and make a follow-up appointment for next week. We'll reassess then, okay?" Lucy nodded and started for the door. "Hey," he called out. "See you at the game tonight?"

Lucy nodded. "Yeah, I'll be there." Beachwood was playing against Hillman Hall. There was no way she was missing it.

"Come on, Beachwood! You call that defense? What? You need a personal invitation to tackle?" Dr. Cane shouted angrily from the stands. He was sitting about ten rows above Lucy but he was so loud, it felt as though he were one centimeter from her ear, yelling directly into it. The only man louder than Dr. Cane was Mr. Mason, Benji's father. Lucy noticed Pickle, Charlie, Max, and Carla sitting on the same bleacher as her, about twenty people down. She didn't even bother to try to make eye contact with them, let alone talk to them. Lucy sighed and tried to be grateful she was here, even if no one was talking to her. Since lying hadn't gotten her very far, she had decided to be honest with her dad, explaining how important it was that she support the team, even if she wasn't on it. Luckily for her, he'd understood.

They were deep into the fourth quarter, and Hillman Hall had just intercepted a bomb from Ryan, running the ball fifty-five yards for a touchdown. The score was now 21-20. Hillman Hall led by one point.

Even from the stands, Lucy could see Beachwood's coaches and players desperately strategizing how they were going to win this game in the next seven minutes.

With less than two minutes to go, the field goal unit jogged out.

"Come on, Benj," she yelled. "You got this!" There was only one minute and forty-nine seconds left on the clock. Any chance of Beachwood winning would now fall onto Benji's narrow shoulders.

Lucy said a quick prayer and crossed her fingers. On the bench, many of the guys—Ryan, Tank, and Cope—couldn't even look. She couldn't either. She held her breath and looked down at her Converse.

"Come on, come on, come on," she muttered to herself. Seconds went by. It felt like an eternity.

*What was happening?* Lucy didn't want to look up . . . until the crowd erupted! Lucy jumped up to see Benji—possibly for the first time ever—being engulfed by his teammates on the field. He'd done it! He'd made it! From the twenty-five! And even though there was still a little time left on the clock, Benji had essentially won them the game! Mr. Mason started hugging people around him and slapping them on the back.

"That's my son!" he said proudly. "My son!"

"Yeah, Benj!" Lucy screamed. "Nice kick!"

On the field, he wiggled out of the arms of his teammates, scanning the crowd. When he saw Lucy, he pumped his fist into the air and pointed to her. She smiled and waved. Coach Offredi wrangled their attention back to the game.

"Let's finish this now," he shouted. "We're not giving anything up in this last minute. I want to see a deep kick downfield!" He sent the kickoff team, Benji included, back onto the field.

The referee blew his whistle. Benji kicked off deep to Hillman Hall. It bounced at their fifteen and was caught by their returner, who ran twenty yards before Tank pulled him to the ground. First down. On the next play, Tank and DeRosa put pressure on the Hillman quarterback as the clock ran down to zero. The quarterback unleashed a sixty-five-yard desperation pass that flew harmlessly over the outstretched arms of Hillman's deepest wide receiver. The game was over, and thanks to Benji, Beachwood had won! Lucy could hear Dr. Cane joyfully screaming behind her.

"Go Wildcats!" he cheered. "Yay, Beachwood!"

On the sidelines, Coach Offredi bellowed, "Way to get 'er done, way to get 'er done tonight!"

Excited, Lucy snaked her way down the bleachers, rushing to get to Benji, ready to celebrate and be happy for him. He ran over when he saw her.

"Lucy!" he said happily. He picked her up and spun her around. "Wait till next week," he told her excitedly. "Wait until homecoming! I'm going to do it again!" Lucy wrapped her arms tight around his neck, making a conscious choice not to mention Dr. Cane's hopeful prognosis, that she might be healthy enough to play in the homecoming game. It just wasn't worth it, she decided. Not if it meant losing her friendship with Benji. Because that was what was most important to her. *Friendship.*

Of course, seeing Benji out there, under the lights, kicking the field goal—she couldn't help but wish she could have friendship *and* football.

She wished she could have it all.

The following Monday at school, gym was particularly brutal. As everyone else played soccer, Lucy sat on the ground, ripping blades of grass in half. She wanted to play; in fact, she had a feeling that maybe Dr. Cane was right. She *could* play. But if she was claiming to be too hurt for the homecoming game, she couldn't very well be out on the soccer field. She watched Pickle take a header, colliding with one of the boys. She won the ball. Pickle was clearly the best player out there—boy or girl.

Lucy stood up to stretch her legs. Every part of her wanted to run and jump into the game. She wanted to give the ball a huge boot upfield, just to see whether she still had any power left inside of her. But she couldn't. Not in front of anyone, especially Benji. But she just *had* to. Just to see what she could do.

She purposefully waited until the whistle blew and Mrs. Sullivan ushered them off of the field and into the locker rooms. Lucy lingered to get a stray ball.

"It's okay, Lucy," Miss Sullivan said. "You can leave it for the next class."

"Oh, that's okay," chirped Lucy. "I got it!" She slowly walked to the ball and when Miss Sullivan went inside, Lucy set the ball down in the grass. She walked two steps back and stepped once to the left. She took a deep breath and then . . . WHACK! She drilled the ball a good fifty yards—it flew so fast and so hard it slammed into the bricks of the school. BAM!

"Nice kick," a voice said. Lucy spun around, caught, not having known anyone else was out there. She came face to face with Pickle, who was holding a soccer ball under each arm.

Lucy gulped. "Thanks." Both girls stood there awkwardly. They were only a few feet apart, but it felt like there was a Grand Canyon–size rift between them.

"I don't want to be late for next period," Pickle finally said.

"Right," Lucy agreed. "Me neither."

Pickle looked at Lucy for another second or two, then dropped one of the balls she was holding and dribbled it inside.

Between classes, Lucy opened her locker and was surprised. Inside sat a folded note that had obviously been stuffed between the slats. She suspiciously glanced over her shoulder, looking for Regan and Kendall ducked behind a column or trash can, spying on her and laughing. But she didn't see them anywhere. She turned back and hesitantly picked up the note, as if it had teeth or could spontaneously combust.

She slowly unfolded it, and as soon as she did, she experienced major déjà vu. It was a note from Ryan. At least, it *said* it was a note from Ryan. Lucy wasn't foolish enough, this time, to believe it actually was. She quickly scanned it.

*Lucy*, it read. *Want to go to homecoming with me? I know it's last minute—and before you think this is another prank from Kendall, I swear it's not. I just thought you deserved a real note from me. Anyway, think about it. We'd have a good time. Ryan.*

*Ryan?* Lucy stared at the words, stunned. Somehow, she just knew in her gut that this was for real. This note was actually from Ryan. She had to call Annie. Quickly, she rummaged around for her cell phone and ducked out of the nearest door. She wasn't supposed to use her phone on school property, but she had to tell someone. She hit 2 on her speed dial. Annie's voice mail instantly picked up, since, even with the time difference, she was in school, too.

"Annie," Lucy said breathlessly, barely able to contain her excitement. "Guess who asked me to homecoming? *Ryan Conner.* He asked me! ME! Can you—" Suddenly, she stopped abruptly. Something caught her eye. It was Pickle, scurrying out of her mom's car and rushing into the building. Lucy watched her head inside and in that moment, she knew what she had to do. If she had any hope of proving to Pickle and the other girls that she was worthy of being their friend, as much as it killed her, she was going to have to tell Ryan no.

# eighteen

"Hey," Ryan said as he slid into the seat next to Lucy in English class. He looked extra cute today in a vintage black Poison T-shirt and perfectly faded jeans. She'd mentioned he was hot, right? And of course now she knew he wasn't *just* hot. He was sweet and kind and incredibly thoughtful.

"I got your note," she said softly.

"Good." He nodded, as he let his backpack fall to the ground. "What d'ya think? Is it a date?"

"Um, well . . ." she answered slowly. "I really want it to be. . . ."

"But?" he asked suspiciously. "Oh no. This isn't the 'it's not you, it's me' speech, is it?"

"God, no. Not at all. It's just . . . um . . . it's just . . ." she stammered, then tried to focus and be semi-articulate. "I mean, I really appreciate your trying to make up for what Regan and Kendall did. You've been, like, so great to me, just in general—like, so supportive. . . ."

"Yeah, right," Ryan said sarcastically, running his fingers through his hair. "I guess that taping you to a goalpost *could* qualify as a supportive gesture."

"No, really," she said, grabbing his arm. As soon as she touched him, it was as though an electrical current shot through her body. This was so hard, but she had to do it.

"You've been great to me," she explained. "Especially because I just moved here and don't really have a whole lot of friends—which is why I can't go with you. To home-coming. Because one of my friends—at least, she used to be—she really likes you. You remember Pickle?"

Ryan smiled behind his bangs, which hung in his eyes today. "You mean the vegetable girl?"

"Yeah. Her name's actually Nicole. You had a conversa-tion with her last year. When she got cut from the soccer team."

Suddenly, Ryan remembered. "Out by the portables. She was crying."

Lucy beamed. He remembered. "Right, exactly," she said. "Well, Pickle's why I can't go with you. And I know you were just trying to be nice by asking me, and I'm sure there are a hundred girls who'd love to go with you to homecoming."

"Yeah, probably." Ryan shrugged. "But I'm not asking them—I'm asking you."

Lucy couldn't help but ask, "But . . . why?"

Ryan smiled. "Joining the guys' football team? That was a pretty gutsy move. I guess I've just never met a girl like you before. You're pretty awesome, Malone."

"Okay, okay," Martie called out. "Let's settle down."

Lucy couldn't help but wonder if she was doing the right thing—turning Ryan down for homecoming when Pickle wasn't even talking to her. She reminded herself that she was. If Ryan really liked her, he'd wait. There'd be more time *after* she made things right with Pickle. She just wondered how long that was going to take.

Ryan tapped her with his pencil. She turned around. "Well, what do you think?"

Lucy considered. She just couldn't say yes to him. "I'm sorry, Ryan. I just can't. Not until I work things out with Pickle." She paused. " Do you think you could save me a dance?" she asked.

Ryan sat back, a little deflated. He smiled, trying to save face. "Yeah," he said. "Sure."

As Martie began the lecture, Lucy glanced over at Charlie, who, as soon as she caught Lucy's eye, quickly looked out the window.

The bell rang. Second period was over. Lucy had received an A- on her *latest* test and was pleased. As everyone hurried out, Martie called her over.

"Can you stay a minute?" Martie asked. Before Lucy could protest, she added, "And I'll write you a pass."

Lucy walked over and half-leaned on Martie's desk. "Yeah?"

"How's your ankle?" Martie asked casually.

Lucy looked down self-consciously. Under her jeans, her ankle was still pretty heavily wrapped. "Um . . ." she said. "I've got the Ace bandage on it still, so—"

"So it doesn't hurt when you nail the ball halfway across the soccer field?" Martie asked with more than a hint of accusation in her voice.

"What?" Lucy recoiled, unsure what Martie was implying.

Martie crossed her arms in front of her chest. "I have it on good authority that your ankle's okay."

"Who told you that?" Lucy pressed.

Martie locked eyes with her. "Does it matter?"

"If people are spreading rumors about me, yeah, it matters."

"Pickle saw you kick the ball today. She said it was like you were never hurt."

Lucy glanced down guiltily. She had fired the ball pretty hard. And it had stung a little. "It wasn't like it didn't hurt," she explained. "I just . . . I wanted to kick anyway."

Martie nodded. "Oh, right. Like . . . work through the pain?"

Lucy shrugged. "I guess. Something like that."

"Then why aren't you playing on Friday?" Martie asked. "In the homecoming game. It's the biggest game of the season. You can't work through it then?"

"I just . . . I don't know," Lucy stammered. "Because my dad won't let me."

Martie wasn't buying it. "He didn't let you the first time and you did it anyway," she pressed. "Why's it different now?"

"It just is, okay?" Lucy insisted, her voice rising a little. "It's different."

"Look, I'm not saying you should sneak around behind your dad's back. I would never advocate that. But if you're *not* playing because of someone—maybe someone *besides* just your dad—you're making a big mistake."

Lucy threw her hands into the air. "Who else would I not be playing for?" she asked, exasperated.

Martie raised her eyebrows. "I think we both know."

Lucy stuffed her hands in her jeans pockets and hunched her shoulders up toward her ears. She waited for Martie to say something, but she didn't. Finally, Lucy had no choice but to admit the truth.

"He's my only friend here," Lucy said softly. "I don't want to lose him."

Martie leaned in close and looked into Lucy's eyes. Her voice was stern. "If you have to be less of a player, less of an athlete, less of a person to have Benji as a friend," she said, "then his friendship isn't worth much, Lucy. It's not worth anything at all."

That night Lucy picked wordlessly at her dinner. It was a strange feeling *not* being drained and exhausted at seven o'clock. Usually she was too tired after practice to lift her fork. Now she was just depressed. She kept thinking of Martie's words.

*If you have to be less of a player . . .*

"So, how was your day?" her dad asked, trying desperately to make conversation. They'd been sitting in total silence for about ten minutes.

Lucy mumbled a slight response and continued pushing rice around on her plate.

*Less of an athlete . . .*

"Are you ever going to speak to me again?" he finally asked. Lucy wasn't paying attention. She couldn't stop hearing Martie's words in her head. She didn't know what to do. Play and lose Benji? Or keep Benji and not play?

*Less of a person to have Benji as a friend, then his friendship isn't worth much.*

She so wanted to ask her dad what to do. She wanted his guidance, his advice, his life experience—but she knew that all she'd get was his wrath if she so much as mentioned what she was thinking about doing. So she said nothing.

"Lucy?" he asked again. "Are we ever going to talk about this?"

Lucy shrugged. She was through being accommodating and not standing up for herself.

Her dad sighed and turned his focus back to his breaded chicken.

Lucy set her fork down, determined. "I want to talk about mom," she said matter-of-factly. "I miss her."

Her dad nodded. "Of course, you do."

"But do you know why?" Lucy asked. "Because there are a million reasons. You know, I miss how she used to scratch my back at night, to get me to go to sleep. I miss how I used to hear her whistling in the kitchen in the morning, just when I was waking up. I miss the way a hug from her made everything better. . . ." Tears were forming in Lucy's eyes as she spoke. "But the thing I miss the most," she said, her voice wavering, "was that she wasn't afraid to just . . . you know, let me grow up and make my own decisions and be my own person." Lucy mustered the courage to say what was on her mind. "She didn't treat me like this fragile little girl that needed protecting. Mom saw how strong I was. And I wish you'd see it too."

She got up from the table and headed toward her room. She quickly shut her door behind her. She noticed the school directory on her bookshelf. She ran to grab it, then locked the door behind her. Quickly, she flipped to O.


It was fourth period. The bleachers were filled with every student at Beachwood. Paper banners were taped to the wall, reading everything from GO BEACHWOOD and WIN FIGHT WIN to OAKWOOD SUCKS and BEAT THOSE WEENIES. The cheerleaders were already leading the crowd in cheers where different sections were screaming, "Go!" "Fight!" "Win!" They were pitting different classes against each other, and so far the sophomores and juniors were definitely the loudest. The freshmen were too insecure and meek to yell, and the seniors were too over it to bother. Because of their different ages, Charlie, Pickle, and Max were each relegated to their own class and couldn't sit with each other.

The entire football team sat together in the bleachers, as Principal Truex gave a speech about Beachwood integrity, good sportsmanship, and pride. The students cheered as the music was cranked up and the cheerleaders, led by Kendall and Regan, did round-off back-handsprings across the gymnasium floor. Then it was time for Coach Offredi to speak.

He took the microphone, which blared feedback as soon as he held it. Some of the more obnoxious sophomores groaned in horror.

"Hello, students," Coach Offredi said, sounding more stilted and formal than he did on the football field, as if he were trying to sound like a calm, rational individual instead of the crazy, victory-obsessed maniac that he really was. "Thank you all for coming here today—"

One of the obnoxious sophomores screamed, "We had no choice." A bunch of the sophomores around him laughed.

"We—myself, the fine coaching staff, and most of all, these dedicated players—appreciate all the support. We hope you'll come out for the game tonight. And I'd like to introduce Ryan Conner, for those of you who don't know him. He's our quarterback and team captain—he'd like to say a few words."

Ryan jumped out of the bleachers to great applause and cheers. Coach Offredi passed off the mic, looking relieved to be finished speaking in public.

"What's up, Beachwood?" Ryan yelled. "You ready to watch us kick Oakwood's butts?" Even the seniors erupted in cheers.

"Tonight's game is gonna be crazy. We're gonna go all out, hold nothing back—and it's going to be especially good because we've got someone back with us. . . ." He looked into the bleachers and smiled. There was Lucy, sitting right above the team. "She missed a couple of weeks of games after making a great tackle, but she's back tonight and we can't do it without her. Malone, come down here!"

Lucy looked around nervously, then stood up tentatively. *Had Coach Offredi already told everyone?* All eyes were on her as she snaked her way through the team, past Benji. From the look on his face, no one had told him. But Lucy couldn't worry about disappointing Benji anymore. And she couldn't worry about defying her dad. She had to do this—for herself.

"You're gonna need this," Ryan said, tossing her her home jersey. Lucy took it and slipped it on over her head.

No surprise. It was a perfect fit.

• • •

After the pep rally, she approached Benji at his locker.

"Hey," she said softly, afraid he was mad.

"Hey," he replied glumly.

She nervously fiddled with her hair, wrapping a strand around her finger. "I guess I owe you an explanation—"

He cut her off. "You know what, Lucy? You don't owe me anything."

Lucy shifted uncomfortably. "I just . . . I, um . . . I talked to Martie. . . ." Lucy trailed off. It was so hard to just be honest. But she had to be. "And she kind of . . . she helped me see . . . that the only reason I wasn't playing, wasn't pushing through my injury, was because of you."

"Me?" he asked, not getting where she was going with this.

"Yeah. I was afraid that if I did, you wouldn't be friends with me anymore."

Benji stopped rummaging through his locker and looked at her as if she had just said something so out there that it was beyond comprehension. Like that the sky was green, or that orange juice was made from bowling balls. "Why would I not be friends with you?"

Lucy shrugged. "It seems like you're only friends with me again now that you have my spot. And I know that sounds really horrible. I mean, I don't want to hurt your feelings, 'cause you've been such a good friend to me."

Her words seemed to hit Benji like a slap across the face. "Right. Good friend," he said in a hostile tone.

Lucy was taken back. "What? What'd I say? What's wrong?"

Benji slammed his locker shut. "Just forget it."

As Benji stormed off, Lucy watched him go. And suddenly something caught her eye. Coach Offredi. He'd been watching.

"Lucy?" he said sternly. "A word?"

"Um, I have to get to . . . um . . . bio," Lucy stammered.

Coach Offredi folded his arms across his chest. "Now."

Lucy sat on a hard wooden chair in Coach Offredi's office, unsure of why she was there. She had called him last night and told him she was cleared by Dr. Cane to play. And surprisingly, he had seemed happy—relieved, even.

"I want to talk to you," Coach Offredi said, his mustache twitching a little. "About Benji. I want to talk about why he's upset."

"Because I'm kicking tonight," Lucy explained. "And he really wanted this position. Badly."

"That's not the problem." Coach Offredi sat down and picked up a pencil. He tapped the eraser against the desk. "The problem is that he likes you."

Lucy almost did a double take. "Huh?"

"He likes you," Coach Offredi said, a little louder. "Listen, I know from experience. I was a teenage boy once." Lucy almost giggled. It was hard to think of Coach

Offredi as a boy. "This isn't about you kicking farther than him, and it's not about beating him in a drill. It's about liking a girl who's probably way out of his league and is all drooly and moony-eyed for the quarterback."

"I'm not drooly and moon-whatever over Ryan!" Lucy exclaimed defensively.

Coach Offredi raised his eyebrows.

Lucy sat back in her chair. "Well, maybe a little," she admitted.

"Give the kid a break, Malone. He likes you. We all lose our heads a little when we like someone. Now get to class."

Lucy stood up. "Yes, Coach," she said obediently. As she opened the door, he called after her.

"Oh, Malone?" He looked up from his desk and smiled. "Welcome back."

## nineteen

Beachwood exploded through the paper banner as they barreled onto the field, ready for a fight. Speeches had been given, ankles had been tightly taped (Lucy's especially), and prayers had been said—now all that was left to do was play ball. Beachwood won the coin toss and opted to start on defense, wanting to send a message to Oakwood's offensive line right away: "We're shutting you down."

BAM! Lucy kicked the ball off solidly to Oakwood. It bounced at the twenty and was quickly picked up by their kick returner, who angled down the right sideline behind a vanguard of Oakwood blockers. Tank literally ran over one of the smaller blockers and brought down the ball carrier with a jarring tackle at the Oakwood thirty-two. The Beachwood section of the crowd roared, as Coach Offredi sent the defensive team onto the field.

Both teams huddled on their respective sides of the line of scrimmage.

As soon as Oakwood broke, Tank looked for signs of what play they were going to do. Seeing Oakwood's tight end move right, he shouted, "Strength right! Strength right!"

As the ball was snapped to Oakwood's quarterback, the Beachwood defensive line charged forward. Big Jimmy came out of nowhere to pick off the pass.

"INTERCEPTION!" Lucy cheered. Big Jimmy faked left, then cut back right, finding a small opening through the surprised Oakwood offense. The crowd roared!

With Tank and DeRosa as blockers, Big Jimmy sprinted straight up the left side of the field, looking as though he had rockets on the bottom of his shoes. Several Oakwood players tried to grab him, but each fell out, one after the other. Triumphantly, he crossed into the end zone, spiking the ball dramatically before chest-bumping his teammates.

On the bench, Lucy went crazy, cheering loudly and thumping several nearby teammates on their shoulder pads with her fists. The game had just started and Beachwood was already up 6-0! She went in for the extra point, which, thankfully, she made with ease. It was now 7-0. Her ankle stung a little on the impact. With all the warm-up kicks, the kickoff, and now the extra point, she was definitely feeling some soreness. But she didn't care. All she cared about was that she was playing.

"That's it!" Coach Offredi bellowed. "That's the momentum we needed." He grabbed Lucy with the play. "Into their end zone for a touchback. We need a big kick!"

On the kickoff, she followed Coach Offredi's instructions, nailing the ball as high and hard as she could, her ankle protesting on contact.

A totally juiced-up Beachwood defense roared onto the field and successfully shut Oakwood down on the next three plays. Oakwood had no choice but to punt on the fourth down. Oakwood punted a short kick to Beachwood that Sascha caught on the Oakwood forty-nine-yard line. On the sidelines, the offensive unit was ready for their turn.

Coach Offredi grabbed Ryan by the shoulders. "Okay, son, let's do this. Read the field, now. Read the field."

Ryan and the offensive team ran onto the field as if they were on fire. The energy and excitement in the air were almost palpable as Ryan tossed a quick pass to Kevin, who cut straight up the middle, gaining ten yards and enough for a first down.

On the next play, Ryan did a pump fake to the right but then sent a low bullet pass to Little Jimmy, who cut back, turned, and caught it at ankle level, before being immediately tackled at Oakwood's twenty. Another first down. Beachwood was clearly dominating.

Anticipating what was coming next, Lucy warmed up her leg on the sidelines, expecting to kick again soon. She was right. Cope caught a line drive right at his gut in the end zone and Lucy was up again. Caleb snapped the ball, Benji held it and BOOM! Lucy nailed it between the uprights. Beachwood was up 14-0.

Caleb knocked Lucy in the head excitedly. "Nice kick," he said, banging her helmet. Her head rattled around inside. She had a moment to regroup on the sidelines as Coach Offredi gave the kickoff team instructions.

"Now, remember the film from earlier," he reminded her. They'd briefly looked at film after their ritual pregame meal at Sizzler. "Let's a do a right return. The wedge slides right! Let's pin their man back!"

Lucy gave a solid kick to the right, just as she'd been instructed, but Oakwood's kick returner was fast and, with the help of his teammates, was able to get by Beachwood's first set of defenders, getting all the way to the Oakwood forty-five before he was brought down. On the sidelines, Coach Offredi threw down his clipboard, obviously angry. He marched over to the assistant coaches, strategizing defensive plays—but nothing Beachwood tried was enough to stop Oakwood's push for a touchdown. The momentum had quickly shifted.

Oakwood scored. Then scored again. And as the quarters passed and the clock ticked down, they scored yet another time. And by the time the game was deep into the fourth quarter, Oakwood was leading 23-14. Although Oakwood's kicker missed one of his three extra point attempts, he had also gone on to nail a field goal from the twenty-five-yard line. Things weren't looking good for Beachwood.

Lucy watched Coach Offredi pacing up and down like a

caged animal about to unleash his wrath on anybody in his way. He yelled at Ryan. He yelled at Tank. He yelled at the ref. At one point, Lucy thought she heard him yell for a hot dog, but she must have been imagining that. Who could eat at a time like this? She looked at the clock. There were only two minutes left in the game. They had to score now.

"Crossfire . . . Idaho . . . Idaho," Ryan shouted on the field. "Hut!" He took the snap from Caleb. The receivers took off running, deep into Oakwood's territory. Just as he was about to be taken down, Ryan fired a thirty-eight-yard bomb to Kevin. The ball spiraled so fast Lucy couldn't even see the laces. It fell right into Kevin's outstretched hands. The entire Beachwood team jumped off the bench, screaming, as Kevin sprinted the final ten yards into the end zone. TOUCHDOWN! The team exploded on the field and sidelines! The coaches hugged! The crowd went wild! Suddenly, Beachwood had a shot. Oakwood only had a three-point lead. They were back in the game!

Lucy looked up at the clock. It read 1:32. She jogged out to kick the extra point. BAM! The ball split the uprights. Another point was added on to Beachwood's side of the scoreboard, which now read BEACHWOOD 21, OAKWOOD 23.

"Huddle up!" Coach Offredi shouted, bringing the kickoff unit closely around him. "Okay," he said. "This is it. We need to get the ball back. They know we need to get the ball back. Ten yards, Lucy. Right in front of you. That's what we need. You kick it, you run after it, and you fall on it. Go to that ball, and whatever you do, hold on to it! Hold on like your life depends on it!"

Lucy tried not to look horrified at what Coach Offredi was instructing her to do. "Wait—I'm supposed to kick it *and* fall on it, too?

"You're not supposed to," Coach Offredi challenged. "You will." He looked her in the eye. "If you can't do it, you tell me now. I'll put Benji in there." Lucy looked over at Benji on the bench. They hadn't exchanged more than two words since their locker fight. And the two words had been *go* and *Beachwood*.

"No," Lucy said defiantly. "I can do it." She looked around at her teammates. "Really," she said, trying to convince herself as well. "I can. I want to."

The kickoff team lined up on the field on either side of Lucy. Fully suspecting that Beachwood was planning an onside kick, Oakwood matched their formation, leaving only one player deep in their backfield on the slim off chance that the kick went deep.

Lucy took a deep breath. She knew she could do this. She tried to ignore the throbbing in her ankle. She could do this. She was tough. She raised her hand. The whistle blew.

BAM! She kicked the ball hard on the ground. It toppled end over end a short ten yards. Lucy ran behind it as her teammates ferociously blocked so that Lucy could pounce on it. And she did!

She hit the ground with the ball and curled around it protectively, holding onto it as if her life depended on it. Suddenly, WHAM! She felt as if a piano had been dropped on her . . . and then another piano . . . and then a concert grand piano, as Oakwood dogpiled on her at the forty-five-yard line, frantically trying to jar the ball loose from Lucy's arms. At the moment the referee blew his whistle and signaled a recovered onside kick, the cleats of one of the Oakwood tacklers in the pile forcefully jammed into Lucy's recently injured right ankle, sending a wave of searing pain and then nausea through her body.

*Oh, please, God,* she groaned to herself. *Please don't let me puke here.* Puking was bad enough. Puking in public was beyond traumatizing.

On the sidelines, the team went crazy. In the stands, the fans stomped and clapped and cheered. The band blared and the cheerleaders bounced as the Oakwood guys were pulled off Lucy, one by one. Her own teammate, Aidan, helped her up, practically peeling her off the ground. She felt as if she'd been flattened by a Mack truck. As soon as she stood up and tried to put any weight on her reinjured ankle, her leg gave out. It hurt so badly she could barely stand it. Aidan helped her clear off the field and led her to the bench.

Coach Offredi rushed over. "Are you okay?" he asked. Lucy took off her helmet.

"Yeah . . . it just . . . it just really hurts," she answered with tears in her eyes.

Coach Offredi beamed at her. "Nice job, kid."

Lucy forced a smile. "Thanks." If it hadn't been for the searing pain, she would have been able to appreciate the magnitude of what she had just done. She looked up at the clock. It read :54.

As the Beachwood offense took the field for what would be their final possession, Coach Offredi shouted to Ryan. "We just need to get inside the thirty. Just inside the thirty. We need fifteen yards right now! Fifteen yards! Let's go! Let's go, Beachwood! Time is now!"

A handoff to Little Jimmy advanced Beachwood seven yards, and a lateral pass to Nick, who dove for the three yards, gave Beachwood a first down. The clock read :28.

The Beachwood team huddled on the field. This was it. Their last chance. They had to get close enough for Lucy to kick. But the question was, would she be able to? Her ankle had swelled so much, she'd just taken off her shoe. The trainer rushed over.

"What's going on?" he asked. "You okay?"

"It's just my ankle. . . ." Her voice wavered. "I think I need . . . I don't know . . . maybe to retape it?" The trainer grabbed his bag and frantically started retaping Lucy's ankle.

On the field, Ryan called out the play. "Green light . . . green light . . . seventy-four." The ball was snapped. Ryan took the snap and faked a handoff to Kevin, who ran off-tackle, drawing the attention of most of the Oakwood defense. Ryan then took one step to his right and sprang through the hole created when the Oakwood defensive tackle went after Kevin, diving for seven yards and another first down. They were within field goal range!

Hurriedly, the trainer finished taping Lucy. Coach Offredi ran over. "What's wrong? *What's wrong?*" he asked, adamantly, his mustache twitching like mad. He looked at Lucy trying to pull her shoe over her swollen ankle. "No, NO!" he yelled. "What's this?"

"I'm fine!" Lucy said, rushing to tie her laces.

"Fine? Your ankle's swelled up to the size of Texas!"

Coach Offredi motioned to the ref for Beachwood's last time-out.

One of the assistant coaches said, "Make the call. You want to put in Benji instead?"

Coach Offredi put his head in his hands. It wasn't what he wanted, but he had no choice. Lucy spoke up.

"I can go in," she said. "I want to go in. This one's mine."

Coach Offredi looked at her, amazed. "You sure?"

She nodded vigorously. She needed to finish this. She had something to prove. To her coaches, to her teammates . . . to herself.

She stood up. "Okay, let's go." Throbbing pain shot through her ankle, as if someone had just hit her anklebone with a hammer. Limping, she jogged out onto the field. She glanced at the clock. It read :14.

Beachwood took their positions for what would

certainly be the last play of the game. Lucy said a quick prayer. *Mom, please help me do this,* she thought to herself. *Please help me.*

The crowd waited in breathless anticipation. Everything became still. Benji gave Caleb the signal. Caleb snapped the ball back . . . but it was off-line. So off-line that Benji had no chance to catch it cleanly.

Horrified, Lucy watched the ball tumble to the ground at her feet.

"Oh my God," Lucy said aloud. She glanced around, panicked. She couldn't let Oakwood get their hands on it. Without even thinking, she scooped it up and did the only thing she could do.

RUN!

Benji sprang up, blocking for her. His action allowed her to cut through an open hole. She was careful not to go over the line of scrimmage as she headed toward the sideline. She tucked the ball into her body and was so terrified she didn't even notice the throbbing pain in her ankle.

She saw the Oakwood defensive end and two linebackers barreling toward her, and she knew she was never going to make it to the end zone. If they hit her, she might not even make it to tomorrow!

Suddenly, out of the corner of her eye she saw Kevin in the end zone in front of the goalpost. Seeing her frantic scramble, he cut across the end zone back toward the left sideline, trying to get open.

The clock ran down. Six . . . five . . . four . . . three . . . two . . .

Lucy hurled the ball as hard as she could in Kevin's direction.

He lunged for it, reaching out just as his body—WHAM!—hit the ground. For a moment, Lucy couldn't tell what had happened . . . and then Kevin reached up, holding the football triumphantly in one hand! The referee raised both arms over his head! They had done it!

Lucy sank to her knees, collapsing with relief.

Beachwood had scored! They had won!!!!

On her hands and knees, Lucy tried to catch her breath. Pain shot through her ankle, but she didn't care. She was in complete and utter shock. Had she really just done that? Had she really just won the game?

The entire team rushed onto the field in celebration. Caleb ran over, hitting Lucy so hard that she almost fell over. She stumbled to keep her balance. He grabbed her arm, steadying her.

"You saved it," he gasped. "I can't believe it. That play—it won the game."

Suddenly, from the back, Ryan picked her up and spun her around.

"What?" he asked, still in shock from what had just happened. "You're a quarterback now too? Unbelievable pass, Malone!"

Lucy beamed as her teammates hoisted her up on their

shoulders. All the fans had rushed the field as well. As she balanced precariously, she felt like she would remember this moment for the rest of her life-the cheering, the fans, the light shining down on her. She watched as Cope and Sascha poured the huge plastic container of water over Coach Offredi. Even dripping wet, he had a tremendous smile across his face. Water droplets gleamed in his mustache as they caught the light. Lucy let out a loud "Go Beachwood!" Then looked around. *Where was Benji?* She scanned the crowd.

And from above everyone's heads, she saw something that nearly made her topple off the shoulders she was perched upon.

"Put me down," she said, tapping Tank's shoulders. "Please, put me down." The guys obliged.

She took off her helmet, hoping her eyes were playing tricks on her. Her dad was walking toward her. Lucy's heart sank. After everything that had happened, was this really how her night would end? Getting yelled at and grounded for life? Again?

But then she saw something in his hand. Flowers. She realized he had a huge smile on his face.

"Dad?" she asked hesitantly, as if this were too good to be true.

"Kid, you were amazing out there." He smiled proudly.

Lucy was stunned. "You're not . . . mad?"

Her dad shook his head. "I'm so proud of you, Luce."

She couldn't believe it. "How did you know I was playing?"

"Martie called," he admitted. "She said there was something I needed to see." He looked at the field, then had to ask. "Did you plan to pass the ball like that?"

"Not exactly," Lucy admitted.

"I didn't know you could throw like that." He laughed, impressed.

"A pretty great guy taught me," she reminded him.

Her dad smiled and pulled her into an enormous bear hug. "You were right, kid. About everything. And I'm—" He stopped. It was hard to get the words out.

She smiled. "I know."

"Your mom would have been so proud of you tonight," he told her. "You're just like her. She never listened to me, either . . . and nine times out of ten, that was a good thing." Lucy couldn't help but laugh; then she hugged her dad tightly. He finally understood. He finally got it.

Suddenly, Coach Offredi's voice boomed loudly above the noise.

"Gather around, everyone!" Everyone on the field—players, fans, and parents—stopped what they were doing. Dr. Cane, evidently a fixture at every game, quieted the crowd.

"Normally, we'd do this in the locker room," Coach Offredi admitted. "But in the spirit of the night, of homecoming, of this great win . . . I'd like to congratulate the entire team on their victory and their heart . . . and announce tonight's MVP." He raised the football he was holding and fired a pass to Lucy, who miraculously caught it.

"Lucy Malone," he announced. "MVP. You were tough out there tonight. As tough as any guy. I speak for everyone when I say we're proud to call you a Beachwood player. I know you've had to overcome a lot to be a part of this team . . . but tonight, in front of everyone, I'm happy to say, you *are* a part of this team, Lucy. So here's to you."

Lucy felt her eyes well up with tears—this time, happy ones.

Part of her wanted to laugh. After all, the other players were considered "part of the team" simply by making the cut. She'd had to do so much for the same rank. It was ironic, really. But in the end she had proved herself—and it was worth it.

"Thank you." Lucy nodded, choking back her emotions. "Thank you so much." And she meant it, from the bottom of her heart.

As she accepted the applause of everyone around her, she reveled in this feeling. This was what it felt like to actually belong. She glanced around.

The only thing missing from the moment was Benji.

Saturday night was the homecoming dance.

Lucy's dad waved as he dropped her off at school that night. "Call me when you're ready to be picked up," he instructed. "And kid?" He smiled. "Have fun."

Lucy grinned. "I will." She decided to leave her jacket in the car so she wouldn't lose it. Now she hurried into the school, her bare arms covered in goose bumps. She walked into the gym and suddenly felt tentative. She told herself that plenty of people were probably going alone . . . but it didn't make it easier to *be* alone. However, she quickly realized she wasn't: Morbid was heading her way.

"Hey," Morbid said, looking down at her shoes and keeping her voice low.

"Hi." Lucy smiled.

Morbid looked around, as if she were worried about people seeing her. When she seemed satisfied that no one was looking, she admitted, "You were great last night. You know, at the game. I got some good shots of that pass. I could e-mail them to you if you wanted. You know, the pictures."

Lucy smiled, grateful. This was only one of two times that Morbid had been in her vicinity without growling. "Thanks, that'd be cool," she said.

Morbid shrugged, "You're welcome. Anyway, okay . . . well, I'm going to go find my friends." Lucy couldn't help but be surprised—and envious. *Wow.* Even Morbid had friends.

"Hey, Lucy," Cope said, walking by. "You look great."

She smiled and glanced down at her little black dress. "A step up from cleats and pads, huh?"

Cope laughed. "I'd say." Then he pointed across the gym. "The guys are over there. Wanna come?"

Lucy nodded and followed Cope over. As she snaked her way through the gym, she passed by Regan, who was slow dancing with Kevin. She turned to get past Kendall, who was in the arms of . . .

. . . Ryan?

Lucy's eyes widened. She blinked twice. Surely she was seeing things. *What would Ryan be doing with Kendall?*

Suddenly, Cope answered. "Oh! Those two? They've been hooking up on and off since eighth grade. He always likes other girls, but somehow Kendall pulls him back in every time." Lucy realized she'd accidentally asked the question out loud.

She couldn't believe it. Kendall and Ryan? KENDALL AND RYAN? Now *everything made sense.* No wonder Kendall hated her so much. And suddenly, she wasn't sure how she felt about Ryan.

"What makes sense?" Cope asked. Lucy realized she'd done it again.

"Never mind," she muttered. She looked around and saw the soccer girls huddled together across the gym. Charlie was gesturing to Lucy and saying something to Pickle. Lucy sighed. They were talking about her. She wondered how she was ever going to make things right.

Suddenly, she was elbowed in the side. Hard. Lucy stumbled back.

"Oops," Kendall said loudly as Cope patted Ryan on the back.

"Hey man," Ryan said to Cope. "Who're you here with?" The boys turned toward each other, caught up in their own conversation.

"Oh, I thought I hit someone," Kendall remarked. "But all I see is a big, giant nothing, in desperate need of a new hairstyle."

Next to her, Regan giggled loudly.

Lucy took a deep breath. This was going to be so satisfying.

"You know what, Kendall?" she said. "You're a bitch. And Regan? You're even worse than that. What you do to people—to me, to Charlie—all for the sake of what? Getting in with *her?*" Lucy pointed to Kendall. "As if that's so great. What exactly do you love about it? Getting her drinks? Doing her dirty work? That's not a friendship. It's a dictatorship."

Lucy shook her head. Regan looked as though she were about to cry, as if this were the first time these thoughts had dawned on her.

"I feel sorry for you," Lucy continued. "You had Charlie as your best friend. You gave up a really good thing with a really great person. And here's a news flash, Regan: Once you're out of high school, no one gives a crap how popular you are. People care about what kind of person you've become. And next year? Kendall won't be here. We will. So think about that. Think about where you're gonna be then." Lucy smiled, satisfied. "And enjoy."

Lucy turned to go, but Ryan grabbed her arm. "Malone, wait—what about that dance?"

Lucy looked him in the eye. "I think you have your dance partner already."

She hurried off, leaving Ryan. Kendall sidled up to him, threading her arm through his, but he just wiggled out of her grasp.

Meanwhile, Lucy headed for the door. She didn't know where she was going. Just out of there. She liked Ryan. She really did. But if he could take a girl like Kendall to homecoming, a girl who thrived on humiliating other people . . . what did that say about him? She'd been so busy seeing all the things that he was, she hadn't noticed what he wasn't.

Besides, as great as Ryan was—and he *was* great—as the quarterback of the team, wasn't he practically genetically programmed to hook up with the head cheerleader?

Lucy kept her head down as she rushed to the exit. Suddenly, Ryan Conner was a lot less interesting. When she thought that by going to meet him under the bleachers, she'd given up her friendship with Pickle . . . it just killed her.

Suddenly, a voice interrupted her spinning thoughts.

"Lucy, wait!" a voice called. She turned around, and Pickle was standing there.

"I heard what you did," Pickle admitted, her voice

wavering a bit. "Charlie told me how you turned down going to homecoming with Ryan for me. . . ." Tears sprang into Pickle's eyes.

"You have to forgive me, Lucy," Pickle pleaded. "For holding a grudge, for being jealous—for everything."

Lucy shook her head. "No, I did everything wrong. I should have been honest. I just wanted you to like me—to be my friend—and I was afraid that if I told you I liked Ryan, it would be a huge mess . . . which it was anyway."

"It was my fault. I never should have yelled at you like that. It's just . . ." Pickle stopped for a moment, thinking. "It's just . . . look at you! Why wouldn't Ryan want to be with you? You're such a great girl and he's a great guy—"

Lucy interrupted. "A great guy who's here with Kendall."

Pickle did a one-eighty. "Ew!"

Lucy laughed. "Yeah!"

Pickle giggled. And Lucy smiled. It felt so good to be laughing with her again.

Pickle shrugged one shoulder and looked like a shy little girl. "Lucy . . . do you think we can we just start over and be friends again?"

Lucy nodded. "I think I'd love that."

Pickle smiled broadly and engulfed Lucy in a hug.

"See, Charlie," Pickle said, turning around. "I told you she was one of us." But suddenly, Pickle realized Charlie wasn't there.

They looked around and were stunned at what they saw. Regan and Charlie were actually talking!

Pickle and Lucy both gasped. From the looks of things, Regan was apologizing. Charlie looked down at her shoes uncomfortably and then back up at Regan. The girls watched as she gave Regan a slight smile. Which for Charlie meant a lot.

"Oh my God. Where's Morbid?" Lucy asked. "This is definitely a Kodak moment."

"I see another one." Pickle smiled and nodded over to Benji, who was lingering by himself at the punch bowl. It was the first time Lucy had realized he was there. He looked adorable in jeans and retro-striped polo shirt under a suit jacket. His curls were out of control.

Lucy stared at him as if her eyes needed adjusting. There was something about him. Standing there, not caring what anyone else thought. It was as if she had just put huge, thick glasses on and everything had gone from being fuzzy and blurry to crystal clear. *Benji.*

Lucy smiled. "I'll be right back. Don't leave without me."

"I won't," Pickle promised. "I wouldn't even think of it."

Lucy tentatively approached Benji. "You're here," she commented.

He nodded. "You too."

They were both quiet for a moment.

"You look nice."

He nodded again. "You too. Less footbally than usual."

She smiled; then there was more awkward silence.

Lucy spoke first. "I looked for you after the game but—"

"My dad—I didn't want to deal with him, so I hid out in the locker room till the excitement died down."

"He was disappointed you weren't kicking?"

Benji sighed. "Understatement of the year." He shook his head. "Dads can be such . . ." He searched for the word.

"Dads," Lucy stated.

Benji laughed. "Yeah. That."

"Benji?" Lucy took a deep breath. "You want to dance?"

Benji looked around. "With who?"

Lucy hit him playfully in the arm. "With me, stupid!"

A broad smile spread across Benji's face. His braces gleamed under the lights. Then he remembered. "What about Ryan? Isn't he the guy you want to be dancing with?"

"Not really," Lucy admitted. "He was . . . but now . . ."

"Now what?" Benji asked.

"There's someone else. Someone else I'm interested in."

Benji deflated. "Oh."

Lucy held out her hand. "Someone who's been great to

*Playing*
*WITH THE*
*Boys*

me since the first day I set foot in this gym."

It slowly dawned on Benji that she meant *him*. But still, he had to joke. "Morbid?"

Lucy laughed and shook her head. She reached out for Benji's hand. He placed his hand in hers.

She led him onto the dance floor. A slow song played. She wrapped her arms around his neck and he gently let his hands rest on her hips. They swayed to the music. She glanced around at Pickle and the girls giggling in the corner, giving Lucy the thumbs-up.

"So . . . next week's game against Branford," Benji said. "Should be a good one. Hopefully you didn't screw up your ankle too bad last night."

Lucy looked Benji in the eye. "So do you think I still have a chance?" she asked.

"To play? Sure! If you wrap it tight, put some ice on it—"

Lucy interrupted. "That's not what I meant. I meant, do you think I still have a chance with you?"

"With me?" Benji asked, surprised. "For what?"

Lucy smiled. "For this . . ." And slowly, in front of everyone, she leaned in and kissed him. And at that moment, under the shimmering light, surrounded by her friends, Lucy finally found that missing *K*. In the company of the right friends and with the right boy, knowing she had made the right decision, for the first time since as far back as she could remember, Lucy Malone felt truly *lucky*.

# acknowledgments

Thank you to all the people who helped make this book a reality.

First to Jane Schonberger and George Morency, whose lives are committed to empowering young women through sports. Thanks to Carole Rosen, Andy Barzvi, and Jennifer Joel of ICM who have been supporters of this book and series from the beginning. Thanks to the amazing, talented, detail-oriented, most insightful storyteller and note-giver, Kristen Pettit, who this couldn't have happened without.

A huge thank you to football players, experts, and friends Jason Wilborn, Nick Offredi, Mark, Sascha, and Caleb Tymchyshyn, who taught me everything I know about football. Thank you to Gretchen West, my laughing potato-in-crime, who kept me "sane" while writing. And most of all, a thank you to my family, Bob, Mary and Kate, who read every word, every chapter, and every draft and are always the inspiration for everything I write. I love you.